THIEVES' MARKET

THIEVES' MARKET

BY

A. I. Bezzerides

Foreword by Garrett White
Afterword by the Author

UNIVERSITY OF CALIFORNIA PRESS
Berkeley • Los Angeles • London

University of California Press
Berkeley and Los Angeles, California
University of California Press, Ltd.
London, England

First California Paperback Printing 1997

Library of Congress Cataloging-in-Publication Data

Bezzerides, A. I. (Albert Isaac), 1908–
    Thieves' market / by A. I. Bezzerides.
        p.   cm. (California Fiction)
    Includes bibliographical references.
    ISBN 0-520-20746-7 (pbk. : alk. paper)
    I. Title.
PS3552.E898T48   1997
813'.54—dc21   97-18530
                                                        CIP

Printed in the United States of America
        1   2   3   4   5   6   7   8   9

The paper used in this publication meets the minimum requirements
of American National Standard for Information Sciences—
Permanence of Paper for Printed Library Materials,
ANSI Z39.48-1984. ⊗

FOREWORD by Garrett White

Long, long ago, when I saw what the produce dealers did, and what
the engineers with their swindle sheets were doing, I knew that the
world was going to end.

— A. I. Bezzerides, 1996

Best known for his free-form adaptation of Mickey Spillane's crime
thriller *Kiss Me Deadly*, the apocalyptic film noir masterpiece directed by Robert Aldrich, Albert Isaac "Buzz" Bezzerides published
three novels: *Long Haul* (1938), filmed by Warner Bros. as *They
Drive By Night*, starring George Raft, Humphrey Bogart, and Ida
Lupino; *There Is A Happy Land* (1942), about a family of rural
drifters; and *Thieves' Market* (1949), which Bezzerides scripted for
20th-Century Fox as *Thieves' Highway*, directed by Jules Dassin and
starring Richard Conte, Lee J. Cobb, Valentina Cortesa, and Millard
Mitchell.

Despite notices in *Time* magazine and elsewhere, the first novel,
which he had begun to write in 1932, sold modestly, as did the second. But by the time Scribner's published *Thieves' Market* in 1949,
Bezzerides was a highly paid screenwriter working free-lance for all
of the major studios. He had spent five years during the war as a
contract writer in the Warners stable, where he became one of
William Faulkner's closest friends in Hollywood, and had earned a
reputation as a writer of tough, gritty action pictures. The novel
was widely reviewed: "Harrowing . . . appalling!" —*San Francisco
Chronicle*. "Taut, fast-paced . . . violence, sex, intensity." —*New York
Times*. "Full of violence and suspense, definitely not for the squea-
mish . . ." —*Book-of-the-Month Club News*. "Crude and elemen-

tary . . ." —*New York Herald Tribune.* "Hard-boiled! Crackling! Races
like a truck going downgrade!" —*Saturday Review.*

Records in the Scribner's archive at Princeton University indi-
cate that the first edition sold out within several weeks, and two
mass-market paperback editions followed. Warner Bros. offered
$100,000 for the motion picture rights, but Bezzerides's agent had
already agreed to sell the book to Fox for $80,000—a small fortune
in 1948, when the rights were sold. Lasting success couldn't be far
away.

Bezzerides was born in Samsun, Turkey, on August 9, 1908, to
an Armenian mother educated by Presbyterian missionaries and a
Turkish-speaking Greek father, a merchant twenty years her senior
with his own train of donkeys. As an infant in 1909, he was
brought into the large Armenian community in Fresno, California,
where his father worked first in agriculture, then as a trucker hauling produce. The richness of the drama in Bezzerides's extended
immigrant family has always been the source of his creative life. As
he tells it,

> They came straight to Fresno because my mother had relatives
> there. My grandmother had been widowed with five daugh-
> ters, and she had to marry them all off. My mother's marriage
> to my father had been arranged in Turkey, but my mother's
> sister, my aunt, had been sent here to marry a guy she had
> never even seen before, a runty Armenian with red hair and
> green eyes. Not only that, but the man with whom my mother
> was really in love had moved here. He had moved here before
> the turn of the century and had a six-hundred-acre plot of
> land. She had grown up with him. He was her age. A hand-
> some guy. He wrote a letter to her saying, "I've got a piece of
> land in California. Leave your husband and come here. You
> can get a divorce and we'll get married," but she couldn't go.
> She was pregnant with me.[1]

Bezzerides began to write while still a student at the University
of California, Berkeley, taking literature courses on the side and
planning a career in Communications Engineering. His first pub-

lished story, "Passage Into Eternity," about a prank for which his
grandmother never forgave him, appeared in the February 1935 is-
sue of *Story* magazine. Others were published in *Scribner's, Esquire,*
and *Harper's.* When *Long Haul* was published by Carrick & Evans
in New York in 1938, Bezzerides was living in Hollywood with his
first wife, Yvonne, and working for the Los Angeles Department of
Water and Power. The couple had moved to Hollywood when
Bezzerides was given a job at Electrical Research Products, a divi-
sion of Western Electric for which he had worked in San Francisco.
He had quit in disgust over what he viewed as unethical conduct at
the company, and was about to do the same at the Department of
Water and Power. He had already been through a string of odd
jobs: sound mixer, installer of public address systems, electrical engineer for Mitchell Camera.

On March 20, 1940, Bezzerides signed a contract giving Warner
Bros. Studios the right to make a motion picture from *Long Haul,* a
bleak, fast-moving story about two independent truckers trading
crops for their share of the American Dream. The agreement gave
the writer $2,000 for the rights to his novel, enough at the time to
make a down payment on a decent house. The original contract for
the deal is preserved in the Warners archive at the University of
Southern California, along with the official budget for the film:
Screenwriters Jerry Wald and Richard Macaulay: $11,167; Direc-
tor Raoul Walsh: $17,500; George Raft: $55,000; Humphrey
Bogart: $11,200; Ida Lupino: $10,000; Alan Hale: $10,000; Ann
Sheridan: $6,000.

Ever since signing the contract, Bezzerides has claimed that when
he first walked into producer Mark Hellinger's office, Hellinger covered a script on his desk titled *They Drive By Night.* Although
much else has been lost, one internal memo survives in the archive
with the contract, a brief note from Warner Bros. producer Hal B.
Wallis to Walsh green-lighting Walsh's request to begin shooting
a few road shots for the film when the weather is right. The memo
is dated March 15, 1940.

Bezzerides had already been involved in one questionable Hollywood transaction. He was standing in front of Stanley Rose's book-
shop on Hollywood Boulevard, marveling at his own book in the

window, when a man who had seen his picture on the book jacket stepped up and asked, "How much of an advance did you get?" Bezzerides told him. "Could you loan it to me?" Always generous to a fault, Bezzerides gave it to him. Months later, after many promises and in need of the money, Bezzerides reluctantly went to the man's wife. She was surprised and angry, since she had already given that amount to her husband on at least a couple of occasions to cover the debt, but she paid him immediately. The debtor was novelist John Fante, who became a lifelong, if difficult, friend and sometimes collaborator.

Sensing a talented source of authentic material—and, as Bezzerides sees it, attempting to placate him after stealing his book— Warners hired him into its stable of contract writers, paying him $300 per week, more than four times his salary as an engineer at the Department of Water and Power. His first assignment was *Juke Girl*, a long-buried film in which Ronald Reagan and Richard Whorf play Florida drifters who become involved in a dispute between packing plant owner Gene Lockhart and grower George Tobias. The liberal Reagan character sides with the growers, his hawkish former friend with the packers. In a scene that will be echoed years later in the spectacular truck crash in *Thieves' Highway* as a metaphor for wasted labor, the savagery of capitalism, and the general stupidity of the human race, packing plant scabs destroy tons of tomatoes. The film did well, and Bezzerides kept writing.

Bezzerides lives in a magnificent, decaying Rudolf Schindler house at the western end of the San Fernando Valley. Since 1955, when he bought the house from actor Albert Dekker, he has lived here with his second wife, Silvia Richards, a screenwriter (*Ruby Gentry, Possessed, Rancho Notorious*) who worked closely with Fritz Lang and King Vidor. Accessible by a short, steep dirt road, and partly hidden by massive eucalyptus trees, the house sits atop a hill that once overlooked vast orange groves. Surrounded by abandoned cars and rusting machinery, it seems a monument to the entropy in the film noir universe that has been the subject of his life's work. ("A house should age with its owners," Schindler told him.)

For the past ten years, we have been meeting in coffee shops on Ventura Boulevard. We met first at Ryons, a '50s diner where he used to sit and write in a corner booth at all hours of the day and night. When it was closed and remodeled under new management as a garish retro '50s diner, we moved down the street to Denny's. "[Bezzerides] converses like a force of nature," Lee Server once wrote, and there's no better way to say it. He is tough, blunt, often emphatically profane, deeply pessimistic as to human nature and the future of humankind, yet also amazingly sensitive and trusting.

His conversation ranges over the topics that have obsessed him since he first sat down to write nearly seventy years ago: man's self-destructive programming ("tragedy is etched into the genes"); the destruction of nature; the mystery and superiority of women; the exploitation of labor; education; addiction as a metaphor for American consumer culture; the "sanity of the insane and the insanity of the sane." He has spent a lifetime figuring out who he is, what happened in his family, why people do what they do. Except about Faulkner, to whom Bezzerides has an abiding attachment (he wrote a feature documentary, *William Faulkner: A Life On Paper*, for PBS in the late '70s, and appears in all of the Faulkner biographies), he rarely reminisces, about family or film, unless it's to make a point about the present.

"Boy, what a business, I'll tell you! Producers!," he says, sitting in a booth at Denny's one afternoon. "They think they understand writing. But there's nothing, no picture, until a writer, even a bad writer, sits down and writes a story, beginning with the first letter of the first word."

Bezzerides likes to pretend that he disdains his writing for film, but this has less to do with his view of the craft than with a subject dear to all screenwriters: the way good writing can be ruined by the process of filmmaking. Behind even his most respected films there are many stories of what might have been. In an interview by Lee Server, Bezzerides recalls,

These non-writers think they can do what they want to a carefully constructed script and it won't turn into a piece of crap. They're wrong. But nobody tells them that. Fox bought . . . *Thieves' Market*. They didn't want to use the original title because "San Francisco objects to it." So, *Thieves' Highway*. So who cares? I said okay. Then the director, Julie Dassin, says, "For the prostitute, I want Valentina Cortesa, so rewrite it for her." He was going with her. We were going to have Shelley Winters, who would have been perfect. This Italian, Cortesa, what would she be doing in this story? I said, "But . . . Julie! But I rewrote it. And we go to the meeting with Zanuck—and already the picture is getting fucked up before that . . .

Now in my story the father is dead at the beginning. The kid starts trucking because he's trying to make his father's life valid. The first thing Zanuck says is, "I want a new beginning. I want the father still alive. He's crippled, that's why the kid's trucking." It was bullshit. But I said, "Yes, Mr. Zanuck." I write another beginning, this revenge business. The picture didn't do real well. There were good things in it, but it wasn't the picture I wanted to do, it wasn't the story I wanted to do. I had the producer's chickenshit changes, the director's girlfriend, and Zanuck's ideas. I only knew that story from my life, my book, my script. But that didn't matter. Oh, I tell you, once you give in a little bit you're finished.[2]

Filming of *Thieves' Highway* began on November 8, 1948. As for *On Dangerous Ground* and *Kiss Me Deadly*, Bezzerides was on the set during the entire shoot and personally scouted all of the locations, which included Highway 99, San Francisco, Oakland, Sebastopol, Calistoga, Santa Rosa, Hueneme, and Oxnard. At the time, Richard Conte was one of Fox's most dependable actors and had just been awarded a new seven-year contract after the success of *Cry of the City* and *Call Northside 777*. (On March 3, 1948, the *Los Angeles Times* had announced that Victor Mature would star in the role.) National and local reviews were favorable: "A gripping presentation of stark, heavy drama," *Fortnight*, September 30, 1940. A reviewer for *Cue* wrote, in what now seems a forced nod to Dassin's documentarist style, "Filmed with astonishing realism . . . *Thieves' Highway* comes çlose to being—in addition to whopping good melodrama—one of the best documentaries about food distribution ever filmed." The *L.A. Examiner*, in a review published September 21, 1949, noted the "triteness of the bad girl with the heart of gold"—

failing to grasp the novelty of the hero's decision to leave his bour-
geois fiancée and remain with the prostitute—but went on to call
the film "a slice of life cut cleanly on all sides and pinned on the
screen with unrelenting realism."

Thieves' Highway grossed $1.5 million in domestic rentals, plac-
ing it 89th for the year—a fair showing, given that the average
take for all but the top twenty was just over $2 million. The top
grosser for the year was *Jolson Sings Again*, at $5,500,000, followed
by *Pinky* and *I Was A Male War Bride*. The top-grossing actress in
1949 was Jeanne Crain.

Hovering always above the consuming work of supporting his
family by writing screenplays was Bezzerides's yearning to write
fiction, but family obligations kept him busy into the television
era, and he has not published another novel since *Thieves' Market*.
In the '40s and '50s, he wrote fourteen produced screenplays. Included in that number are four pictures for which he is sometimes
given partial credit or to which he made substantial uncredited contributions: *Action in the North Atlantic* (1943), a film credited, after
arbitration, to the more powerful John Howard Lawson; *Northern
Pursuit* (1943) and *Background to Danger* (1943), both credited at
times to either Bezzerides or to W. R. Burnett; and *Desert Fury*
(1947), credited to Robert Rossen.

Bezzerides's big break in television came in the mid-1960s,
when he created the series "The Big Valley" for Barbara Stanwyck.
As an antidote to "Bonanza," he developed a role for the main character's daughter, and as he originally conceived it, the series would
have included many stories about immigrants in the Central Valley.
In another common Hollywood transaction, the producers saw to it
that the series—one of the most popular syndicated shows in history—never turned a profit on paper, and Bezzerides was denied
a share in what had certainly been a lucrative four-year run and a
successful launch into syndication. (According to Bezzerides, Stanwyck threatened to sue for her share of the profits—an option
Bezzerides could not afford at the time—and received a settlement
out of court.)

Three of Bezzerides's films are included in nearly all of the film
noir anthologies: *Thieves' Highway, On Dangerous Ground* (1951), di-

rected by Nicholas Ray and starring Robert Ryan and Ida Lupino, and *Kiss Me Deadly*. All three were made by directors who have received a great deal of attention, with the result that Bezzerides's contributions to many aspects of each film have often been overlooked. Although the latter two were based on popular novels (*On Dangerous Ground* was written from Gerald Butler's *Mad With Much Heart*), each has the unmistakable stamp of his interests, from car culture to the psychology of male violence. The most personal of his films—including *Thieves' Highway*, which though based on his own material was nevertheless restricted to a very specific milieu— is *Kiss Me Deadly*, one of the most influential American films in the postwar era. Sitting at his typewriter at home, bored with the formulaic motivations for murder in Spillane's novel—money, drugs—he simply set the book aside and invented a movie out of his own thoroughgoing revulsion at humanity's race toward annihilation.

With *Kiss Me Deadly*, as with many of the films that now form the permanent center of the otherwise fluid film noir canon, French critics hit the mark from the beginning. In a review of *Kiss Me Deadly* in Jean-Jacques Pauvert and Michel Laclos's surrealist literary revue *Bizzare*, Louis Seguin wrote:

> The hero of a film must always, as certain "moralists" argue, meet with our sympathy, if not our estime. Mike Hammer is no exception, not because he will be saved by the action of a mysterious grace that happily is rigorously absent from *Kiss Me Deadly*, and not by his final submission to a police force that has no idea what to do apart from spew insults and whose least reprehensible representative is a self-righteous homosexual, but because, while everything collapses around him at the death of Va-Va-Voom, he finds the sympathy of a barman and a wonderful singer, both of them black. The single fact, moreover, that in an American film the only human characters are a Greek, therefore a "greaseball," and "negroes" should give pause to those who are so quick to scream sadism and immorality against it matters not what film noir, this one of Aldrich's included. This choice of characters is far preferable

to the ethic, standard in such films, of the weak-man-victim-ized-by-the-evil-woman.

I might also add, in favor of its ethic, that Aldrich's film is profoundly feminist. The tortured Christina dies without divulging her secret; Velda, her face wet with perspiration, sacrifices herself in a way that is altogether rare to find; and who could forget the ravaged voice with which [Lili] Carver murmurs, before killing and dying, "Kiss me, Mike."[3]

What Seguin was saying—to conservative French critics—is that the film is profoundly moral. Behind everything Bezzerides writes is an apprehension of what the world could be but isn't. In the moral universe of the film, everyone is degraded, men and women, but also empowered to carry their prescribed roles to extremes. Lili Carver, of her own will—the only freedom allowed in the film—chooses, like all of the men, including Hammer, to pursue the Great Whatsit. Beneath the shockingly brutal misogyny apparent on the film's surface, a seeming hatred of women that is all too undeniably genuine in most films of this kind, is Bezzerides's belief that the system we have created is an equal opportunity destroyer. There are no *femmes fatales* in *Kiss Me Deadly*, just as there are no heroes. The only people in the film outside of this loop of destruction, and the only ones to show kindness, are the servants—immigrants and the descendants of slaves.

Shortly before he died, Aldrich phoned Bezzerides. "He wanted to tell me," Bezzerides recalls, "that he had just reread my script for *Kiss Me Deadly*." When Bezzerides asked why, Aldrich replied, "I wanted to see how I could've shot it in three weeks. You know what? It was all there."

All three of Bezzerides's novels have been called proletarian, although they do not appear in most of the literature on the subject. Given the writers he collaborated with over the years—Meyer Levin, John Howard Lawson, Alvah Bessie—and the salient themes of his writing, he would seem to have been an inevitable candidate for the Hollywood blacklist. *Thieves' Highway* was Jules Dassin's last film in America (preceded by *Brute Force* in 1947 and *The Naked City* in 1948) before he was blacklisted and moved to London,

where he made another noir classic, *Night and the City*, in 1950.
Bezzerides did, in fact, narrowly escape the blacklist. In the late
'40s, he was teaching at Hollywood's famous "Little Red School-
house," where many Communist Party members taught. "I said to
that whole class," he recalls, "if you think writing a story about a
bunch of union workers going on a strike is a story, you're mistaken, because it's how you write, not the subject that you pick,
that I'm interested in. And half of the class got up and walked out.
They were Communists. I was left with about thirty students, and
they stayed and had fun while I was teaching."[4]

Although not a Communist, as Bezzerides tells it, his name was
placed on the blacklist merely for having taught at the school. In
1950, MGM was about to buy the film rights to an unpublished
Bezzerides novel, *Not Too Big A Dream*, about his father's belief that
he would get rich in America. When he showed up at the studio to
sign the contract, he was notified by an MGM executive that his
name was on the list, and that the film would not be purchased.
Bezzerides told the executive what he had told his students, that he
had never considered joining a party of any kind, Communist or
otherwise. MGM bought the novel, and subsequently, although
the picture was not made for other reasons, his name disappeared
from the list, demonstrating once again the capriciousness and cul-
pability of the studios in the imposition of the blacklist.

Like *Long Haul*, *Thieves' Market* was written directly from Bezzerides's experiences as a trucker with his father and in the fields
and packing houses of California's Central Valley—the breadbasket
of the world—and in the markets of Stockton, Oakland, San Francisco and Los Angeles. His personal experience of the unbridled
cheating and brutality that characterize the novel is the basis for his
politics, and for whatever resemblance his characters have to others
in film noir.

A passage late in *Thieves' Market* provides a key to the bleak view
of human relations that Bezzerides learned as a young man and that
continues to inform his writing:

He had started so bravely, quitting his job and buying the

truck and venturing to find a load, but now it was all gone, all
the fine bravery gone. You had to be hard and shrewd, very
hard and shrewd, more shrewd than he could ever be. It was
not buying and selling. It was standing toe to toe and slugging at each other in a combat of such ferocity that he knew
he would never be able to beat anyone down, but would always be the first to drop his arms, more in awe than in defeat
that his opponent could put up such a fight for money, just
money, not much money, not more than hardly enough for a
person to live decently, if one had the time to live at all . . . [5]

Far more despairing than the film, which ends with the dramatic
arrival of Cortesa with the police before Conte has a chance to finish beating Cobb and perhaps kill him, the novel opens with broken dreams, after the death of an immigrant father, seen through
the eyes of an assimilated son who has yet to make good, and
through the eyes of a disappointed immigrant mother who hated
the father because of his failure to realize the American promise of
wealth and prosperity. Family values have evaporated in the face of
survival and greed, and mother and son have turned against one
another, bickering not only over what's left—insurance money that
has become the old man's only real accomplishment in the new
world—but also over the memory of the father as a representative
of old world honesty, which was his undoing.

For the mother, this is evidence of failure—the father had the
dream and the talent, but wasn't cunning enough—and for the
son, another kind of failure, because he knows that the new world
is corrupt, that the ruthless succeed, and that old-world values are
the values of weakness.

A. I. Bezzerides's *Thieves' Market* is a fitting addition to the University of California's valuable California Fiction series. Looking
back, it is tempting, especially given Bezzerides's reputation as a
screenwriter, to view the novel only in the tradition of hard-boiled
fiction of the 1940s. In fact, it was an attempt by the author to ex-
plore his real experience as a young California trucker in a work of
serious commercial fiction. His influences were those of many writ-

ers at the time: Hemingway, Faulkner (to whom Bezzerides once introduced himself in a Hollywood restaurant years before working in film), Katherine Mansfield. His themes—California as a land of opportunity, the clash of immigrant values with those of America and the resulting loss of innocence—are as current now as then.

Garrett White
Hollywood, January 1997

1. Taped interview with Garrett White, Woodland Hills, CA, 1995.
2. Lee Server, *Screenwriter: Words Become Pictures, Interviews with twelve screenwriters from the golden age of American movies* (Pittstown, New Jersey: The Main Street Press, 1987), 40–42.
3. Louis Seguin, "Kiss Me Mike," *Bizarre* (Paris, October 1955, No. II), 68–71, my translation.
4. Taped interview with Garrett White, Woodland Hills, CA, 1996.
5. P. 224, below.

THIEVES' MARKET

1

NICK awoke, shivering.

A sound had wakened him, he did not know what. Outside,
high up, the moon was shining. It filled the night with a luminous
glow that made him feel airy and weak. He tried to rise, but he felt
trapped in bed. He pressed his hands on the mattress, but he could
only raise his head.

The sound came again and he lay quietly, listening. Box cars
slammed together in the freight yard far across town. Crickets
chirred in the rose bushes beside the house. Their song gave him
a memory of big red roses blossoming in Spring. But now it was
Autumn and the roses had long since blown and in their place were
the golden rose hips, swollen on the thorny stem. In these first cold
Autumn days, the trees were changing color, dropping leaf, pre-
paring for Winter. In the harvested vineyards and orchards of the
San Joaquin Valley, another season had ended.

A car passed, rattling its fenders. Mice scratched on the raw
side of the wall. He could hear them chirping, and a memory of
mice came over him. How long have we been living in this house,
he thought. A long time. I was a boy then, seven maybe; my grandmother was with us, and then she died. It was in this house. He
remembered the scamper of mice in the walls, the scratch of their
feet on the floor, the clatter of a pan they had overturned in the
kitchen. I used to think it was my grandmother's ghost, he thought,
coming back every night to tidy the house. He remembered the
sharp snap of a trap and the next morning finding the dead mouse
and flushing it down the toilet and the body of the mouse sliding
through the underground maze of pipes to the sewer farm
clear across town.

1

Was it the house that had awakened him? Year after year, the house creaked and thumped, settling on its foundations, adjusting itself to the earth that was settling too. Or it could have been the toilet on the back porch. Something was wrong with the float and it flushed itself regular as breath, day and night water cascading through the pipes, then the sighing of the reservoir as it filled again.

It was none of these sounds that had wakened him, for whatever it was had made his face pucker and his eyes burn and filled him with an indefinable sadness. The paralysis had left him now and he could rise, but he felt dizzy and faint. All the night sounds were far away, as though in a dream, and his head swam as he sat on the edge of the bed. The sound came again.

It was his mother crying. Now that he was able to identify it, he wondered why he had not recognized it before. She was crying softly in the dark, saying a word over and over, caressingly, finding comfort in it, but what she was saying, he could not tell. He had an impulse to run to his mother and comfort her, as though something within him were unguarded for a moment; but it alerted instantly, and the hatred he felt for his mother reasserted itself.

He stood up.

Far across town, a train bell rang, making a church sound in the night. As Nick stood listening to the slow tolling of the bell, his eyes spurted tears, and there came upon him a memory of his father. The old man, seventy-three, had died and been buried more than a week ago but for a moment Nick forgot that he was dead and not lying on his cot in the living room. "Pa?" he started to call out, but he choked the cry. He thought of his father, Yanko Garcos, full of piss and vinegar, as good a man as any man. He had been sick over a year, never getting well, but steadily ailing until toward the end he could not get up and had to be fed and panned in bed. He could not be given a proper bath and his body broke out in sores and he began to smell of the sweet smell of decay. He had been a big man once, walking loud, talking loud, trying to make his scratch upon the world, but he grew older and older, shrank smaller and smaller until one day the stride that had been hard and vigorous faltered and tripped him into the cot in

the living room where the wood stove burned all night to keep his
thinning blood warm. His head shrank until it became a death's
head, but his eyes grew bigger and bigger until all that seemed left
of him were his shining eyes looking feverishly about the room.
He could not sleep. He would toss for hours on the cot, sighing
endlessly, and call out softly in the middle of the night:
"Nikko?"
"What, Pop?"
"Nikko, I just think."
"What are you thinking?"
"When I get well, we work together, huh?"
"You said it, pop."
"No good working in packing house. Waste your life. If you
want to get somewhere, work for yourself. You hear me, Nick?"
"You bet. We're going to work for ourselves."
"That's right. We going to work together. Yanko Garcos and
Son, fruits and produce. We're going to buy truck." A shrewd look
would come into Nick's father's face. "Nikko, why you don't ask
where I'm going to get the money?"
"You'll get it, pop."
"You bet I get it. I find somewhere. Someday we're going to be
bigger than Tartarian Brothers."
"You're frigging right, Pa." Nick would look down on his
dreaming father. He was always dreaming. That's the way you do
things, the old man used to say. First you dream and then you
make the dream come true; but first the dream.
It was hard for Nick to believe that his father was gone, his
earthly possessions gone, the mattress burned and his clothes given
away, the iron cot sold to the junk man and all that remained of
him was the smell of man, seventy-three years of living and nothing left but the smell of tobacco and pipe and old socks and sweaty
clothes. Nick had only to shut his eyes and he could see his father
lying on his death bed, his breath rattling. Pa, Nick had shouted,
but the old man could not hear. His mouth hung open. His eyes
were glazed and he kept flapping his hand. Interminably his breath
rattled as he drowned in his spit, but suddenly he sat bolt upright,
his eyes bright and young, and he shouted, in a voice full of joy,

his wife's name, Parthena! and fell back and died. My old man, trying to put his scratch on the world, Nick thought. He scratched it all right, six feet deep. He thought of his father lying in his grave, not as a body embalmed and preserved to eternity, but as a small cardboard box full of ashes. It had rained the day he was buried, a hard soaking rain that flooded hills and fields until surely by now the box had dissolved and his father was a sodden lump of ashes.

The ringing of the train bell, small and distant in the night, smothered Nick in its clangor. He went down the hallway to his mother's room.

He stood at the door, trying to hear what she was saying, but he could not hear and he leaned over the bed and he could see her broad gross face, puckered with crying, saying the word over and over again, and now he could hear it, his father's name, Yanko! asking him to come back so she could be forgiven, so he could know it, if he could only know it, how much he was loved and how much he was needed.

Another memory came on Nick, of his father working in the coal yards of the town and coming home black with dust, of him unloading lumber from the flat cars over in Helbing's Mill; working in the farms, the vineyards and orchards of the valley, working in the packing houses, in the wineries, buying a wagon and a horse and peddling fruits and vegetables in the streets of Fresno, shouting, Fresh orangey, peachy, trying hard to make money to buy a farm, to buy a truck, not for himself but for wife and child, to make a foothold for them in the world. And in all this Nick saw his mother's sullen face. The only time it wreathed into smiles was when his father gave her money or bought her a gift or complimented her on how beautiful she was. You got pretty mama, boy, she make my heart sing, he would say to Nick, or he would say to Nick's grandmother, How do I touch this girl's heart, Mother? It's like stone, how do I touch it? And his grandmother would say, I don't know, my boy. You love her too much. You shouldn't love her so much, or if you do, you must not show it. And his father would say, But how can I help it, Mother?

Nick wondered how his father could love this petty, wicked

woman who loved only herself, and if she ever showed any affection for Nick it was only to prove to her husband that she was capable of affection. She had shown the old man nothing but cruelty all their married life, but after he died she displayed an unusual concern. Are you going to have him cremated, she had said. No, Mom, Nick had lied, "He's going to be embalmed and buried; and I got a plot for you, just like you said, so you can be near him when you die."

Good, she had replied, but what she did not know was that he had made arrangements to have her cremated too. Two lumps of ashes in the ground. The fire had purified his wasted father, and it would purify her too, burn away the evil and leave only clean ashes. He thought of it every time he looked at her, burned and reduced to ashes and clean. If she could only come alive while she was burning and know that she was being cremated, if he could only tell her how it was going to be. He continually played with the idea. Somehow he was going to tell her. He thought fiercely, you bet I am, as he remembered his father going quietly to her bed, his heart full of love and longing, the creaking of the bed as he got in beside her and his mother waking and saying in a voice full of loathing, Don't you touch me, and his father protesting in the mild way that he had and his mother screaming, You're not going to touch me, I don't want you to touch me, and his father slapping her and she cursing and saying in a voice hoarse with loathing, Don't you touch me, and his father saying, All right, girl, all right, be quiet, you'll wake the boy, I won't touch you, and returning to the sofa where he lay awake, heaving sighs.

Nick felt such a pity for his father, for the life that was wasted, all that breathing and living wasted, the dreaming wasted, the doing wasted, the loving wasted. His poor father, loving a woman so hard and only loathing coming of it, being loathed with every pore of her body, the way she tightened at his touch, the way she spat on him and the look that came upon her face. What had he done to deserve all this? Nothing. Just lived, the way men live, committed a few sins, a few thoughtless violences, but she had no capacity for forgiving, just a capacity for loathing, her life consumed with loathing.

"Hey, Mom," Nick said.

His mother gasped as she sat up in bed. She snapped on the light. She was a tremendous woman with thick flabby arms and a round puffy face. Her eyes were small and crafty and her mouth was thin and cruel. The bed was a huge brass bed which she filled completely, the ends leaning together under her weight.

"Oh, how you frightened me," she said in Greek.

"What the hell you bawling about?" Nick said.

"Your father. Why else would I cry?"

Nick thought of his mother taking care of his sick father. She begrudged him the least glass of water. She cursed him every time she brought him food or gave him medicine or gave him the pan. "You filthy old man, why don't you die?" he remembered her saying. "What did I do that God has to torture me like this. Why doesn't He take you. Dear sweet God, why don't you take him and clean this house of his filth!" and spat on him.

"I loved him," she said.

"Don't give me that crap," Nick said. "You hated his guts. You miss him because he ain't around for you to step on."

The mother's face became ugly, her voice nasty with the sibilances of Greek. "Yah! I miss him because he isn't around for me to step on. Is that it?"

"Don't feel bad, Ma. You'll have me around for a while. Step on me."

"I had a dog for a husband and now I have a dog for a son," the mother said, her voice charged with the familiar loathing. "That beastly father of yours, he had to go and die and leave me in your worthless hands."

"And I've got a bitch for a mother, so that makes us all dogs. Yanko, Yanko," Nick mocked his mother. "He died of a broken neck, the way you used to step on him."

"Listen to you, listen to you," the mother said. "You're no better than your father, you devil!"

"I'm glad he's dead," Nick said. "It was the only way he could get out from under you. The way you used to yell at him and slap him down. All his life he had your foot on his neck. That's your kind of love."

"The thoughtless beast, he had to go and die and leave me destitute," the mother said. "How am I going to live, who's going to take care of me?" She began to cry again, clapping together her hands and shaking her head. "Yanko, Yanko," she said.

"Ah, for Christ's sake, cut it out, Ma," Nick said. "You know you're glad he's dead. Just think, if he lived, you wouldn't have four thousand bucks."

His mother instantly stopped crying and her eyes became suspicious. "What four thousand?" she said.

"The money you got from his insurance," Nick said. "You think I don't know, but I do."

"It's my money."

"Sure it's your money. You took out the insurance and prayed for him to die, but he wouldn't die, and you had to pay on it for years."

"You think you're going to get it, but you're not."

"Where do you keep it, Ma?"

"It's in a good place. You'll never find it. The worthless old man. I thought he was never going to die. It's my money, all of it."

"Why don't you keep it in the mattress? Maybe it'll hatch. Is that where you've got it, Ma?"

The breath hissed from his mother as she darted a quick look toward the closet.

"Pa knew all about it," Nick said. "You know what he told me? He said it was mine. He said if he died, for me to take it. Will you give it to me, Ma?"

"I won't give it."

"Okay, spend it on yourself then. And you'd better hurry, because you're not going to live forever."

"You think I'm going to die, but I'm not. I'm going to live and I'm not going to spend my money, not any of it. You're going to take care of me. You're my son."

"Sure, Ma; and you're my sweet mother." Nick reached over to switch out the light, but his mother caught his hand and clutched it to her cheek. "He never listened to me," she said. "He treated me as though I were a stranger."

"Okay, Ma," Nick said. He tried to free his hand, but the

more he pulled, the tighter she pressed it into the spongy, tear-soaked flesh of her cheek.

"I'm alone in the world," she said. "I haven't anyone. What will become of me?"

"You've got yourself, Ma," Nick jerked his hand free.

"Don't leave me, Nikko," his mother said. "You're all I have now. Lie with me, like you used to when you were a little boy. Let me hold you so I can sleep."

Nick looked at his mother. As he stepped from the room he heard her say in Greek, hissing the words with the hatred that filled her, "You're not my son, you're a devil, that's what you are."

Nick returned to his bed. The sheets, moist from perspiration, had turned frigid and he shivered as he drew them over him. It was still early morning, hours until daylight. His mother turned off the lamp, and the night sounds which had retreated in the light, now came forth in the darkness. The busy singing of the crickets, the box cars slamming together in the freight yard, the footsteps of some night walker echoing and hollow in the silence. Far off a train whistle blew and he could hear the swift rattle of steel wheels on steel rails, going and going, diminishing into the long night cave. His mother began to cry again, saying his father's name over and over.

A picture of his father came into Nick's head, his face smiling. At first it was very clear so he could see his tobacco-stained mustache and yellowed teeth and his friendly brown eyes. Then it drew away, became very small and finally faded.

2

"NIKKO!" a voice said, in Greek, and a hand tugged at him, dragging him through the syrup of sleep. "Nikko, it's after six, you'll be late. Get up!" The hand whipped the cover from him and he lay cringing on the bed.

Ah Christ, Nick thought. He ached at the prospect of dressing and eating and going all the way through town to Gugenheim's packing house where he worked in the fig sheds. The season's crop of dried Calymyrna figs was beginning to come in and the trucks would be lined up, forty in a row, waiting to be unloaded. "Leave me alone, Ma." Nick groped for the cover to pull it back, but his mother had thrown it to the floor and he could not find it.

"Don't think I don't want you to sleep," his mother said in Greek, her voice persuasive and affectionate. "Of course I do, but it's getting late and you have to be on your way. Come along, lamb, you'll feel better once you get up. There's my boy, there you are, that's it."

Nick felt himself helped to the edge of the bed, and a robe being thrown over him. He held his head a moment, poisoned with the thought of going to work. The packing house with its slippery floors and clatter of machinery and stench of wet figs revolted him. When he had first gone to work, he found pleasure in watching the women at the packing benches, the way their bodies filled out the blue dresses that were the packing house uniform, but that pleasure was gone now. Most of the women were old, with shapeless, breastless bodies and coarse unattractive faces. Even the young ones had no appeal for him, they were so busy grading, culling, cutting, packing, forgetting to be women in their haste to make money.

Nick quivered with the longing to kick his mother from the room, pick up the bedcover and return to sleep, but somehow he discovered the resolution to dress and he threw off the robe and swiftly began to put on his clothes: the gummy socks, the heavy sweat-soaked shoes, the soiled jeans, the shirt that was still caked with the salt of yesterday's perspiration. His clothes gave off an odor that stunned his senses.

His mother had poured coffee and was breaking eggs into a frying pan when he stepped into the kitchen. She had made great clumsy slices of toast from homemade bread, and a saucer of fig jam, thick with nodules of seed, was on the table. His mother smiled at him. One of her front teeth was missing, and it gaped through her smile. "Sit down and eat, Nikko," she said, pleasantly.

You bitch, Nick though, you're scared stiff I'm going to take your money and you're trying to sweet me out of it. She had always exercised this capacity for being affectionate on one hand, but cruel as a butcher on the other. She kept her objectives always in mind and worked toward them with whatever weapon she could use. It never failed to work on his father who could not see his wife for what she was but always viewed her as what he imagined her to be, this devious, scheming woman whose plans had become so transparent to Nick; at any cost to have shelter for her ugly body, money hidden in a safe place simply for the possession of it, and food to eat, with no thought or consideration for others.

"I'm not hungry," Nick said.

"But Nikko, my lamb, you have to eat," his mother said. "You work hard, you get tired. It's all ready for you."

"I'm not hungry." Nick started to go out, but mother blocked the door. She searched his face, but Nick avoided her eyes. Outside, the sun had come up and its light was fresh and strong on the bright yellowing leaves of the poplar tree. He could see the old chicken fence with its broken planks, clumsily mended with slats from lug boxes. His father's handiwork. Beyond the fence the chickens were singing and for some reason he saw his father, rushing among the squawking hens, catching one and stretching its neck on the wood stump he used as a chopping block. Raising the axe. The gleaming edge of the axe, the terrified eye of the chicken, the swift descent of the blade that never cut cleanly but always half severed the neck so that chicken and head went flopping, scattering blood over his father and the ground and the fallen leaves. My mother's neck, Nick thought.

"Why do we always hurt each other?" his mother said. "Why do we, Nikko?"

"You know why," Nick said quietly, and a cold frozen look came into his mother's face as though somewhere within herself she were tightening something into stone. She had changed in a subtle way. Her face was the same, she wore the same dress with the soiled front, its sleeve torn at the shoulder, her flat feet wore the same worn shoes which his father had cut out at the big toes to relieve pain, but all the same she was changed. There was an expression in her eyes, a quiet look of agony as though from some deep hurt. The look made Nick doubt his feelings about his mother and for an instant he passed through the fringes of shame for thinking so cruelly of her.

"Okay, Ma," he said.

The old woman shook her head. She sat at the table continuing to shake her head, caught in some great misery. She held out her hands helplessly, her mouth tightening to hold back a cry. She resembled a grotesque doll, one that could laugh or cry or sit soberly lost in thought, depending on Nick's whim. He had always blamed her for what she was, but for the first time he knew that she could not help it. She did not do the things she did deliberately but from some secret compulsion which even she did not understand. Nick began to laugh and his mother looked up, startled. He clapped her solidly on the shoulder, feeling the mass of flesh under his hand, and kissed her roughly on the neck. "Ah, what the hell, Ma," he said.

"Why are you laughing, Nikko?"

"You're some joker, Ma. Come on, get my eggs. You want me to be late?"

His mother got up and brought his eggs and Nick gulped them down and ate two slices of the toast, heavily buttered and piled high with jam, drank three cups of coffee and before he knew it, he was sitting in his jallopy, belching the hastily gobbled food as he went down Broadway, heading for work.

There was a boil of traffic on the street in front of Tartarian's gas station. It was a semi blocking the road. The big red van had on its side the sign *Tartarian Brothers, Fruits and Produce*. It was waiting for another truck, parked on the sidewalk, tractor at the pump, to pull out of the way.

The station was a big yard, jammed with trucks, all with the same sign on their sides, and over the pumps was an enlargement of the sign which said *Tartarian Bros., Truck Service*. Men walked briskly, pushing carts, carrying batteries, delivering manifest sheets that fluttered in the morning breeze. There was a great activity over the grease pits that were lined with trucks, and in the garage at the back four men were lifting with great labor an engine from a gutted truck, while on the ground lay the new engine waiting to be installed.

Someone in one of the cars shouted, "Hey, get your ass out of the street," and horns blew, but no one in the semi or on the lot paid any attention. They had no regard for the traffic in the street or the workers who were anxious to get to the packing house, but were concerned only with their own activities, taking their holy time.

As Nick waited, the car shaking beneath him with the idling of the engine, he counted the trucks on the lot. Seven, not counting the ones that were probably rolling the highways, hauling north and south to the big cities, Oakland, San Francisco, Los Angeles, and Portland and Seattle, lugging bulging crates of lettuce and celery from Salinas or spinach and asparagus from Stockton, or corn down from the north. Tartarians, the lucky bastards, Nick thought. Fifteen years ago, old Haig Tartarian, a lean spit of a man who was always smoking badly rolled cigarettes that came apart in his mouth, with a peculiar way of holding them, clumsy fingered, as though in all the years of smoking he had not learned to manipulate the cigarette, this old man from Bitlis, with the green shrewd eyes of the Bitlistsi had started with no more than Nick's father, less than two bits in his pocket and an old model T,

worm-drive Ford truck. He had started with even less, for it was
Nick's father who had provided the idea that the thousand acres
of vineyards which had already been harvested could be made to
yield still another crop. So on a gray day late in Autumn, with the
sky loaded up with the first fall rains, Haig and Yanko had gone
through hundreds of acres of Malaga vineyards, at a time when
the crop pickers had departed and the field trucks were put away
and already the pruners were cutting the vine tentacles and throwing them into steel sided wagons to be burned; and they had
harvested the stray bunches of grapes which the pickers had passed
by. They had not even asked for permission, but had driven their
two trucks down the vine rows unmolested, for who would believe that loads of grapes could still be culled from vines that were
yellowing and dropping leaves. The two men had cropped two
loads of Malagas at a time when there were no grapes and prices
were high. But Nick's father had failed, while old man Tartarian
had taken this simple beginning and expanded it to prosperity
until he owned fleets of trucks, and old Haig, retired these days,
went around in pointed shoes and tight pants that bulged at the
crotch and pink silk Armenian shirts, soiled under the armpits;
and his five sons, who were once lean and tanned black, had retired too. Instead of striding about fiercely, cursing and making
their way, they ran the outfit from desks or shining cars, every
year a new one for each of the whole crew. They lost their hawk-
ish looks and sported sleek wives in stone marten furs and spent
their idle time fishing or racing speed boats in the lakes or playing
poker at Ambrose Brothers Cafe while others did the work that
once enslaved them.

Why? Nick thought. Tartarian's wife Ahna was the answer.
She was one of these black Armenians with coarse black hair, thinning at the crown, and live dark eyes that brought an indefinable
beauty to the thin ugly face with its scrawny muscular neck and
sinewy body. There were secrets between Tartarian and his wife,
in the way they looked at each other in the house or in the yard
or clear across the meadow at the river picnics, secrets that made
Tartarian strut and stroke his mustache and lighted a fire in his
eye. The moistening of eye, the erection of spirit when they were

together, these two who kept each other in a continual state of heat
simply by knowing one belonged to the other. "What's that scratch
on your face?" Nick once heard a man ask Tartarian, and Tartarian laughed a mysterious laugh and replied, "My woman. When
I give it to her, she screams and bites and sometimes when I give
it to her hard, she claws my face like a cat." The men looked at
each other and one of them asked, "What about the children,
don't they hear?" And Tartarian said, "The pillow in her face.
That keeps her quiet."

When the women discussed their frustrated sex lives at ladies
aid socials, Ahna Tartarian always smiled and when women asked
her, "Ahna, why do you smile in such a way?" she replied, "My
Haig gives me all I need. I have no complaints." It was always "my
Haig." She was endlessly exalting him, boosting him, building
him up. It was Ahna and the bed and the success in the bed that
brought success to Haig's life and gave him five lusty, vigorous,
profane sons who were the embodiment of this success. A happy
family, man and wife always touching each other in the proper
places with a look or a thought or the hands or the body or all of
it together at night in a bed that had been reinforced to take the
onslaught of loving, the springs of which had been greased in
broad daylight in the yard, with the sons helping, so they would
not squeak in the dark, as though such a tumult could ever be
silenced.

Over by the pumps, Frank Tartarian, in a tailor-made, double-
breasted imported tweed suit, the coat of which was opened because of the morning heat, was testing a new trout rod, springing
it whip-like in his hand.

"What have you got there, Frank?" one of the drivers said.

"New pole," Frank said. "Telescopes instead of coming
apart."

"Where the hell you gonna catch trout this time of the year?"

"Canada."

Canada, just like that. The whole frigging outfit could move
out of town, hell bent on vacations, and the business was so worked
up it would run itself, loads picked and hauled and sold and the
money pouring in. Nick burned with envy. Somehow he felt that

what the Tartarians had might as well have been his, but something had gone wrong, somewhere his old man had slipped up. He had dreamed just as loftily as Tartarian, worked just as hard, but the dream had died, and it was Nick's mother who had killed it with the way she had of sneering at her man, cutting him down, cursing his life with her hatred.

The semi cleared the street and traffic began to move.

The packing house whistle blew just as Nick pulled into the parking lot. He was late. He parked his roadster and as he hurried down the long row of cars, he thought how much these cars with their banged up bodies and torn fenders and broken bumpers, the upholstery worn through to the stuffing, the battered tires booted and vulcanized and retreaded until they disintegrated on the wheel when they were not thrown aside but cut into curving lengths to be burned in the living room stove during Winter, how much these cars resembled the workers who owned them. Their engines knocked and their exhausts blew oil and for fuel they burned not high octane gas with tetra-ethyl lead, but the cheapest gas that money could buy at rickety stations that said on big signs, *SAVE FOUR CENTS,* forget the anti-knock quality.

At nights when the cars were gone and the lot was empty, the ground was seen to be caked with grease and oil and patches of rusty water. But the lot was never completely empty, for there were always one or two jallopies that had quietly given up the ghost while standing in the sun, and their drivers could be seen, arms black with grease up to the elbows, trying to goose them into starting.

Nick went up the steps to the time clock. The planks that made the steps and platform were cracked and splintered and where the trucks had backed into the dock the beams were smashed. At the far end of the packing house, men were unloading trucks, moving with the deliberation that said, we work straight time, four bits an hour and we've got all day. But in the packing house where the women packers stood in a long line on pedestals in front of the packing benches, the work was more urgent, for here the work was by the piece, and their hands flew, wielding the little knife, the blade of which was taped so only the glittering point was exposed, carving the wet figs, trimming, culling, rejecting in swift nervous movements that bewildered the eye.

Nick punched in. Ten after seven. This meant that he would be paid for the half hour instead of the hour. Thirty-six dollars a week, less the income tax deduction, less the old age security and unemployment insurance. And now less whatever he would be docked for being late. Some day it'll be less the whole thirty-six bucks and the hell with it, Nick thought, as he entered the roaring space of the packing house. It was dark in here, lighted only by the raw light of globes that dangled on long cords from the ceiling that looked to be infinitely high. There were dark passages filled with the thunder of machinery, turning, shaking, pounding, the whir of belts smacking stickily on pulleys, the acrid smell of live steam on metal, the deafening hiss of it. Shadows drifted about, pushing hand trucks on which were boxes of figs piled to an unbelievable height. All of it soaked in the stench of wet figs.

He passed the long line of women dressed in shapeless blue dresses who stood on squarely planted feet, completely immobile except for the hands which worked as though possessed. They had been at it for only a few minutes, but already their dresses were splotched with sweat at the armpits, across the shoulders and at the backsides, and this was discounting the sweat that flooded down their necks, soaked their breasts and streamed down their braced thighs. There was an odor of female bodies. The sight of the women set something to palsying within Nick and he thought of his mother working in the packing houses too, making the circuit from Gugenheim's to Rosenberg's to Setrakian's to Sun Maid, in raisins and peaches and apricots and figs, but never on fancy pack, she was not good enough for fancy pack where the real money was, she was too clumsy, her hands were too big, she was always slicing the fat of her thumb into a million little cuts that became infected and remained red and irritated and never healed until the Winter lay-off. There were women who made eight, ten dollars a day, women with powerful arms and clever eyes who could coordinate eye and finger and knife so they wasted no motion except

now and then to cast a glance at their neighbors to see if they were
going faster; and if so, their hands went faster still. It was
as though these strong women from Germantown and Russian-
town and Armeniantown and Woptown were holding a contest to
see who could pack the most crates and make money. The winners
were the elite who ate in a little group, devouring their sandwiches
and spending the rest of the lunch hour rubbing down their arms
with olive oil and flexing their thick stubby fingers that were cal-
loused where the knife was held and where the blade had cut. The
jealousies, the intrigues, the quarrels. The women were always
spying on each other and reporting the crates that were carelessly
packed to the forelady, who would bring them back thirty at a time
to the woman who had packed them, causing her to lose precious
time.

There was ever present in the packing house a feeling of sex,
the men watching the women, nudging each other and pointing out
some big bottom or breast or mouth, finding the one beauty in
women who were coarse and unbeautiful and showing their arms
up to the elbow. *Oh boy, would I like to ram it to her.* And the
women, not unmindful of this, but from their places on the pedes-
tal, watching the men. *That Joe, that hair on his chest, ummmmmm!
Them big feet, you know what that means. What does it mean,
Esther. You know!* The leering eyes, the broad smiling faces of
the men and the ready hot responses of the women, as though they
were not human beings with the usual restraints and frustrations
of human beings but wild animals continually in heat and endlessly rutting. During lunch hour the men gathered together on
the platform and told dirty stories: *This guy wanted to marry this
girl, but he was worried about her being a virgin so he asks his
friend how he can find out and this friend says, well, get her to go
to a hotel and when you get her there, you undress and when she
says*—The ribald laughter, deep from the gut. Or the women in
their groups near the women's rest rooms would be eating their
lunch and a shrill excited voice would say: *Me and Harry, we goes
out last night over to Corbett's and we get some drinks, God did I
get cockeyed and he wants me to go up to his room but I wasn't*

*that cockeyed. So what did I do, so I went to his room, so what
did he do. Oh, My God, what didn't he do.* The women leaning
together and listening to what Harry had done, with gestures, and
suddenly that wonderful lusty deep-bellied laughter, and the men
stiffening as they listened to it. Them God damned women. Sometimes it got so you couldn't stand it and you wanted to grab one
and run to the shook shed where were stacked the fresh pine pieces
of unmade boxes, way in back on the sawdust floor, and tear off
her clothes, like that time that guy Stephen Jauss, a squat, pug-
nosed man with squinted merry eyes, and that woman Clara Schu-
man, a big shapeless blob of female, so much female that it was
her virtue, with a way of bouncing around, constantly peddling it.
One of the hand truckers saw them and gave the high sign and in
two seconds a mixed crowd of men and women was standing
behind the shed, watching until the observers were observed and
Jauss got up with his fly open and the woman with sawdust sticking to the moist patches of her back and they were both fired to
work in some other packing house.

When Nick's mother would relate these experiences at the
dinner table, his father would be jealous. The men are always
touching us with their hands, when they pass behind us, she would
say and Nick's father would say, Do they ever touch you? and his
mother would say, Of course they touch me, and Nick's father
would sit quietly, with the jealousy sharp in his face. And do you
like it? he would say, and Nick's mother would say, Sometimes I
like it. Sometimes I get a feeling, why doesn't somebody pick me
up and carry me behind the shook shed.

Nick's mother never made more than three dollars a day. She
would come home, complaining, Ahk, my hands, what's the matter
with them, they won't move? And she would take the taped knife
and go through the motions of packing, moving her hands so
rapidly that they blurred before the eye, but it was not fast enough,
never fast enough.

An Armenian woman named Markarit shouted without pausing
at her work, "Nikko, how's your mama?"

"She's fine," Nick said.

"She's rich, now your father die, huh?"

"I wish my old man die," one of the women said. "I collect all his insurance and buy myself a young husband."

"What you going to do with young husband, Esther?"

"I take care of him in daytime and he take care me at night," the woman said, and Nick emerged from the packing house through the hearty roar of bawdy female laughter.

Here in the yard, the sun was hot. There was a sudden spinning quiet in the air, a sensation of reeling backward. At first, in the brilliant light, there was a feeling of blindness but as he stood waiting for his vision to clear, the sheds burst into sight. He would be looking into space and suddenly a post would pop into view. The spaces between buildings would be empty, then he would see that a tractor had been hauling three yard trucks loaded with sweat boxes. He would look down at his feet and see nothing but blankness. Then the steps leading down into the hot yard would burst into view. He waited until the packing yard with its sheds and paths and men and tractors and the interminable stacks of boxes had materialized completely before he stepped carefully down the steps and traced his way along one of the paths.

The sandy soil burned through the soles of his shoes. The soft sand held his feet, retarding his steps as though he were walking in a bad dream. It was always hotter here in the yard than anywhere else in town, probably because of the ashy soil that caught the sunlight and bounced it against the galvanized tin walls of the storage sheds which bounced it back to the ground again, back and forth in a circuit that set the space between buildings into a blazing heat that was not dissipated with sunset but kept on, torrid and sweltering, long after night had fallen. Occasionally the intense heat started spontaneous fires and everywhere, along the ridges of the buildings and beside the walls were red, moss crusted barrels of water that evaporated under the sun and constantly had to be refilled.

A tractor passed, towing three yard wagons loaded high with sweat boxes filled with Muscat raisins. Nick hopped a ride on the last wagon and reached for a handful of raisins. The raisins were fresh from the vineyard, soft and not completely dry. A month in the sheds and they would be dry, hard and brittle on the filigree of stem.

He dropped off at shed F.

The shadowed inerior of the shed looked to be cool, but when Nick entered it was like stepping into an inferno. Intense, suffocating heat. The sun was like a torch on the metal walls and roof of the shed. There was a frenzied sense of choking, of catching for breath, of being smothered, as though the air were under pressure. Nick waded through this heat down a narrow passageway between high tiers of boxes into a space in the center of the vast cubicle of the shed. Here in the darkness that gradually became relieved as his eyes became accustomed to it, a gang of men, stripped to the waist, was working in pairs, picking up sweat boxes from a roller ramp that brought them in from the yard trucks outside, swinging them, onetwo*three*, up to men higher still who relayed them still higher to men on top of the tier of boxes. Box on box, the workers were slowly filling up the space.

As Nick stepped to his place, he saw that his partner Fanstock was working with a new man. Ganso, the shed boss, a paunchy old man with a beard like the jaw of an old dog, stepped out from behind the ramp. "Hey, you," he said to Nick, "what time you got?"

"About a quarter after seven," Nick said.

"That makes you late, don't it?"

"So it makes me late."

"If you'd cut out jacking off all night, maybe you could get up in the mornings and get to work in time."

"So dock me. It won't cost you a cent."

"Okay," Ganso said. "You work up there today."

"Where?" Nick said.

"On top."

On top was high on the tier of boxes, directly beneath the galvanized tin roof where the heat was terrific. Nick had spent four months on top. It was the place new workers went and graduated to the floor as old workers were fired or quit. A day up there and a man came down wrung dry, exhausted to the marrow. He came down parched, for Ganso would not permit the men to go for water, but forced them to drink from a common jug that tasted of spit by the time day ended, so that by quitting time you were so thirsty you had to bury your face in your hands cupped under the faucet and drink the way a horse drinks, sucking it in until you ran out of breath and you raised your dripping head for a gasp of air and plunged it back into the water.

Ganso pinched Nick's arm. "Okay, up you go," he said.

"I already spent my stretch up there," Nick said.

"Well, you're back for another stretch," Ganso said.

"The hell with you," Nick said.

"Go up or quit."

"Okay, I quit."

Nick started to walk off, but Ganso grabbed his arm. "Like hell," he said. "You work up there until I find somebody to take your place." He gave Nick a shove.

Ganso stood before Nick, blocking his path and Nick said, "If you don't get out of my way, I'm going to walk right through you."

The men stopped working and Ganso braced himself, waiting for Nick, who stepped steadily toward him, as though he were not there, with a look on his face that said, Don't move, you son of a bitch, stand right there because there's nothing I'd like more than to walk right through you. But at the last moment Ganso stepped aside and Nick went out into the sun-blasted yard. The sudden light blinded him and small white spots danced fiercely before his eyes. He felt very tired and he wanted to lean against the building, but the feeling passed and he went to his car.

He sat in the car, thinking, Now I'll have to get another job in another packing house or get in the crops somewhere, but the season was ended. His head buzzed with plans which he discarded before he had thought them through and in the midst of it the feeling came to him that this was a thing that had happened to him before, a strange familiarity to it, as though in another life he had been caught in a similar trap and struggled just as now to get out of it. Escape. His father, perhaps, yes it was his father who had sat in a wagon and tried to plan his life, way back when he was a young man with a wife and child. He had a feeling that his father had gone through the same thing and he thought, Not me, it isn't going to happen to me. By now the sun had mounted into the sky and the dry air withered the rims of his nostrils as he breathed it in. Hot. But he was spared the day beneath the galvanized tin roof. Not me, he kept thinking. His head felt as though it were being clamped. I can go away, he thought. He sat speculating the distances he could go, but the fact was he had never been away from home except for a few trips he had taken with the track team when he was a kid in high school. Running the quarter mile, the runners walking around nervously at the starting line, not looking at each other, and if they did, shaking hands and wishing each other luck, Good luck, Jackson, I hope you win, after me. The starter checking his gun and saying, All right boys, and the runners getting into their holes, down on one knee. Now take your time boys, no hurry, if you break the gun, I'll penalize you five yards. On your marks, the long pause, get set, the long long pause as you got off your knee and leaned forward with your back level with the ground, balanced on your hands, waiting for it, then BANG, and sprinting forward, driving hard with your spiked shoes, swinging in to catch the pole and running in a big circle, that wonderful circle, winning or losing the circle, the endless circles he used to run and was still running and would continue to run if something did not happen in his life. A kid, he thought. Not so long ago. A kid still, tied by the umbilical cord which was cut but continued to connect him in many subtle ways to his mother. He thought of the way she used to slap him around, the hard words, the venomous looks, all things which should have driven him away from home long ago but which created in him instead a feeling of dependence, a need for her that was like a disease. He thought of the abused sense of responsibility which he felt for her. What would she do if he were gone, how would she live? It did not help to think of the money she had collected from the old man's insurance, four thousand dollars, which she hoarded somewhere in the house, the closet perhaps, high on the shelf, beneath the bundles which contained the worthless old treasures of the family. Why did he feel so responsible for his mother when the truth was that it was he who needed her? In the midst of those depressing thoughts there came to him one bright thought: *the money*. It had been in the back of his mind all the time. He had toyed with the idea of taking it, buying a truck, buying loads, hauling, the way he had planned with his father. Four thousand dollars. He could go South and pick up a truck cheap at one of the War Surplus sales, then scout around for a load. He had teased himself with the idea, but had always rejected it out of guilt, but now the plan stood up clearly, the one brilliant thought he had had in a long time, beautifully stated, with all the rationalization marshalled behind it, justifying, prompting. It's your money, Pop wanted you to have it, so take it, do what Pop wanted to do, try once again and in all his life of failure make for him his one success; for you, sure, but for Pop too, mostly for him. He knew he was going to take the four thousand dollars and it frightened him to think that he was going to do it. Some timid part of his nature said, Don't do it. But I'm going to do it, he thought. Frig Mom, let her try to stop me.

But the timid part of him said, Talk it over with Polly. It was too much guilt for one to take. Share it with Polly. It was not nine o'clock yet, she would just be going to work. He could catch her at the door and discuss it with her.

He started the car. The engine came to life with a sudden rattle of exhaust, its bearings knocking until the oil had worked into them.

3

AT THIS hour of the morning, Fulton Street was quiet. There were a few people walking around, a few cars parked at the curbs, the day just beginning. There was not the bustle of early Summer, with crops ripening in the vineyards and orchards, and kids fresh out of school invading the town. The sky was not blue, as in Spring, but gray, as though the dust of Summer, from the commotions of plowing and discing and harvest-gathering had mounted into the sky and was waiting there for the first rains to wash it down. The tramps, who had been working up to now in the crops, were back in the south end of town, sitting in doorways or at the gutters, with nothing to do, the whole empty Winter before them. Soon the few dollars they had in their pockets would be spent on wine and once again they would be on the ready charity of the town, singing for a handout at the Full Gospel Tabernacle, or hitting people on the streets for a dime, or not a dime, not in these days, but a quarter, brother, can you spare a quarter, two little bits.

By now, after the long hot Summer, the country all through the Valley was tinder dry and quick to burn. Fire in the mountains, snakes in the grass, the old man died with a bug up his ass. It was the season of forest fires, smoke filling the sky, and at night you could see the distant sullen glow and people would be standing on their porches, pointing out the remote blaze: Must be around Bass Lake, hell of a fire, hope it ain't over by Eagle Shit Peak, was goin' deer hunting up there this year. Old Jim Collier says he seen eleven bucks last Winter. Ah, that Jim, he can't see his own pecker to pee.

Nick's eyes sought the mountains, but the haze was too thick. Fresno was surrounded by the haze of Autumn, like a city lost in

24

space. But he did not need to see the mountains to know how they were, dark humps in the distance, towering very high. In the Winter they would be white with snow, the snow melting through Spring until all that remained by the end of Summer were white caps on the loftiest peaks. Then the caps too would melt and it was Autumn. Nick remembered his father standing on the front porch and looking toward the mountains. High Sierras. Huntington Lake. Crown Valley. Friant Dam. Kerchoff Dam. All the rivers, Kings and San Joaquin, Three Rivers, the headgate, the big flume. His father would look toward the distant mountains and say, Good snow this Winter, plenty water next year. Nick remembered his father's farm at Wahtoke. One hundred acres of Zinfandels, wine grapes, harvesting the crop and hauling it to the Great Western Winery. The yeasty smell of the winery, the dusty grapes being crushed, the juice of the grape pouring frothy and red into the vats. Irrigating the vines with the water that came down from the mountains and flowed among the rivers and canals and ditches, to the vine rows. Standing knee deep in mud, tending the rows, working all day under the sun and all night in the moonlight. He thought of how hard he and his father used to work, and how his father had finally lost the farm. No more farm, no reason to worry about next season's water, but the old man continued to stand on the porch and measure the snowfall, or watch the Spring rains. *Good rain, good for the crops.*

Nick stopped in front of the S. H. Kress store where Polly worked. An old pick-up pulled in ahead of him. The truck body was crusted with dust, and the two men in it, one young and one old, both wiry and hard looking, burned red from the sun, were cattle ranchers from the West Side. They got down and walked past Nick with stiff-kneed strides, their legs accustomed to riding horses, unfamiliar to walking.

Although the store was not open, a line of women was waiting before it. Nick went past the line to the door and pressed his face to the glass. In the wide space of the store, girls were readying the counter for the day's business, replenishing the goods that had been sold the day before. Over at the candy tables two girls were emptying a wooden bucket of hard candy into a glass showcase, spread-

ing the mound with their hands. A sign in the window said,
CANDY SALE.

Polly worked at the stocking counter. She always wore sheer
black stockings that showed her legs with the black curling hairs
flat against the white flesh. She had good strong beautiful legs
that gave Nick a clean hot feeling. But Polly was not in.

Nick saw the floor supervisor, Rose Ash, of the peach orchard
Ashes, and he knocked on the glass. Behind him one of the women
said in a nasal Okie voice, "Seems like some folks'd git in line."
Nick rapped again on the glass, trying to catch Rose's attention. She
had worked in the store over twenty years, ever since she was a kid
out of high school. The store had become her life. She worked in it
all day and talked about it all night, always telling stories about people: There was this guy come in, and he wants to know if we got
any toys for kids and I says to him, you're too old to have kids,
Pop, and he says, ain't for mine, lady, they're for my great-grandchildren. I got forty-seven great-grandchildren, twenty-one grand-
children, fourteen children, all of 'em spanking alive. He bought
one hundred and sixty-three dollars worth of toys because he figured he wasn't going to live until next Christmas. He was over
ninety-four years old, so he was getting his shopping done early.
She had worked so long for the store that she was not working for
it any longer, but it was the store working for her, filling her life
with the adventures of the people who came into town.

Nick looked steadily at Rose through the glass, willing her to
see him, and he knocked again and Rose saw him and smiled. She
came to the door, smiling that big smile. "Hello, Nick," she said in
a languorous voice. "What's up?"

"Nothing's up," Nick said. "Polly in yet?"

"I think she's in the back. What do you want to see her about?"

"Just want to see her. I thought maybe she wasn't working yet."

"Didn't you see her last night?"

"Yeah, but I've got to see her again."

"I wish I had a boy friend who couldn't wait until tonight."

"You've got a lot of boy friends."

"Sure, but not any who can't wait."

"Will you get her?" Nick said, impatient.

"How long will you keep her?"

"Not any more than five minutes."

"Then I won't get her, not unless you promise me you'll keep her half an hour. An hour would be better."

Nick started to laugh. "Get her, will you?" he said.

"Oh, all right," Rose said.

She went away and Nick saw that the women in the line were smiling at him. They made him feel uncomfortable.

Polly came to the door. She was a short stocky girl with big breasts, an extremely narrow waist and broad full hips. Her backside was not flat, but big with firm well developed cheeks. She was an athletic girl and her body was not flabby but solid and hard. She looked to be all woman, good warm woman, one that could give as well as take. It was in her face that the woman stopped.

When you saw that face, you knew that the woman that was in the rest of her body was wasted. It was a good face, plain and round, but attractive. She had black hair, combed straight back, and her face had a good even tan, silky to look at, silky to touch. She had a wonderful mouth, the lips full and rounded, a good kissing mouth, and a strong tongue. Her eyebrows were a startling coarse-haired black that glistened, and her eyes were big and clear, beautiful brown, wonderful eyes. It was all fine, even to the eyes, marvelous in the eyes, but at the look it stopped. The look was cold. Where the rest of her drew Nick, suffocated him with longing, the look repelled him. He stopped at the cold look.

The first thing Polly said, when she opened the door, was "Nick, you knew I was working." She said it, unsmiling.

"Yes, but I had to see you."

"What about?"

"I want to talk to you."

"Well, go ahead and talk. What is it?" Polly's voice was unfriendly. She had a way of being disapproving, never sympathetic, never willing to anticipate his feelings and to make some effort to comfort him. She always made Nick feel that whatever he did, it was the wrong thing. "I'm in a hurry," she said in a testy irritated voice, "what do you want, what do you want?"

Nick squirmed under her questioning, feeling furious.

"Why aren't you at the packing house?"

"I quit my job."

"Oh, Nick, you didn't. What on earth for?"

"Because I wanted to."

"You make me sick. You're always quitting. Now look, you call 'em back and tell them you're sick, that you'll be to work in the morning. You do that, now. I've got to beat it. I'll see you tonight."

Nick looked quietly at Polly, his face set and angry.

"Oh, cut it out," Polly said. "If you could only see yourself. Cut it out and do what I told you and I'll see you tonight."

Nick stepped from the door. The women in the line had heard the argument and were smiling at him. They understood the game Polly was playing. He stepped toward his car parked down the street and he heard Polly call out in a voice that sounded annoyed, "Nick!" and the quick rattle of her heels as she ran to him and slipped her hand in his arm, trying to stop him. "Nicky." Her voice was better now, more tender and affectionate. "I'm sorry if I hurt you."

Nick did not answer. She had a way of turning on affection when being dominating did not work. The sensitive organism she had in her which told her when to be soft and when to be hard, always working under tension so it was one way or another, but never a relationship that was relaxed so they could be normal with each other. He always felt ill at ease with Polly, like a dog too often booted and never knowing when a pat was going to turn into a kick. He could hear her plugging along on her high heels beside him and without looking at her he could see her mother, Helen Faber, a woman with a sure loud manner of talking, big, bosomy, beautiful in a massive way, opinionated, the way she had of ramming her ideas into everyone's head. If she cooked a dinner, a strange dinner, devoid of spices or of any of the creative quality that good food has, such as the judicious use of tomatoes as in Armenian cooking, a dinner that was as colorless as it was tasteless, she would say, Wasn't that a wonderful dinner? It was a wonderful dinner, old man Faber would say. Or if they went to a show, and she said, Wasn't that a marvelous picture? this trite crap that Nick had seen a million times and would see a million more because there were only three theatres in town and you saw what they showed you, or else. It was a great picture, great, Mr. Faber would say. Nick could see this imperious woman lying in bed, covered with the tent of silk and lace that was her nightgown, nudging her husband with a heavy hand and saying, Harry, make love to me. And old man Faber complying and afterward Helen Faber saying, That was a wonderful love, Harry, and Harry, still un-consummated and smothered with the flurry of breath and massive breast and arms, would say, Yes it was, it was, dear. The poor old duck lying awake long after she had fallen into a snoring sleep, and wondering how he had got into this life with this woman who was day by day absorbing him until all that was left of him was a lean little lick of a man.

She had a quality of demanding the pay check, commanding de-votion, running old Faber's life, of being pleasant to get along with just so long as she got her will, but thwart her and what a female she became.

The game she was playing was a child's game that had got out of hand somehow and was no longer a game but a vicious chemical process in which one ego etched with acid another ego. Or it was a tactic that was endlessly flexible, adjusting itself to every situa-tion. If Mr. Faber came home full of fury and indignation then Helen would become sweet and affectionate until Mr. Faber low-ered his guard which was Helen's cue to stop the role of pretend-ing to be a loving wife and begin once more to wield a heavy hand, varying her behavior with fiendish cleverness, with one unvarying objective, to be cruel, to hurt Mr. Faber. But poor old Faber was beyond indignation. It was obvious in the quiet way he looked at his wife that he thought, My wife is a bitch, but what do I do about it? Nothing. The house and the wife and the child and the life, unsatisfactory though they were, were a web in which he was caught, and he was past struggling. So in another ten years or twenty or maybe a week or, who knows, within two days or tonight or possibly this day, August fourteenth, 1948, eleven A.M. this instant, right now, I'll die and it will be ended.

It was a new idea to Nick that old man Faber probably wished continually that he were dead. Thinking this cleared up a lot of things, the man's silence, his inability to protest, the way he sat in a chair, his thoughts far off while his wife talked in that all-knowing way. A quiet little man with a small cramped face, the beaten look in his face from the bludgeoning of the invisible weapon which his wife wielded so expertly. Nick remembered the way the woman would stop talking and say, You're not listening to me, dear, and Mr. Faber would say, Yes I was, love. Dear and Love, the wonderful language. Why didn't he look up once with his eyes smouldering and say, just once, No, I'm not listening so why don't you shut up, sweet?

Somewhere back in her childhood, Polly had watched her parents dueling, each with his weapon, and she had selected Helen's with absolute confidence that it would work. Hadn't it worked on her father all these years? So now she was working it on Nick, practicing it, refining it. Sometimes Nick wondered what Polly would have done if Mr. Faber ever turned on his wife and gave her a cracking blow on the jaw. What weapon would Polly have picked then?

"Well, what's bothering you now?" Nick heard Polly say beside him. "Go on, tell me, aren't you going to tell me?"

The hell with you, Nick thought. He considered what he was going to do when he got home and he decided that the guilt of stealing his mother's money was something he would have to bear himself.

Walking as he was with Polly, down the street, she was one thing, but when he was away from her, alone in his room or lying in bed thinking stray thoughts, she became something else, not Polly any longer but the girl he wanted her to be, someone who loved him and wanted to hold his hand and fondle his head, eager to listen to his plans, to encourage him. Such plans he had, to buy a truck, to buy loads, to sell them, not important in themselves except that they led to doing something for himself, to being on his own, which was very important. But how could he tell all this to this hard-headed, cold-eyed girl? She would laugh at him and ridicule his plans, try to force him into her own schemes. And she had schemes, Polly did: Work, save your money, put the down payment on a house, get married, have a child, just one because one would make it a tight knot, and live the long life tied down to the futility of a job, any job. It put lumps in Nick's head just to think about it. Well, what's wrong with it, Nick thought. Millions of people do it. What makes me think I'm so good that it shouldn't happen to me? But somewhere, somehow he had been poisoned and he could see through it all in a kind of swift pure wordless logic.

Polly's hard voice said beside him, "Are you going to tell me or aren't you, because if you aren't, I'm going back to work."

Nick pulled his arm away from Polly's hand. No, I'm not going to tell you, he wanted to say, so why don't you beat it? But he could not say it. He knew that she would walk away from him in a moment and that he would go on to his car and drive off, but he would be back, he would always be back. He needed her in the same perverse way that he needed his mother. They were two of a kind, his mother and Polly, attached to his vitals in a way that meant death to be parted.

"Okay," Polly said, and as her footsteps retreated behind Nick, such a lassitude came over him, such a feeling of helplessness and of being alone and unwanted in the world. Poor Nick, a voice said within him and he felt so heartsick he could hardly walk. Poor little Nikko, the voice said, in mockery, and such a wave of loathing for himself washed through Nick that miraculously he was purged of his self-pity and he felt resolute and strong. The hell with her, Nick thought. I don't need her. All I need is me and I've got me. I know what to do. All I've got to do is do it, so what about that?

4

NICK stopped the car in front of the house and got down. At this hour his mother was never home. She liked to walk downtown in the morning and pass through the stores where she never bought anything. Sometimes she would meet her old woman friends in the ladies' rest room at Radin Camp or at Gottschalk's where they sat and gossiped. Or she would go into Kress' and sit at the soft drink stand with Rose and have a malt. An old woman wandering about the town. But Nick was afraid to go into the house. A feeling came over him of being watched and he looked down the street which was empty. He searched the porches of the houses down the block. Even old man Buford, who was usually in his rocker where he kept an eye on all the doings in the neighborhood, was gone. The tennis players were swatting balls back and forth in Dickie playground.

Nick started to go up the steps when a voice called to him from the house next door. "Hello, Nick." The voice startled him so he could not answer. It was Mrs. Atkinson, sitting in plain view, easily seen, but Nick had not seen her. Her husband had made his money in mining, Alaska. Gold. Very rich. But he had lost it in land now. Very poor. But plenty of memories. He was always talking about the old days. A wirey old man, with the flushed cheeks of a drunk. He liked to smoke cigars and there was always the smell of whiskey on his breath. He was a permanent fixture on the porch, another geezer like Buford, keeping his finger on the pulse of the neighborhood from the perch of his rocking chair. He liked to snag Nick from the porch, calling out, "Hey, boy—" continually arresting him in his flight between porch and car to tell him stories of the old days. "Hot day today, boy. 'Minds me of the time when

it was hot like this up in the Yukon. You know, folks think it's
always cold in the North, but that ain't so. Well, on this hot day,
was late in Spring—" on and on, pouring the concrete of his story
around Nick's feet so he could not move. But the old man had
died. All the old folks in the neighborhood were dying off like
flies with hearses making trips late at night and carrying away their
corpses, these old people who lived through Spring and Summer
to die in Winter, passing away quietly in the middle of the night
so all you saw was an empty porch chair, or a lawn that had been
well tended suddenly continuing to grow until it dawned on you
that death had taken its tender. Or an old widow or widower standing behind a window with that lonely abstract look in their eyes.
Nick had last seen Mr. Atkinson sitting in his bathrobe on the
porch, looking pale and not long for this world and he said,
What's the matter, Doc, been sick? and Atkinson said, Yeah, had
a pretty narrow squeak, boy. But if I pull through this Winter, I'll
be okay. Can't wait to get me some of that old sun. But he had died
and here was old lady Atkinson sitting alone on her porch, snagging
him the way her husband had, "Hello, Nick."

"Morning, Mrs. Atkinson."

"Back from work so soon?"

"Yeah, things were kind of slack today."

"I think I'll get me a job. This sitting home all day."

"It must get kind of boring."

The conversation died away and Mrs. Atkinson's attention
wandered into space. Things must be kind of goofed up for her,
Nick thought. He used to hear the old couple quarreling in the
house. Now Clyde, you know that ain't so. Sometimes I think you
got mule blood runnin' in your veins, the old woman's voice
strident and sharp but the old man's never heard, because he
whispered when he was angry, and the quarrel had a curious one-
sided quality from the street. Or they would sit together on the
porch, in silent company, never saying a word, and she would say
after a while, I guess I better be getting dinner, and if he nodded,
in she would go. In all their long life with each other, they had
talked each other out until by now she knew all his jokes and had
heard all his stories and there was nothing more to say. Somewhere

a guy met a girl and love made a hot little blaze, Nick thought, but after a while old age set in and now they waded around in its ashes.

Nick went up the stairs to the door which was locked. But the key was in the mailbox. He unlocked the door and swung it open, but just as he was about to go in something made him stop. This voice that always kept talking to him, telling him what to do, bewildering because what it said was always contradictory, suddenly shouted in him, Don't go in the house. It was like a hand pushing him in the face. He waited until the feeling had passed and quietly stepped into the house. The instant he shut the door he felt the presence not of his mother, but of his father, as though he were still in the living room, smoking his pipe. That odor of pipe. The presence mounted on him until he wanted to shout, "Pop?" but he restrained himself. His impulse was to go at once to the closet in his mother's room, but he resisted it and went on through the living room, through the kitchen, stood a moment on the back porch, then returned to the living room.

The floor of this room had a worn rug with a rose pattern woven into its fabric. At the doors, where there was a continual passage of feet, the rug was frayed through the roses, and paths were worn to the stove, the sofa, the easy chair, the table. Behind the stove, where no one ever walked, the rug was still new, the roses complete and beautiful, but faded, and where his father's cot had been, a rectangle of dust had set into the pile which no amount of sweeping could get out, the ghost of the cot making a dust shadow on the rug; and where his father had leaned his head against the wall were the smears of grease from the oil in his hair.

Nick stood before the spot where the bed had been and his father came to life again. Two o'clock in the morning, he thought, my old man getting up to go to the market. Dressing quietly so no one would be wakened, going out to the truck, cranking it. The buzzing of the spark coils as he whipped the crank. Starting it and driving off to market.

Nick remembered going to the market. What a big place it was in the dark. Long rows of stalls. Mounds of vegetables. Crowds of whiskery, rough-looking men. The shouting and cursing, buy-

ing and selling. Nick and his father loaded the truck, but
before they went out on the grocery store route, they went to
a restaurant. Cups of coffee and stacks of hots. After the hot cakes,
his father had a bowl of soup. The hot soup made the old man's
nose run and he kept blowing it on the table cloth and Nick kept
looking away, to avoid seeing it. Once he said, Pop! mortified, and
his father said, What is it, what I'm doing son? and Nick said,
Don't blow your nose on the table cloth, and his father said, Why
not, that's what it's for. After they had eaten, he told Nick to bring
in a box of tomatoes. He wanted to trade the tomatoes for the
breakfast and this too mortified Nick. He was easily mortified in
those days, but his father made him go. Go, go, he said, in Greek,
What a shit of a son you are. Are you going to get it or am I?
Nick got the tomatoes and Gianaclis, the proprietor of the restaurant
said, What's that? and Nick's father said, Two breakfasts, one box
tomatoes, and the proprietor said, No-no, I want the money, and
his father said, Ah, shaddup, you take the tomatoes. The argument
sent Nick out to the truck and his father came too, after a while,
without the tomatoes, and he said, That's the way to get rich. Keep
the money, give them the tomatoes. Oh, his old man knew how to
get rich, all right, this old man of his who was broke every day of
his life, as far back as Nick could remember.

Nick stood thinking about his father, all the things they had done
together, the life they had lived. It had none of it seemed very
exciting at the time, but now seen back through time it was like
an adventure in a book. The day in the river country, up around
Minkler, buying frostbitten oranges because they were cheap, and
cheating everyone in order to sell them. Or the journey to the
honey farm with its tall gum trees and its white beehives like a
little village in a clover field. The early morning trips to buy
produce at the Chinese market across the tracks. Or the year they
made the haul to Frisco. It was all unreal and far away, as though
it had happened in another life. The pictures ran swiftly through
Nick's head, his father smiling the way he did when things went
right, like turning on a light. The way his father could laugh, right
out of the belly, or turn it off when things went bad.

When he thought of it, it seemed to Nick that his father was

continually fighting an enemy, as though his life were endlessly
pitted against an invisible adversary, the way he had of doing things
with a chip on his shoulder, his hands tightened into fists, slugging
it out. Nick knew this feeling well, for he had it himself, all the
time, more and more as he grew up, this clever opponent who kept
well hidden and waited for the chance to trip him down, but never
openly. If it would only come out into the open, come on him
visibly and at once, then he could battle it with muscle instead of
wit, but it opposed him so insidiously that at times he forgot there
was an adversary that was subtly, cleverly eroding him, wasting him
away until before he knew it, he would be exhausted, all done, all
finished, all worn and grown too old, rotted for the grave.

Nick went quickly to his mother's room. The blinds were up and
he became frightened that he could be seen from the street, and he
drew them down, but now the room was too dark and he turned
on the light. He went into the closet before he discovered that the
bedroom door was open, and once he had reached the door, it
occurred to him that the front door was not locked. He went to it
and locked it from the inside, and as he stood listening to the
house, once again the guilt of what he was about to do swept over
him and the voice said, You'll be sorry. There were implicit in
this warning all the things his mother would do when she learned
the money was gone. Don't do it, the voice said. It commanded him,
but by now he was without volition and he could not have stopped
if he wanted to. He found himself going into the bedroom and
feverishly taking down the bundles from the shelf in the closet
and groping after the money, but it was not there. He opened the
bundles and went through them, but the money was not there. One
of the packages contained a stack of photographs, taken in the old
country of people, men and women, young a long time ago, but
most of them dead and gone, and those who were still alive, very
old, waiting for death. The ovals and squares of these pictures
mounted on heavy cardboard, portraits of wedding couples, men
in black suits, standing behind seated women in white, folded or
torn through and laid face to face. The stack slipped in his fumbling
hands, and from the pile of pictures emerged a picture of his
mother; a young woman, looking at Nick with a steady unsmiling

face. He gathered the pictures together and hastily tied the cloth about them and threw the bundles back upon the shelf. He went through the closet, searching every coat, looking into every corner without finding the money. Try the bed, the voice said, helping him now.

Nick went through the bed, searching under the three mattresses upon which his mother slept. He looked for rips in the mattress and places where they might have been sewn together and when this failed he punched the mattress from end to end, feeling for the money. It was not in the bed.

The dresser, the voice said. Nick went through all the drawers in the dresser. He pulled the dresser away from the wall and looked behind it. He looked for places in the wall where the money might have been hidden. He tore down pieces of wall paper to see if they concealed an opening.

The money was not in the room. I'll have to search through the whole house, Nick thought in despair. He stood thinking about the most likely place where the money would be. It had to be in this room.

The closet again, the voice said. Nick returned to the closet where once more he brought down the bundles and groped his hand along the shelf. He was not surprised when he did not find the money, but he felt prompted to get a chair and get up on a level with the shelf. There was a board at the back. He touched the board. It was loose. He drew it away and exposed an opening in the wall. He reached into the opening and his fingers touched a cloth. He brought out the cloth and it was another bundle which he opened without stepping down from the shelf. In it was the money.

He piled the money on the bed, four thousand dollars in packets of hundred dollar bills, and looked around for a book to wrap in the cloth and found the Greek bible in which was the record of the family. It was about the right size and he wrapped it carefully and placed the bundle in the hole behind the shelf, replaced the board and returned all the bundles to their places in the closet. Then he returned to the money. The bills were all new and crisp, and made a good clean feeling in his hand, not like the dollar bills one gets in a store, bills that have travelled from hand to hand and purse to purse and in and out of the cash registers of the town until they were frayed and worn and had collected the taint of each person who had handled them.

The money was in four packets of ten hundred-dollar bills. Holding it in his hand, it was difficult to understand that it could buy a truck, buy loads, buy his future, alter his whole life. He placed the sheafs of bills in his back pockets, two in the left and two in the right, and stood looking about the room to see if anything was misplaced, so his mother would not know the money was gone. Everything was in order. He saw that he had tucked the bedspread under the mattress along with the sheet and he pulled it out and smoothed it down. And the pillows were not right. He rolled them into cylinders and tucked the bedspread neatly about them. He was doing this when he heard a sound outside on the walk, of feet on gravel, and he stepped quickly to the drawn blind and looked out. It was his mother.

She had walked two blocks from the bus on Blackstone Avenue and she was tired. She came to the steps and paused a moment to rest, breathing hard through her open mouth. Seen this way, through the chink of blind, she looked very sad, her round face, which could be so jolly when she was not crossed, set in some painful melancholia. She caught her breath and came slowly up the steps with the labor as of climbing hills. She was a big woman and it was very difficult for her to move. She came up, one step at a time, her hand reaching out for the porch column, and when she was on the porch, she rested again.

She would be in the house in a moment and catch Nick in the bedroom. He went to the kitchen where he poured himself a glass of milk and got the box of crackers from the cupboard and sat down to eat, waiting for the sound of her entrance. But she could not enter. He had forgotten the door. It was locked. She rattled it and he heard her say to herself in irritation, "Now what's the matter with the door?" She rattled it again and he heard her say in surprise, "Why, it's locked. Nikko? Are you home?"

Nick got up and went to the back porch, prepared to escape, but he knew that Mrs. Atkinson would tell his mother that he was in the house. There was no escape. He had to unlock the door. He went to the front room. "Nick," he heard her say, "open the door. Why don't you open it?" She was becoming angry, but he hesitated. The guilt of what he had done was so strong in him that he knew she could detect it in his face. He stood trying to calm himself while his mother rattled the door and kept shouting, "Nick, Nikko. What is it, my boy, why don't you open the door?"

For a moment Nick wanted to return the money to the closet, to get rid of the object of his guilt, but quickly, before he could think any further, he stepped to the door, unlocked it and opened it wide.

"My God," his mother said, "Why didn't you open?"

"I was in the kitchen," Nick said. "I didn't hear you."

"Why couldn't you hear me? I was shouting. I don't know, but I was so frightened." She waddled into the room and Nick closed the door. He felt calm, very sure of himself, completely secure; he knew there was not a trace of guilt in his face. She could not tell from him that anything was wrong.

"The doors were shut," he said. "Your voice didn't come through."

"Oh, how hot it was downtown," she said. "I couldn't stand it, I had to come home." She tried to remove her coat, but her thick arms caught in the sleeves. She stood grunting and struggling to free herself, both arms trapped in the coat, and Nick watched her, unmindful of her predicament until she cried fretfully, "Don't stand there, help me," and Nick stepped behind her and tugged at the sleeves. The lining had twisted on her arms and he had difficulty getting his mother out of the coat. For some reason she began to cry and Nick said, "It's okay, Mom, take it easy." She went into the bedroom and Nick returned to the kitchen. Once again the impulse to run from the house passed over him, but he resisted it and forced himself to sit down and finish his milk. He did not know until he had raised the glass to his mouth, that it was empty and he got up and went to the icebox and refilled the glass and sat down again. Get the hell out of here, the voice said, but he continued to sit, frightened now. He tried to drink, but his hand trembled, slopping the milk to the table. His mother had removed her black dress by now and had put on her old house dress, the one with the torn sleeve, and he could hear her coming through the house to the kitchen. He could feel her heavy steps shaking the floor.

His back was to the door, but the moment she entered, he felt her eyes upon him. She went to the sink and poured herself a glass of water and drank, then sat at the table. Nick continued to avoid looking at her, but the sensation of being watched became stronger and stronger until he had to look and he did and he saw her watching him with her small eyes narrowed suspiciously. He drank the milk, swallowing slowly.

"Nick, my boy, tell me something," she said. Beneath the calm of her voice, she was very excited.

"What is it, Mom?"

"Why did you pull down the blinds in my room?"

"I didn't pull down the blinds. What for?"

"They were up this morning, and now they're down."

"Maybe you did it when you were dressing."

"No. I always leave them up. I like to see the trees in the morning, the way they move. I know they were up."

"You must have forgot."

"Maybe," his mother said, and Nick felt a surge of relief, but he knew she was not finished. There was the presentiment of danger ahead and the necessity for being careful. "I didn't pull them down, but supposing I did, what the hell difference does it make?" he said.

His mother did not answer. She sat looking at him. After a time she said, "Then why did you lock the front door?"

"I don't know, I just did," Nick said. "I felt tired and I thought I'd lie down, so I locked the door. Maybe that's why I did it."

"That's not why," his mother said. "You didn't go to work this morning. You waited in the car until I left the house and then you came back."

"Why would I want to do that?"

"So you could steal my money. You took my money, didn't you?"

Nick stood up in sudden anger. It was such a good anger that he could believe in it himself. "You and your God damned money," he said. "You waddle around all night hiding it in different places. Fat chance I'd ever have of finding it. You've moved it around so many times, I'll bet you don't even know where it is."

"You took it, didn't you?" his mother said.

Nick shook his head sadly at his mother. "Look, Mom, if you think I took it, why don't you go see if it's gone." He thought, by the time she gets up on a chair and looks behind the shelf, I'll think of some way of getting out of this. He thought of her forcing a chair into the closet, laboriously mounting it, moving aside all the bundles, removing the board and feeling into the space in the wall and touching the package. It would take a long time.

"If you took the money, it would be in your pocket, wouldn't it?" his mother said. "Can I search your pockets?"

"No," Nick said. "You go look where you hid it."

"I want to look in your pocket," his mother said. "If it's not there, then I'll know it's still in the house and my heart will be at ease." She got up and came toward Nick and Nick found himself retreating before her.

"Nick, come here," she said. She spoke forcefully.

Nick stepped aside so the table was between him and his mother. "Look, Mom," he said.

"You've got my money," she said. "I want it, I want my money."

"Your money's where you left it. Go look where you hid it," Nick said.

"Afterward," she said, "but first I want to search your pockets. I'm going to do it, Nick."

"Don't you touch me, Mom."

Nick tried to escape from his mother, but this woman who could hardly walk down a street, who found it so difficult to mount the porch stairs, who became exhausted simply by washing the dishes, who could not get out of a bathtub when she took a bath but had to be helped up by Nick, instantly became surprisingly agile. She darted to the back door and Nick ran to the swinging door into the living room, but she was on him in an instant and had him by the shirt. He tried to tear away from her, but with astonishing strength she wrapped her arms around him and held him tight. Nick squirmed free, but her hands caught his hair and held him. He twisted her wrists, so thick with layers of fat that he could hardly grip them and she gave a scream of rage as he got free once more and ran to the kitchen, where he stumbled over a chair and went down, his mother on him, fastening him to the floor with her weight.

"I want my money," she kept saying, "I want my money." She clawed like a witch at Nick, feeling him for the money.

"Mom," Nick said. "Get off me or I'll dump you on your ass." He caught his mother's arm and twisted it hard and when she rose in agony, he rolled clear and stood up, but now she hugged him tight and since her arms were occupied with holding him, she began to snap at his face with her teeth like an enraged animal. Up to now Nick had been intent only on escape, but now he became frightened. "Okay, Mom," he said. "Okay, Mom, I'll give you the money." But she had become deafened with fury and she could not hear him and kept trying to bite him. Nick did not know how he did it, but he reached into his back pockets and threw the money onto the table, showed her he was throwing it, and when she saw the money, she released her son and ran to the table and began counting the bills and Nick stood rubbing his arms which ached from the struggle. His whole body ached, and there were bruises on his wrist simply from the strength of her grip.

All his life Nick had been contemptuous of his mother, never afraid of her, but now he was completely intimidated. There was no way to get at her. He knew it as his father must have known it. He stood watching her huddled over the money, counting it, bill by bill.

"Your filthy father," she said. "It was the only decent thing he ever did, dying and leaving me all this money, and you want to take it from me. He was a trash and you're his son, you're a trash too, the same trash. God punished him and he'll punish you too, some day."

"And you're a sweet old lady, Mom, who believes in God," Nick said.

"Go, go," his mother said, "go and don't ever come back. You rubbish. You trash."

"Thank you, Mom, thank you for letting me go," Nick said.

He felt calmer now, for all at once he knew that he was going to get back at his mother—how he did not know—but he was going to do it. It was in something he was going to say, but what it was was not yet clear.

"Mom," Nick said, letting it come from him without knowing what he was going to say, "remember the day we buried Pop?"

His mother looked up and there was a look in her eye that told him he was on the right track. The night the old man died, she had gone from the house, terrified in the presence of death and Nick had to bind up his father's jaw so it would not set open, and weight his eyelids with nickels so they would remain closed and conceal the sightless eyes. She stayed at Mrs. Atkinson's house until the body had been removed, weeping hysterically not because her husband had died but because she had seen death, this was how it was going to be with her. All the next day she spent purging the house of his father, burning and throwing out and giving away.

As the day for the funeral neared, she said, I'll need a black dress, Nick. I want to look nice for the funeral. Later, after she bought the dress, she said, Do you think I'll need black gloves? Should I wear a black veil? And the night before the old man was to be buried and the house was full of relatives from Reedley and Sanger and Del Rey and Orange Cove, she said, Dearest God, I'll have to mourn him for a year. How dreadful. But she put on a beautiful display of grief before the little old men and the withered old woman who were his father's brothers and sister, crying noisily all night so the wives had to comfort her. The next day, late in the afternoon, she fainted dead away at the church door and sat in a coma in the pew before the coffin. She interrupted the preacher's oration several times with loud gulping sobs and afterwards, during the singing of "Nearer, My God, to Thee," she achieved a climax, slapping herself in the cheeks and swaying from side to side and groaning as though at any moment she too would die and join her husband. When the time came to pass by the open coffin, she was inconsolable and Nick and one of the brothers named Aris had to support her.

The sight of Nick's father in the coffin was a sight never to be forgotten. Here was the man who had never shaved himself completely, but always forgot to touch the razor somewhere, either under the chin or a corner of the cheek so that there was always on his face a week's growth of beard. Here was the man who never combed his hair but laid it back with a brush of the hand, who never straightened his mustache but let it droop over his lip, who never wore a tie, let alone buttoned a collar or wore a clean shirt, lying in his coffin with his hair neatly combed and parted, his mustache neatly trimmed, wearing a new shirt which was buttoned high and a colorful necktie around his neck. He had been carefully shaven and made up to look pink in the cheeks. This was not the careless, unneat man that Nick knew, but a stranger in the coffin, and when Nick's mother saw him, she forgot her grief for a moment and stood up straight, unaided. Ahk, Yanko, Nick remembered his mother saying, why weren't you a man like this when you were living?

As Nick stood looking down at his mother seated at the table, with the money in her hand, waiting for him to go on, he remembered how she bent over the coffin and for a moment he thought she was going to kiss him goodbye, but instead she did a strange thing. She thumped his skull with her knuckle, so it made a hard knocking sound. Mom! Nick remembered saying. And later he asked, Why did you do a thing like that, Mom? Do what, Nick? And Nick said, Knock on his head the way you did. And his mother said, I wanted to see how it felt. But it was more than that, it was the fitting farewell, better than a kiss or a tear, the only thing a woman who had abused her husband all his married life could possibly do, send him to his grave with a blow in the head.

"Remember that tall chimney, over by the trees, when we came out of the church. The black smoke coming out of it?" Nick said.

"What are you saying?" his mother said.

"That was the smoke of bodies being cremated," Nick said. "Maybe it was even the smoke from Pop's body."

"You didn't have him burned!" his mother said.

"Yes. I told you I wasn't going to do it, but I did. I had him cremated and it isn't his body buried at the cemetery, but a little box of ashes."

His mother arose and the money dropped from her hands. "You told me you weren't going to do it," she said. "You said you wouldn't."

"That's right, but I did it anyway, and you know what else, Mom? When you die, I'm going to have you burned too."

"You're not. I won't let you."

"You won't be able to do anything about it, because you'll be dead."

"No, Nikko. Don't do it." She clasped her hands together in a gesture of prayer and began to cry and Nick said, "Why not? You're going to burn in hell anyway. You might as well burn here on earth too, and I'm going to stand outside and watch the smoke come out of the chimney."

His mother fell to her knees and clutched him around the legs. "No, no," she said, "you can't do that, not to your mother, Nikko. I'm your mother, don't burn me."

Nick freed himself from his mother and stepped toward the door, but she intercepted him, weeping and begging. "I know I've been cruel, I know I've been bad. I didn't want to be, but I was. Don't punish me, Nikko, don't burn me."

Nick looked stonily at his mother. She got up from the floor and picked up the packets of money from the table and held them out to him. "If it's the money you want," she said, "here, take it. But don't burn me, Nikko, promise you won't burn me."

"You can keep your money."

"No, Nikko, it's your money too, please take it."

She crammed the bills into his pocket. Nick stood looking coldly at his mother. Then he went out. As he walked away from the house, he could hear the wailing weeping of his mother and he was certain that she was clapping her hands together and shaking her head in the way that he knew.

It was not until he had walked to the highway and caught a ride, in a new sedan driven by a travelling salesman going South that he permitted himself to think of what he had done and suddenly he began to cry and the salesman said, "Hey, what the hell's the matter with you?"

5

IN the eight hundred block on Elm Street in Modesto was one house that was different from all the rest. Where the other houses were freshly painted, with crisp curtains at the windows and neat, well tended lawns and orderly paths and gardens, this one house was in total disrepair. Its fences were broken, the palings lying where they had fallen. The garden was a jungle of vines that swarmed over and choked the bushes. The white paint on the clapboard walls of the house was curling and peeling. The porch railings had collapsed, and where the rains had soaked the floor, the boards were warped into hills and valleys. The underpinnings of the stairs had been eaten away by termites and gave to the step when they were mounted. The screen at the door was rotted with rust and the curtains at the windows were drab.

A woman carried a basket of laundry down the back steps. She was in her late thirties, a big broken down blonde with soft shapeless breasts and a big mass of body, gone to pot. Her hair had not been combed or brushed but coiled and piled in a careless way as though pinned up with other things on her mind. Her face was pallid and her lips were pale and chapped. She wore a dingy housecoat that was too long and its hem was soiled with the dirt it had collected from the floor and the earth of the yard. She lived in the coat. On her feet were an old pair of satin slippers crushed down at the heels. She wore no stockings and as she carried the basket to the clothesline, one of the slippers fell off, but she did not bother to slip it back on, but walked ahead, barefooted. She had big feet, with prominent ankle bones and strong structures of the toes, which seemed broken.

The woman, Mabel Kennedy, began to hang clothes on the line, the shirts and jeans of a boy, the blouses and dresses of a girl, the garments worn and faded and patched. She hung them carelessly, draping them on the line without pins to hold them in place. As she worked, she could hear the boys of the neighborhood playing ball in the street. "Peg it here, Jimmy," she heard the piping voice of a kid, "Right in the groove, atty ole boy."

The boy, Jimmy, cocked back his arm to throw the ball, aiming it at Chuck Cochran down the block. He was fourteen years old, already fitting into the leanness of the man he would be one day. He had a strange narrow face with cold, dead eyes, as though the eyes were one place where he could be seen and he was glazing them in order to hide. He heaved the ball with a quick wiry motion, and stood on his toes, watching its flight. His shoes were old and run down at the heels. He had outgrown his shirt and it kept bursting its buttons, revealing the hungry body, with its gaunt pattern of rib cage and collar bone. The back pockets of his jeans had been removed to supply material for patches in the knees, and where the pockets had been was the unfaded square of blue denim.

On the green clipped lawn next door was a group of little girls, playing house. One of the girls was a little blonde named Barbara. She was not more than six years old, and she had a plump soft body and a round open face in which were wide blue eyes. She sat playing with a doll that had been made from a stocking. The other girls played with store dolls with golden hair and eyes that moved. This opening and closing of the eyes seemed to fascinate the little girl, and though her doll's eyes were chalk marks on the stocking, she kept standing it up and laying it down and saying, "Wake up, baby, go to sleep, baby." The other girls had clean scrubbed faces and shining well combed hair, but Barbara's hair was in snarls and her face was dirty in an irregular line that curved down her cheeks and beneath her chin where she had neglected to wash. The other girls had new cotton dresses, freshly starched and ironed, but Barbara's dress had not been ironed, and it was old. It had once been pink, but it had been washed so often that it was now almost white, except under the collar and within the pockets. She looked pale and tired as she played with her doll, and her eyes had a quality of looking but not seeing.

Chuck had missed the ball and it bounced down the street. Just as it rolled into the intersection, a truck turned from Fern Avenue into Elm. It was a big truck with broken-down side racks and a dented cab. The engine needed repair and it ran noisily, with an irritating gnashing sound. The tires were worn smooth and the left rear axle was bent and the dual wheels wabbled slightly as the truck passed down Elm and came to a stop in front of the dilapidated house.

The instant the driver, Ed Kennedy, stepped from the cab, it could be seen that the truck, the man in the truck, the boy in the street, the girl on the lawn, the woman in the yard, the clothes on the line, all belonged to the house.

"Jimmy, it's daddy," the girl said from the lawn. She came running to the truck. The boy looked with a checked animosity toward his father, his eyes smouldering.

"There's a couple of boxes of oranges in the back. Get 'em in the house," Ed said to his son in a hard clipped voice. His hair was red, but it had turned white at the temples. He had a mean intense face with a mouth that was set in a tight line. He was a man slightly past forty but looked to be much older, very tired and going along on nerve.

Father and son had the same gaunt body, the same meanness of face, the identical veiling of eye. They looked at each other in a kind of duel, and finally the son came reluctantly toward the truck and the father, knowing he had asserted his will, turned to house.

The girl trotted beside him, crying, "I want a kiss, Daddy. I want a kiss." But Ed paid no attention to her. He seemed not to hear. Mabel called out from the clothesline, "Ed?" but he went up the front steps without answering.

Ed went through the house, looking at the rooms. He had been gone two months and nothing was changed. There were newspapers on the floor. Comic books were spread open on the sofa. The two bedroom doors were open and the beds could be seen unmade, the blankets on the floor. Barbara had wet her bed, and there was the pungent smell of urine. Dirty dishes were piled in the sink, dirty pots stood on the stove and the residue of the noon's lunch was still on the table. As Ed saw the condition of the rooms, his face became tighter and his mouth more firmly set.

He went into the big bedroom and began to remove his clothes and while he was undressing, Mabel came in. Barbara was bouncing on the bed and she pulled her from it and pushed her to the door. "Go outside and play, honey," she said.

"I want to be with daddy," Barbara said.

"Now, be a good girl and go outside," Mabel said.

"But, Daddy, I want to be with you," Barbara said.

Ed did not answer. He continued stripping off his clothes, balling them in his hand and throwing them onto the floor. Mabel pushed Barbara into the living room and shut the door. Ed removed his shorts and stood in his socks and shoes.

His arms up to his elbows and his face, down to his neck, outlined where the collar had been opened, was burned red from the sun, but the rest of his body was dead white, the red bunch of pubic hair startling against it. He had a flat, hard belly and muscles were laid in bands on his arms and his shoulders and across his gut and back. He had a long narrow body with the spine lost in the folds of muscles that rippled when he moved. The white of his legs had a transparent quality so the blue tangle of veins could be seen in the flesh.

Mabel stood watching Ed remove his shoes and socks. After he had taken them off, his feet continued to wear socks of dirt. Outside, she was glad when she saw the truck come to a stop before the house, but when Ed went up the steps instead of coming to her, she was hurt and now, watching him, she let herself go good with feeling glad again, the gladness flushing through her.

Ed stepped toward the bathroom, but she stopped him, and when he turned, she opened her housecoat and took him into it, holding him tightly. She was naked beneath the coat. His body, except for a tuft on the chest, was practically hairless. The hair felt good on her breasts. She ran her hands over his back to press him harder against her, enjoying his sinewy body. She curved against him, holding him. She parted her legs slightly, feeling his knees with the inside of her thighs, and it was all very good with the waves passing through her, and she opened her mouth, waiting for him,

until she saw his eyes, hard and distant. He struggled to get free
and the gladness went from her, but she tried to hold him. It hurt
but she still tried and he had to pry her arms apart to get away
from her. There was a look on his face of panic, as though he were
in a room that was closing in on him. "Get your hands the hell off
me," he said.

"What's the matter, Ed?"

"Nothing. Just get the hell off." He went into the bathroom.
She followed him. It was the feeling of having to hold him when
he did not want her. She had to hold him and she had to follow
him. She turned on the bath water and cleaned the tub which was
ringed with dirt and put in the plug and let the tub fill, the water
splashing and steaming. The steam coiled up, filling the
room.

"Have any luck?" she said.

Ed did not answer.

"I see you came home empty," she said.

"Yeah," he said. He said it angrily.

"Ed, I saw Mr. Harris downtown yesterday," she said. "He
asked me what you was doing."

"What did you tell him?" Ed said. It was not a question but an
accusation.

"He's got a job for you, Ed. Pays sixty dollars a week. He needs
a mechanic."

"Is that right?" Ed said. He got into the tub and began to soap
himself, washing himself vigorously, while Mabel stood watching.
The steam filled the room.

Mabel did not know how to talk to Ed. No matter how she did
it, he was always putting up barriers, freezing her out. If she made
a suggestion, he resisted her. Even silence did not work. He seemed
to enjoy silence and would have been willing to live in it forever,
except that it was so unbearable for her. She had to talk to him,
to get at him somehow. She kept experimenting with different ways
of getting at him, but nothing worked. It was almost better for
him not to come home, except that she got to worrying when he
was gone too long. She began to have bad dreams of him on the
road. The truck would go rolling down a hill and explode into

flames and she would awake, screaming. Lately, he was not home, even when he was home.

She watched him through the curling steam. I wonder what he's thinking, she thought. That hard nut he calls a head, I wonder what's going on in it. I wish he'd talk. Or I wish he'd listen when I talk.

He was trying to wash his back, cramping his arm over his shoulders. "Here, I'll do it," she said. She soaped his back with the wash cloth and the water came away soiled. He had been gone over two months and in all that time he had not had a bath. In all that time, sleeping in the truck. He had lost weight. In all that time, not eating, grabbing a bite from the grub joints along the road.

She had cleaned his back, when she saw that his head had fallen forward. He was asleep. Seen this way, his face was relaxed, the tension gone from it, but in his expression there was a sadness. Oh, Ed, she thought, and she wanted to hold him in her arms and carry him to bed. He was so light, she knew she could, but of course, he would waken and spring at her with his fury. She wanted to cry, but she knew that would not do either, not if he heard, and she got up, but could not hold back the crying. She was too full of it. It spurted from her before she got to the bed and fell on it, crying hard and biting the pillow so she would not be heard.

Jimmy came into the kitchen and he said, "Where's Dad?" Mabel said, "He's sleeping," and Jimmy said, "Why did he have to come home? We have a better time when he ain't around." Barbara said, "We do so, we do so have a good time when he is," and Ed came in and he said, "What do you do so when who is?" and Barbara said, "When you are," and Ed said, "What's she talking about?" Jimmy sat stiff in his chair and Mabel said, "It isn't anything, honey, honest it isn't." Barbara said, "Yes it is. Jimmy says we have a better time when you ain't around, that's what he said, isn't that what you said, Jimmy?" Ed slapped Jimmy with the back of his hand and Jimmy fell off the chair, but he got up and he didn't cry. He started to go from the room and Ed said, "Come back here, you little bastard," and Jimmy went to Ed and Ed slapped him again and Jimmy didn't cry. Ed slapped him several times but

Jimmy would not cry; he stood with his eyes hard and his mouth tight and Ed kept slapping him and Mabel said, "Ed!" Barbara began to cry and when Jimmy heard her, he began to cry too and he ran from the room and Barbara ran after him and Mabel wanted to run too, but she sat and Ed began to eat his soup. He ate a spoon of it and he turned to Mabel and he said, "This God damned soup's cold."

"Oh, Ed," Mabel said, and Ed said, "What's biting you?" and Mabel said, "What's happening to us, something terrible is happening to us, just look at this house, just look at us, just look at me, I'm so scared I'm sick, I wish I knew."

"Not a God damned thing's happening to us that I know of," Ed said.

"That's because you can't see," Mabel said. "If I could only make you see. It used to be I could talk to you, but I can't even talk to you anymore. Honey, I'm not your enemy. I'm your wife and I'm trying to help you."

"I suppose I like to ride trucks. I'm doing it for the fun, not to be of any help," Ed said.

"It's not that you're not trying," Mabel said. "You are, but you're killing yourself, and nothing's coming of it. You just won't see it. You've been trucking all these years and what's it got you?"

Ed did not answer and Mabel said, "If you'd only take that job with Harris. When I met him downtown, he seemed anxious to talk to you. He likes you, Ed. He wants to give you a job."

"You didn't see him downtown," Ed said. "You went over to his garage and seen him. You went sucking around for a job."

"No, of course I didn't," Mabel said. "You know I wouldn't do a thing like that. I know how you are. Honest to God, I saw him downtown, on Main Street, across from the bank and he asked me, 'Mrs. Kennedy, how's Ed doing these days?' and I told him—"

"Yeah, you told him all right. You sure told him."

"Honey, all I said was—"

"Ah, cut out the crap, baby. I don't care what you said. Pass me the spuds."

It was after dinner and they were sitting in the front room. Barbara was reading the comics and Mabel was sitting quietly, lost in thought. What's she beefing about, Ed thought. Long ago he had given up trying to figure her out. He was acutely aware of his own processes. Floods of thought continually passed through him, recounting the successes, the failures, planning the next haul, knowing he would make it somehow, knowing he would and knowing he wouldn't, as in shooting craps, knowing you can win and knowing you can lose more than you will ever win, but playing it out until you came to a hot run in which you passed fifty times and quit winner, sweating it out for that hot run. All Mabel could think of were the failures. She could not see how it was with him, that waiting for a good haul, a run of good hauls so he could wind it up winner instead of loser. He hated to quit any other way. He had to win; then he would chuck it. How did you make that clear to her? It was like two people wearing blinders so they could see only their way and the hell with the other guy. The hell with Mabel, Ed thought. I have to work this out myself. He thought of his family. What a crap of a family it was. But there's nothing wrong with this outfit that a little money won't cure, he decided. A couple of good hauls is all it'd take. He could see himself coming home with a big smile on his face, plenty of green in his pocket, showing the sheaf of bills to Mabel. Hit it right this time, Babe. How sweet he could be to Mabel then, and how loving she would be, might even begin to clean the house and show some interest in the kids. The look would change in Jimmy's eyes and Barbara would be able to kiss him without crying. Jumping Christ, all it would take was a couple of hauls. Well, why don't they happen, he thought, and the fury fired in him at something nameless. Maybe it'd be better if he took that job. Mechanic over at Harris Garage. What was so wrong with Mabel sucking around after it? Why couldn't he work like other guys on a job? Why did he have to be a big shot in a truck, holding out for the big chance. That big chance, something wrong there. The thought touched him lightly and was gone before he could make something of it and he was sitting again in a hopeless muddle, trying to burst out of himself. He was in such a muddle, that he was continually shifting from one plan to another without following any one plan through to its logical conclusion and ending by clinging to the one simple idea he

had always had, to make it go. If it's the last thing I do, I'll make it
go, he thought.

"Where's Jimmy?" he said.

"In his room," Mabel said. "Jimmy," she called.

"Yeah?"

"Why don't you come in here and visit with us?"

"Okay."

Jimmy came into the room. He had removed his shirt and his
hard lithe body with its play of muscles was good to look at. Good
shoulders, Ed thought, good arm, good hands. Someday he'll have
as good a wing, grow up to be a good man, better man than I am.
He liked his son. He remembered the night Jimmy was born. God,
make him a boy and I'll take him hunting and fishing and we'll
go on hikes and I'll talk to him about the way things are and he'll
know how it is. Make it a guy, God, and leave the rest to me. God
had made it a guy all right, but Ed had not taken him hunting or
fishing or gone on hikes or told him anything about how it was in
the world. One of these days, he told himself, I'll lay it right out
for him, the way it is. He sat looking at Jimmy. There were red
marks on the boy's cheeks where Ed had slapped him and when he
saw this he wanted to grab his son and hug him tight and tell him,
I didn't mean it, kid. Honest to Christ. I didn't mean it. It wasn't
you I was hitting. It was all those other things. What the hell I
wouldn't know, but it wasn't you. Understand, Kid?

"How are things, Jimmy?" Ed said.

"They're all right," Jimmy said, his voice firm and his eyes
smouldering.

Good eyes, Ed thought. Looks me right in the eyes, but not
like that, kid. Don't look at me like that.

"How would you like to go out on a trip with me one of these
days?" Jimmy did not answer and Ed said, "Maybe when school's
out, we'll go on a haul up North. Good mountain country. Maybe
go hunting. How's about it?"

"If I have to," Jimmy said.

Ed felt an uncontrollable rage firing within him and his face
hardened. You little bastard, he wanted to say. He wanted to slap
the boy around, obliterate him. "Okay, go on to bed," he said.

Jimmy left the room and after a minute Mabel went after him and Ed could hear her remonstrating with the boy for the way he had behaved toward his father. He could hear the steady mumble of her voice. He could not understand the words, but he knew what she was saying and this made him more angry.

He sat watching Barbara. There had been another girl, Helen, who had died while she was still a baby. Two girls in the house, he thought. That would have been dandy, to have them growing up, wearing bright dresses and putting flowers in their hair. Guys coming to the house, making passes at my girls, taking them out, having a good time feeling them up. He thought of all the things he had done in his time with the girls and a flash of jealousy went through him. No guys messing around with my kids, he thought. But then he thought of himself and Mabel and the things they had done, the nights at the river dances, necking in the car, the awkward clumsy lovemaking, and it had turned out all right. It hadn't damaged Mabel that he could see. The damage had come later.

He wanted to hold Barbara and bury his face in her silky hair. He thought of the shivers it used to send through his spine to feel Mabel's hair against his neck, right under the ear. That wonderful feeling.

"Babs," he said. "Come here and give your old man a kiss."

Barbara looked up from her comic book and Ed knew that she was frightened. "I said come here," he said and Barbara got up and came slowly to Ed and he held her and she shut her eyes to kiss him, but when her mouth neared his face, she burst into tears.

"What's the matter, honey?" Ed said, and Barbara said, "You slapped Jimmy," and Ed could feel his face go hard, tightening so swiftly that Barbara was frightened by it. She tore away from him and ran to the bedroom and Ed suddenly felt how alone he was in his own house.

It was dark outside. The darkness filled the windows. There was a sensation of someone standing beyond the darkness, watching him. When he was alone, the look of tension slipped from him and the same sadness that he wore when he was asleep came into his face. He got up and began to walk back and forth across the room.

After a while Mabel came in and sat down.

"Are they all right?" Ed asked.

"I put them to bed," Mabel said.

Ed sat down too, across the room from his wife, and began quietly to watch her. My old lady, he thought. She's beginning to look like a bat. That blowsy hair, that big can, that fat puss. He thought of how she used to be, a small girl with a bright smiling face and live curious eyes and a quick bird-like way of moving around, always calling him honey or baby or love. The way she had of walking, close beside and a little behind him so he could feel her breast against his arm. What had happened? Ed did not know, but as he sat looking at his wife, she slowly changed before his eyes, became more beautiful until she was once more the person he once knew.

"Babe," Ed said.

Mabel looked up.

"Why don't we go to bed too?" Ed said.

They undressed and got into the bed. It was good lying in clean sheets again. It did not matter that the sheets had not been properly washed and they still smelled of soap and the musty odor of mould. It was good. He felt her body beside him, the thigh, lumpy and fat, not the satin smooth skin of the girl she once was. But he was not repulsed by her. A feeling of longing and tenderness came over him and he laid his hand on her hip.

"Don't let it throw you, Babe," he said. "Things ain't so bad. Sure, I had a rocky time down South, but some good came of it."

"What good?"

"Well, I went over to Hueneme when I was in Oxnard. The War Surplus was selling army trucks and I was just looking around and I met a kid. Guy named Nick."

"What's he got to do with you?"

"Well, he didn't know the first thing about the kind of rig he wanted and I helped him. He don't know the next thing about hauling loads and he wants me to learn him, so we're going in together on a few trips and I'm going to show him the ropes."

Mabel began to laugh. The laughter was like a slap to Ed's face and the rage sprang in him again and he was about to strike her when he realized that she was not laughing, but crying and again the tenderness came upon him and he drew her to him and held her tight. "Ah, come on now, Babe," he said. "It ain't that bad. He's got around four thousand bucks in his kick and he's willing to finance everything and we'll split the take. I know a place where there's some apples, Golden Delicious. They're hot as hell right now in the markets, so I know we'll make a good run."

"I've heard that so many times," Mabel said.

"Yeah, I know, Babe. But this time it's different," Ed said.

"Honey, why don't you listen to me?" Mabel said. "You don't ever listen to me. Why don't you listen just once?"

"I'm listening, Babe."

"Why don't you take that job with Harris? He likes you. He knows what a good mechanic you are. You can make something out of it. Why don't you do that, honey?"

"I can't. This guy's coming tonight. I promised him. He's expecting me to make the trip. I'm on a good thing at last, Babe. I know I am. Anyways, I'm going to take a whirl. What the hell, it ain't my dough. What have I got to lose?"

He could feel Mabel go flat in his arms. Golden Delicious, he thought. He could see a load of them, two loads. They made a fabulous picture in his mind. Thinking about it made him feel good. It's going to be all right, he thought. Everything's going to be fine.

He began to make love to Mabel, but it was bad. Jimmy and Barbara were in his head. And the look on Mabel's face. She did not want him, he could feel it. Her mouth was hard when he kissed her. He tried to break her down, but it was bad. Not like when you're both feeling good and it is endless and wonderful, but quick and unsatisfactory and painful.

He rolled away, and on the point of falling to sleep he heard himself say, "I'm sorry, Babe."

Mabel lay awake thinking where this was going to get them. Nowhere. No good. It was like slow death. She remembered when she used to be a neat young girl, living in a neat little house with her neat mother and father and her brother Charles and her sister Willa. But the house was not neat enough for her and she used to pick on her mother. Oh, Mother, you ought to know better than to wear green earrings with a pink dress. How many times do I have to tell you not to put on so much powder and lipstick? You look like one of those women, you look just awful. And you never arrange the furniture right. This place looks just like a barn, and Ed's coming over tonight. Do you think I want him to see us living like this?

Look at me now, Mabel thought. I know how I look. Like one of those whores from Jamestown. That's me all over. Look at this house. She amended her thought with the word stinking. This stinking house, this stinking life, this stinking Ed, these stinking children. Jimmy started out so nice and clean and now he's getting that same stinking look in his face, and Barbara's getting it too and I've got it and Ed's got it, and the house has got it. What else do I expect? We're all beginning to look the way we feel, even the yard and the truck. That stinking truck. I wish it would get smashed up in an accident and I wish Ed would get smashed. I wish he'd die. Yes I do. If he was dead, I'd be on my own and I'd do something about us, but I can't so long as he's alive. Why doesn't he die? The best thing he could do is die, I wish he'd die. No I don't, not Ed. I wish it was me, I wish I was dead.

Ed was snoring loudly, sleeping hard.

Mabel drew back the covers and got up. She found the housecoat and put it on and slipped her feet into the slippers. The night was cold and she got a shawl from the closet and hung it across her shoulders. The closet door squeaked and Ed turned in his sleep.

The moon was shining and she could see him in the light. The covers had fallen off and she bent over him to draw them into place, and her hair came cascading down, covering his face. She swirled it back, but the touch of hair had roused him and he stopped snoring. He turned again, hunting his face into the pillow as though trying to find her. He looked like an old gray-haired, seamy-faced little boy, very tired. For some reason, as she stood beside the bed, she shivered. When the feeling passed, she went to the kitchen.

The time was nearly one o'clock. There was still some coffee from dinner. As she waited for it to heat, she lighted the oven and stood with her housecoat open before it, warming herself and looking about the kitchen.

The sink was full of dishes, the accumulation of breakfast and lunch and dinner. It was so easy to wash dishes. Ten minutes and they were finished and put away and the dish cloth was drying on the stove. It was so easy to wash the curtains or to sweep the house, or to tidy the garden or burn the papers or do any one of the hundreds of things that needed to be done to bring order out of chaos, but let them go, day after day, and you ended with the biggest chore in your life. It became easier then to die.

The coffee began to boil, sizzling against the hot sides of the pot, and she poured herself a cup. She had seated herself at the table and was taking a sip when she heard the sound of a truck. Headlights swept past the window. The truck stopped.

She went out to the screen porch and she saw it parked behind Ed's truck, a big shadow. The lights went out and a figure stepped from the cab. Mabel watched him go to Ed's truck. He had seen the light in the kitchen window and she knew he was coming to the house. She stepped down to the yard.

He had not seen her and when she came upon him suddenly, he was startled. He was a young man, not much over twenty years old. He must be the one, Mabel thought, Nick, the man Ed told me about.

"What do you want?" she said in a hushed voice.

"Is this where Ed Kennedy lives?" Nick said. His voice was loud in the silent yard.

"Shhhh," Mabel said, "he's asleep."

Nick hushed his voice too. "I met him down South," he said. "We're going to work together on a couple of hauls."

"I'm not going to wake him," Mabel said.

"He told me it was important to get there the first thing in the morning," Nick said.

"I don't care if you never got there," Mabel said. "Why don't you go away and let him sleep?"

"He told me to wake him," Nick said. "He wanted to make this trip."

"I don't care if he don't never make any more trips," Mabel said,

and though she was whispering, her voice sounded fierce and angry.
"I want you to leave him alone and let him sleep."

Nick stood looking at Mabel. He did not know whether to go or
to shout for Ed. He had counted a lot on this trip, and now it was
washing out from under him.

Mabel went up the steps into the house and the kitchen lights
went off. Nick stood looking at the dark house. He returned to his
truck. Somewhere a cricket chirped. It was dark and lonely in the
night soaked street.

Nick started the engine, and backed out, but before he could
go, he heard Ed's voice shouting, "Nick." The front door opened
and Ed appeared on the porch. He was fully dressed and buttoning his shirt.

"Be with you in a jiff," Ed said.

"Your wife said you couldn't go," Nick said.

"Never mind what she said," Ed said. He went back into the
house and Nick waited in the truck. He heard the woman saying
in a voice that was fierce with anger, "I hope you don't find any
apples; and if you do, I hope they're rotten; and if they're not rotten, I hope you don't get 'em to market; and if you do get 'em to
market, I hope they don't sell, and if they sell, I hope you lose the
money."

Then he heard the sound of someone being slapped around and
the hoarse crying of the woman. Ed came out again, slamming the
door behind him. He put on his leather jacket as he crossed to his
truck. "Okay, let's go," he said.

He got into his truck and Nick saw the woman standing on the
porch, huddled in her shawl. Ed started his engine and it roared
and as the truck moved forward, the woman ran into the street.

"Ed," she shouted, "wait a minute, Ed."

She tried to get onto the running board of the truck, but Ed
would not stop. The extended arm of the rear view mirror caught
the shawl and tore it from the woman's shoulder.

The two trucks went off down the street.

As Ed went down Elm, he saw the shawl fluttering from the
mirror. He reached out and gathered it in a silken ball in his hand.
He was about to throw it into the street, but it felt good in his

hand. It made him feel sorry that he had not stopped for Mabel. He held it to his nose and it smelled pleasantly of her. He placed it beside him on the seat.

Mabel watched the two trucks go, one behind the other, the Christmas tree of lights disappearing beyond the trees. After the trucks were gone, the sound of their exhaust could still be heard. Then the exhausts disappeared too and Mabel went up the steps into the house.

6

THE apple farm with its rough planked buildings and its
brambly orchard lay trapped in the hollow between hills and the
river. The road out was steep. Nick swung his truck around to give
himself a run.

He could see the farmer, Josef Polansky, watching from the
yard, his eyes anxious in his face. Behind him, in the doorway, his
wife watched too, her eyes narrowed and suspicious. She was a
squat strong woman with thick legs and arms. Her body was so
broad, her arms stuck out at the sides. Her round face was dark
and sullen. She had straight black hair drawn into a tight knot at
the back. There was one shock of gray over her temple and she had
bushy black brows, not placid but arched over angry eyes. She spoke
in a rapid foreign tongue to her husband, as Nick let out the
clutch and headed the truck for the climb.

The truck got out easily. There was a little trouble where the
ground was still soaked from the early Autumn rains. The back
wheels began to spin and the truck slewed sideways off the road,
but somehow Nick made it to the top and parked the truck on
the shoulder of the county road that ran along the rim of the hollow and got down. He felt like a giant, standing beside his truck.
Where the tires had nearly bogged in the mud the earth was
churned into gumbo. I got her out, he thought. She almost got
caught in that, but I got her out. He felt that the engine had nothing to do with it. I just grabbed her by the tail and pulled her out,
he told himself. He thought of Polly, back home in Fresno. He
could see her standing before him, looking him straight in the eye
with the contemptuous look that he knew so well. You didn't
think I could do it, he told her. You didn't think I could but I

did, I got a truck and I got a load and I got her out of the hollow
and now I'm all ready to roll and you didn't think I could do any
of it, but I did, and I'm going to keep on doing it.

Down below, Ed had squared his truck around for the run. The
engine roared and now he was taking it, heading for the hill, making the climb. He made it to the muck and the tires began to skid
and he went off the road into the raw earth on the hillside. He was
making it, but something snapped beneath the load and they had
to untie the ropes and throw off the tarp and unload the boxes and
haul them out thirty at a time with the farmer's horse and wagon
until they had the whole six hundred out of the hollow and stacked
beside the county road. And now the farmer watched them from
the road. He was not a suspicious man, but he had been waiting two
days for his money. He had thought they would pay him after the
price had been set. He had even planned to throw in free of charge,
thirty extra boxes, because the bargaining had been fair. But they
had not paid and he decided they would pay after the apples had
been picked, and if not then, surely after the trucks had been
loaded and the loads tied down. His wife had kept prodding him to
ask for the money, but he had hesitated, out of a sense of reluctance
to call them thieves. If they did not pay, then they were thieves, but
they would surely pay; especially now when the trucks were out
of the farm and up on the road. Now they would pay. First he
looked at Nick, and then at Ed, trying to tell them with his eyes.
It disturbed Nick to be watched so steadily. He wished the farmer
would go away and he tried not to look at him. He could feel the
farmer's presence there beside the boxes, but Ed took no notice of
him. He passed the boxes steadily up to Nick, asking the farmer
several times to move. After the truck was loaded, the farmer
cleared his throat. "You ready to pay me now?" he said.

Ed was busy opening the tarpaulin and he did not answer. Nick
said to the farmer, "You'd better go down and take care of your
horses. He'll be with you in a minute."

The farmer led his sweating horses down the hill into the corral
and Nick said to Ed, "Why don't you let me pay the guy? We're
all loaded and ready to go and he wants his money. He's been waiting all day."

Ed gave the tarp to Nick. "Get it up and tie her down," he said. "I'm going to get under and take a look at that drive shaft." He dropped to his knees beside the truck.

"What's the matter with it?" Nick said.

"She sounded like she stripped something coming out of that hole," Ed said. He crawled under the truck and Nick was alone on the road.

The road dropped and turned through woods. Beyond the tree tops was row after row of mountains, growing higher in the distance until they became lost in a vaporous mist. The wind made a strong sound blowing through the trees. There were clouds running North, but when Nick looked up through the tall timber growth, it seemed to him that the clouds stood still and it was the earth that fell South.

Ed was banging under the truck. What a hell of a place to break down, Nick thought. He climbed to the top of the load and flew the tarp over the apples and dropped to the ground. He was tying the ropes when Ed crawled out from under the truck. Grease was like mittens on his hands.

"What did you find?" Nick said.

"Universal's shot."

"Oh, Jesus," Nick said.

"That mud hole was all she needed," Ed said. He got a rag from the tool box and wiped off his hands. "She'll hold until we get to Auburn. You want to give me the money? I'll go down and pay the guy."

"How much is it?" Nick said.

"Twelve hundred boxes at two bucks a box adds up to twenty-four hundred dollars."

Nick counted the money from his wallet. It was all the money he had. There were some ones and a five left from a broken twenty. Gas money. The twenty-four hundred left him clean. He handed it to Ed who stacked it neatly in his hand and wadded it into his pocket.

"Maybe I ought to kiss it goodbye," Nick said.

"What's the matter, you getting scared?"

"Seems like a lot of money to pay just for a couple loads of apples."

"You should've thought of that before you got into this racket."

"You're sure we can sell em?"

"We can sure as hell try. We bought 'em for two, we'll try to get six."

"Suppose we don't get six?"

"Then we'll try to get four, and if we can't get four, we'll try two. You start thinking like that, you'll scare yourself so bad you'll piss out." Ed stepped away from the truck. "You'd better check the oil while I pay him off," he said. He went down the hill.

After Ed had disappeared into the orchard, an uneasiness came over Nick. All that insurance, my mother waiting for it all these years, he thought. All gone. All he had was a truck and a load of apples, two loads really, because Ed's load was his too. The presence of the money in his pocket had given him a feeling of security, but now it was gone. Now I've got the two loads, he thought, twelve hundred boxes. If we get six bucks for them that'll make seventy-two hundred bucks. That's a profit of forty-eight hundred dollars. Somewhere at the end of the road that ran through the hills and on through the Sacramento Valley was a market in a big city where some produce dealer would shell out seventy-two hundred dollars. But the thought did not excite Nick. Who the hell was going to buy twelve-hundred boxes of apples? he thought. Somehow he could not associate the apples with money. So much money. Twenty-four hundred dollars. He brought out the oil can and raised the hood and began to pour the oil. He wished he had not quit his job to go on his own. He wished he had not bought the truck. Ever since he had bought it, he had not had a decent night's sleep. Ever since he had met Ed he had not had a moment free from worry. Ed talked too little and thought too much. Suddenly Nick put down the oil can and ran down the hill after Ed.

"Where the hell do you think you're going?" Ed said.

"I thought I'd go along to see you give him the money," Nick said.

"All I'm going to do is hand it to him. You'd better go on

back and check the oil like I told you. If we kill too much time, we're likely to get stuck in the hills with that shot universal."

"It's my dough, I want to see it get spent," Nick said.

Ed looked at Nick with his bullet eyes. As they went down the hill into the orchard, their feet made stumbling sounds over the plowed ground.

The farmer had released the horses into the corral and was crossing to the house where his wife was standing when Nick and Ed came into the yard. He stopped when he saw them. Behind him the horses were nipping each other in the corral. The sweat had dried on their flanks and left a frothy stain. They began rolling in the dust, bathing in it, grunting with pleasure.

Ed brought out the wad of bills and began to count, plucking them from one hand into the other. The woman said something in the foreign tongue and the farmer laughed. "My wife, she say to tell you, one thousand two hundred box at two dollar a box make two thousand four hundred dollar," he said.

"That's right," Ed said. He handed the stack of bills to the farmer. The woman, who had been standing with her arms crossed at the doorway, went to her husband as they turned away. They were in the orchard when Nick heard the farmer call out behind them, "Good lucky, happy trip. Sell good my apples."

Ed looked briefly to Nick, his face saying nothing.

They were almost through the orchard and mounting the hill, when Nick heard the woman call out in alarm. "Papa! Papa!" She spoke rapidly in the foreign tongue. After a silence, the farmer shouted, his voice raised in anger, "Say, you wait, you stop." He ran through the orchard, waving the money in his hand.

"I'll see what he wants," Ed said. He started down the hill, but when Nick went to follow him, he stopped and said, "You go on up to the truck. I'll take care of this."

"The hell you will," Nick said.

They went together down the hill to the farmer, who was coming out of the orchard. The running had made him breathe hard and his mouth was open and his face was red. Nick could see his heart pumping in a vein in his neck.

"You don't count right," the farmer said. "One thousand two

hundred box make two thousand four hundred dollar. You only give one thousand eight hundred."

"That's right," Ed said, "a buck and a half a box."

"No, I don't say dollar and a half. I say two dollar," the farmer said.

"That's me you hear saying it," Ed said. "We'll play hell coming out at a buck and a half."

"You not going to pay two dollar?" the farmer said.

"You got what I'm going to pay," Ed said.

"This only one thousand eight hundred dollar," the farmer said. "I want six hundred more dollar. You pay me six hundred dollar." He had a hot stubborn look in his face. The woman was coming through the orchard. She ran heavily through the broken earth of the yard, stopping to catch her breath and running again. She said something in the foreign tongue that sounded like a profanity.

"What are you beefing about?" Ed said. "Eighteen hundred bucks is a lot of money."

"Is no two thousand four hundred dollar," the farmer said. You say you going to pay two dollar box, I want two dollar box. I want two thousand four hundred dollar."

"I never said I'd pay two bucks," Ed said.

"You lie, you cheat," the farmer said. He grabbed Nick by the shoulders. "You hear him," he said. "You hear what he say."

Nick shook his head.

The farmer gripped Nick in his hands. "You are young fella. You don't be like him," he said. "You be honest, you tell truth."

Nick wanted to be honest and to tell the truth, but he could not help thinking of the six hundred dollars. It was a lot of money, a lot more money than he had in his wallet. "I don't remember," he said.

"Sure he don't remember," Ed said, "because it didn't happen. A buck and a half is all we're going to pay. If you don't like it, you can have your apples."

"What you say?" the farmer said.

"I said if you don't like it, you can have your God damn apples," Ed said. "A buck and a half is all we're going to pay." He went on up the hill and Nick found himself standing with the farmer and his wife. The farmer pointed up the hill and shouted to the woman. He pounded his fist in his hand and raged in a fury. He ran up the hill and the woman turned to Nick.

"He going to fight," she said. "Please, you stop, I don't want fight."

Ed had the ropes off the truck and was pulling off the tarp when the farmer caught him and threw him aside. He moved like an ape in his anger. "Here your money," he said. "You take your money, I take my apples." He threw the wad of bills into Ed's face and began to unload the apples. He threw the boxes to the ground and the apples spilled and went rolling down the hill. They flashed golden as they tumbled down the hill. He tore the boxes from the truck and piled them in clumsy stacks on the roadside. The woman was picking up the money which had scattered in the wind. It was difficult for her to bend over and the wind kept moving the money along the road.

After the farmer had the back row of boxes off the truck, he stopped unloading and an expression of crying came into his face. "What I'm going to do with all this apple?" he said. "I got no truck, I no can haul. They going to rot. Is not too much I ask for what you promise to pay. I don't ask more. I say two dollar, I want two dollar. Maybe if you are my brother is different, but you are stranger. I don't give present to stranger."

"I ain't paying no two bucks," Ed said.

The farmer nodded. "All right, he said. "You dont pay, you dont pay. I give you for dollar and half. But if you sell good, make good money, you come back and I give you next load for two dollars and half."

"I'm only buying one load at a time," Ed said.

The farmer looked steadily at Ed, the anger coming on him again. His mouth trembled and he clenched and unclenched his hands. His eyes suddenly watered and brightened.

Nick touched his arm. "Take my word for it, if we come out right, we'll buy the next load at two-fifty," he said.

The farmer brushed off Nick's hand. "I want to hear him," he said.

"You'll wait until hell freezes over, if you're waiting for me," Ed said. "Come on, let's throw off this crap and get out of here," he said to Nick. He turned to pick up a box, but the farmer grabbed him and cramped him into his leather jacket in such a way that he could not move. "I spit at you," he said, and he spat into Ed's face. Ed kneed the farmer in the crotch and the farmer went down. He went to kick him, but Nick caught him and the woman helped the farmer up and they went down the hill. Ed was like a snake in Nick's arms. After the farmer and his wife were gone, Nick let him go. Ed got the cloth from the tool box and wiped his face.

"I guess that's telling you," Nick said.

"He could spit in my face all day for six hundred bucks," Ed said.

"You've got a spit coming. Do you want to take it now or later?" Nick said.

"How do you mean?"

"The money, I want it, hand it over."

"What money? What are you talking about?"

"The six hundred bucks, give it to me."

"The hell you say. I'm the guy who cut him down to a buck and a half. The money's mine."

"You son of a bitch. Are you going to hand it over, or do I have to take it?"

Ed thought about it. "We'll split it," he said.

"We'll split hell. I want it all."

Ed hit Nick with his eyes, but Nick did not move. He stood with his hand out, waiting for the money. After a while Ed brought it out and handed it over.

Nick found himself going down the hill with the money in his hand. All the way down the hill and halfway through the orchard, he thought of the money not as six hundred dollars but as an injustice to be rectified. When he neared the far end of the orchard row, the money began to assert itself until by the time he had reached the edge of the orchard, it had become six hundred dollars again. He had not thought of the bills as money at all, but now he began to think of it as cash, the things it could buy, the security it could give. Here he was with hardly enough money in his pocket for the gas and oil he would need for the journey to market. He would land in the market, fretting with the worry of being broke. There was never a time in his life when he did not feel panic when he was broke. He was all right as long as he had a dime in his pocket, but when he got down to that last dime, the panic set in. He had a memory of childhood, of an empty icebox, of unpaid light, water, gas, rent, of bill collectors coming to the door every day in the week and his mother hiding in the closet until they went away. His father would have paid them if he could, but he couldn't, and if he could, there were always more debts than money. He remembered how he had resolved never to be broke. There was always going to be the jingle of silver in his pockets. Six hundred dollars was a long way from being broke.

Nick decided to keep the money, but he was already near the yard and he stepped quickly behind an apple tree. It was a tree matted with twiggy branches and dead leaves. The trunk, which carried many knots from such a long time back that they were covered with a woody flesh, was too narrow to hide behind, but Nick crouched against it.

Beyond the tree was the empty yard and beyond the yard was the house crowded against sycamores that bushed the riverbank. The river flowed in a big rush beyond the sycamores.

The farmer was sitting on a box before the house. When he walked, talked or used his hands, he hid his age, but now sitting on the box collapsed in thought, his age settled on him and took him over. His hands shook, his mouth trembled, his head wove slowly from side to side.

The wife spoke from somewhere within the house, but the farmer did not look up.

Why should I give him the money? Nick thought. I didn't hold out on him. Ed did. If he had stuck to his guns, he would have got it, but he didn't, so why should I make him a present of it.

The farmer looked up and Nick narrowed himself against the tree. He stood with his head in the branches and his body hard against the rough trunk. Ants were crawling in a long irregular wavering line through the mottled bark of the trunk. There was a sticky exudation where the tree had been wounded.

The ants began to crawl onto Nick's coat, moving excitedly, as though they had found new prey, and Nick wished he had not come into the orchard.

After a time Nick bent down and saw that the farmer had dropped his head again. What will he do with the money? Nick thought. He can't spend it, he can't even spend the eighteen hundred. He'll be dead before the year is out.

He thought of the year before his father had died. You could tell he was going to die from the expression in his face. There was something sainted, some quiet inner grace that said, this man is not long for this world. And now here was the farmer with the same look, the same sense of staggering through the last days of his life. One morning his strong wife would waken in the iron bed that Nick could see through the window and find him lying cold beside her. He could see the old woman becoming very frightened in the presence of death. When he was alive, she was not alone, but the instant he died she was very lonely. The wind was louder in the trees, and she heard the river running in a way she could not remember. The sky seemed terribly blue and empty. And the simple flies that came from the barn, they were not flies any longer, but something evil feeding on her husband's eyes and mouth. How frightened the old woman would become when she saw the hungry flies. Nick could see her running through the silent woods to the neighbors, and later the farmer, Josef Polansky, being buried on a corner of his farm. And one day the woman would die and be buried too, and there they would lie, with the weeds growing over their graves; and the sun would shine and the rain would fall and the trees would continue to bear crops that would be harvested by some strange family living in the house. And who would get the money? Some heir who would spend it, and if he remembered the farmer and his wife, he would remember them so vaguely as not to be remembrance at all.

Over by the house, the farmer was rising to his feet. He stood with his legs apart, still in pain from the kneeing Ed had given him, supporting himself with one hand against the wall. After the pain had subsided, he went slowly into the house. Nick crammed the wad of bills into his pocket and stepped away from the tree. He headed quickly through the orchard and as he went up the orchard row, he could feel the silence pressing on him all around. Far away a bird sang and beyond the trees the river flowed. One of the horses whinnied in the corral and Nick started to run but the rough ground tripped him and he fell. Sunlight streamed through the flickering leaves of the trees and when he looked up, the bright light blinded him. He felt trapped. He wanted to get up and run but the silence held him and he lay listening for some sound from the house but there was none. He got to his feet and was running again when he heard the slap of a door. After a silence, he heard the farmer's wife say in an excited voice that was like a finger pointed to his back, "Papa!" And after another silence he heard the farmer call out, "What you want?"

Nick stopped. The farmer and his wife were in the yard, looking at him. He wanted to go on up the hill and get into the truck and drive away, but he found himself walking to the yard. He saw himself with the money in his hand, going to the woman, holding it out. Then she had taken the money and he was running across the yard, through the flickering light of the orchard and on up the hill.

Ed had gone under the truck again. He came out with a wrench in his hands and his hands greasy. "Did you give it to him?" he said.

"Yeah," Nick said.

"Do you feel clean?"

"I feel fine."

"That's good, I'm glad you feel fine," Ed said. He put away the wrench and cleaned his hands.

"What I want to know is how you feel," Nick said.

"What do you mean, how I feel?"

"About giving back the money."

Ed did not answer. He stood looking at Nick with his mouth tight and hard. Then he laughed and said, "What do you care how I feel?"

"I thought maybe you'd like to wash up the deal we made."

"Not a chance. You buy the loads and I'll show you where to find 'em. That still goes."

"You don't hold no grudge?"

"Hell no. You just threw away my six hundred bucks, but I don't hold no grudge."

Your six hundred bucks, Nick thought. You crumby bastard. Your six hundred bucks. I'm going to have to watch you, you bastard. "I told the guy two bucks and I like to stick to what I say," he said.

"Sure, your word's good as gold," Ed said. He went to the engine and dropped the hood and clamped it in place. He had oiled up the two trucks, but the can was still on the road. He stored the can in its place on the tire rack.

"How's the universal?" Nick said.

"I tightened her up," Ed said. "She ought to hold okay, but you never can tell."

"I'll tail you in case you break down," Nick said.

"No, you better go on ahead, see if you can find a part in Auburn. Stores'll be closed by the time I get there. I'm going to have to nurse this baby along."

Nick went to his truck and got in. He started the engine and pulled onto the road. He heard Ed behind him, pulling out too.

The trucks had rolled in easily, empty, but now, loaded, it was a hard pull going back up the long grade that wound out of the valley where the farm was.

7

THE grade was steep and the truck climbed straight into the sky, and when it had burst into the clear on the crest of the hill, the woods and meadows were far below. A stiff wind was blowing and the sky was clean. All around were the green woods and far away the snow-covered mountains. Nick forced his eyes to the road.

The road ran a short space along the ridge before it curved into the twists and turns of the downgrade. The truck began to take the grade and Nick rode the brakes until he was out of the curves when he threw it out of gear and let it go. The engine was quiet under the hood, but the tires sang. The singing of the tires on the road made Nick feel good. Here he was on the long road between farm and market and the truck going fast. He felt fine. He thought of selling the apples and of men and women and children in the city buying and eating them and he felt big. He had been to the market before with his father, but not in his own truck with his own load, and it had meant nothing, but now he felt excited. The steering wheel trembled in his hands.

The sugar pines that bordered both sides of the road surged up in tight green swaths. The road ran evenly between them to a long way, falling before him down the hill and across the saddle of valley until it diminished in a thread that rose again into the face of the hill on the far side. Nick looked into the rear view mirror, expecting to see Ed's truck, but the road lay empty behind him. He had lost Ed.

He began to worry about Ed. He cursed himself for going on before him. Now how will I know if he's coming or if he's broken down or if he's turned North up the Tahoe road, he thought.

You dumb sucker, you cripple-brained bastard, he told himself.
That's why he told you to go on ahead. So he could ditch you.
And you fall for it. You've got to cut out letting people talk you
into doing things. You've got to look behind their eyes, listen
behind what they say. He wanted to stop and wait for Ed and
if he did not come, to turn around and go after him, but some
inertia kept him from hitting the brakes; and the truck kept rolling
down the hill, going faster and faster until it seemed hardly to
touch the ground.

Suddenly the air darkened and a shadow fell over the truck.
The air chilled and a lonely feeling came into the cab. Nick sat
up and he could see the giant trunks of the evergreens standing
close to the road. They were like an army of men watching him
and a wave of cold went through him and he felt lost and alone
in the woods.

Fog steamed up from the marshy forest undergrowth. Where
the road shoulder dropped away were beds of frost in the shadowed
meadows. The frost covered the grass and brush and the trunks of
trees. In the hollows where aspen and sycamore grew, the Autumn
freeze had touched the leaves and there were bursts of yellow and
red and brown making spears of color in the green bed of the
forest. But it was all turning gray in the dark. The truck had
descended into the lowland where the sun had set. The slope of
hill ahead was still bright with sun, but it was growing night in
the saddle of the valley.

Somewhere a tree crashed and there was the piercing cry of a
bird. The sight of the forest made Nick shiver. He slapped together
his hands, trying to beat some warmth into them. The tires sang
swiftly as the truck fled along the road that crossed the valley.
I'll be out of here pretty soon, Nick thought. He tried to make
the truck go faster. He could not get out of there soon enough, but
when the truck hit the upgrade again, it began to slow down. It
was as though the valley were trying to hold him. He shifted into
second and then into low and compound. The engine roared,
pulling the load. The trees which had blurred by a moment ago
now fell back like the spokes of a slow turning wheel. At this
moment a frightening thought went over Nick: Suppose I can't

get rid of the apples? He had had such thoughts before, but always he had seen himself selling them for the money he had put out. But suppose the market was flooded and he could not sell them at all?

The slow-moving truck crawled up the grade toward the last rays of sunlight. Night was welling from the forest. He could see it flooding up the slope before him, darkening the hill, and he got out to the running board and looked back into the deepening air of the valley, searching for Ed, but the road was still empty. There was one last patch of light on the crest of hill behind him. Suddenly it vanished. And now with the darkness all around him, the truck seemed to be standing still. The engine thrashed and roared, but the hills were endless. He drove mile after mile, climbing and waiting for Auburn, but Auburn never came. After an interminable time of making the twists and turns of the mountain journey, Nick began to wonder if he had taken the wrong road and was lost.

The time felt to be very late. High up, the night was clear with the clearness that comes with extreme cold. The milky way was a cloudy smear among the stars. Nick drove and drove, the head-lights pronging out into space, then sweeping over stratified beds of rock on the side of the road as he made the turns. His eyes felt numbed and tired and he began to feel that he had been on the road most of the night when he saw a glow in the sky. At first it was faint and far away and it held his eyes without his knowing it, but gradually it swelled and brightened until it became the glow of some fabulous city in the distance. Auburn. There it is, just around the turn, Nick thought, and he wakened and sat up. The light made him feel good, but he passed the turn and many turns, the glow moving before him. When he had given up hope of ever reaching it, the truck rounded a hill and there was the town with its string of lights and its block of buildings below him in the mist. So this was Auburn, this was the town that had been making all that spangle in the sky for all those miles in the mountains. It looked lonely and deserted. Nick steered the truck down the hill and through the underpass and parked at the first gas station on the main street. The station was dark and the town was asleep.

Nick switched off the engine and instantly the muffler began to creak. He sat listening to the muffler shrinking and creaking in the cold.

After a while he got down and began looking for a store where he could find a part to fix Ed's truck, but all the stores were closed. There was one place, Murphy's Auto Parts, on the other side of town where a light burned, but the light was in the back, and when he knocked on the door, no one answered. He returned slowly to the truck, his feet sounding on the empty street. The night was cold. The cold got under his coat and made him shudder.

There was a coffee shop across the street from the truck. Its lights spilled onto the walk, staining it yellow, giving an effect of warmth. Nick walked by and saw only one person in it, the waitress, a brunette, young and vigorously made, with strong arms and legs. She was busy cleaning the malt shakers, making the nickel parts glisten, and her bottom jiggled as she worked her arms. She made Nick think of the waitresses in Ambrose Brothers in Fresno, the way they brought the menus and plates of French bread to the table, saying, What will you have? as they bent over the table; and the farm hands and ranchers and the guys from the railroad yard two blocks away on J Street with their cloth caps and leather sleeve protectors, eyeing the girls, leg, thigh, hip and breasts, and sometimes the waist if it was very slim, speculating about encircling it with arms, or laying open hands upon the broad fleshy cheeks of rump, watching the waitress, and finally one of the men saying to a girl, Hey Irm, what you doin' tonight? And Irm saying, Oh, I don't know, Sam was going to pick me up, we was going out to his ma's place, Why? and the man, Paul Finley, perhaps, cat wrestler from the Wiley ranches, living with his wife in a shack, but actually months without a woman, saying, I'll be around about ten o'clock, parked out front, and Irm saying in a slow drawling voice, Okay, and as she walked off one of the other waitresses saying, Poor Sam, and at this all the men at the bar and the waitresses standing at the kitchen counter and even some of the diners in the booths exploding into laughter.

Nick went into the restaurant and sat down. The waitress looked over and caught him investigating her body, about and around and

above and below, going gently and sweetly and lingeringly over
her.

"What'll it be?" she said.

"Coffee," Nick said. He watched her as she poured the coffee.
She was hot and sweaty from working near the stove and she had
a narrow waist and flaring hips. Nick thought of the men who had
no doubt had her. Men passing through. Great town, Auburn, he
thought of them saying. There's a dame there, works in a coffee
joint on the main drag. Hard to get at, but once you get it, Oh Joe!
Yeah, what a town. How the town was the girl. The sweat glued
her dress to her body and she kept picking it off. He could see
every curve on her, the outline of brassiere, the outline of pants,
even to the band holding it to her waist and clasping it high on her
thighs. She was hot and sticky and odorous, and that was the way
Nick wanted it. He got a whiff of her when she placed the cup
before him and it was wonderful, that sweet, musty, body smell.
He wanted to bury his nose into her as into a bouquet of flowers.
He sat slowly drinking his coffee and watching her, and because
she resented it, this watching had in it some of the quality of
pulling a resisting woman to him and tearing off her clothes. Rape.

When he had tired of watching her, he laid a dollar on the
counter and went to the door.

"How about your change?" the girl said.

"You earned it," Nick said.

The girl crushed the bill in her hand and Nick went out and
crossed the street to his truck. He walked back and forth beside his
truck, waiting for Ed. He tried not to think of Ed. Ed would come,
he had to come, unless he broke down.

He had waited over an hour, when Ed's truck nosed quietly
through the underpass and drifted to a stop at the station. The
universal was thumping. Ed got down. His hair stuck up wild all
over his head. He looked to be tired.

"Jesus Christ. I just about gave you up," Nick said.

"What's the matter, didn't you think I was coming?"

"I thought you were broke down or something. Where the hell
you been?"

"Where the hell do you think I've been?"

Nick did not answer and Ed smiled. It was a thin, frigid smile, as though he were cursing inside. "You weren't afraid I ran out on you?" he said.

"Hell no," Nick said. "Why would I think that?"

"Oh, I don't know," Ed said. "What would you do if I had run out?"

"I guess I'd have to go it alone," Nick said.

"You'd last just about two trips."

"You think so?"

"You're God damned right I think so. You don't know those wolves at the market. They're waiting for suckers like you." Ed turned up the collar of his coat and buttoned it high around his neck. He had not shaved in a long time and his beard was thick on his face. For some reason Nick felt sorry for him. He did not like him, he had no friendly feeling for him, but still he felt sorry.

"Did you think to look for a universal?" Ed said.

"I checked around," Nick said. "They're all closed. There was one place with a light on, but I couldn't shake 'em up."

Ed nodded. "Where is it?" he said.

Nick took him to the store. The lights were off now, but Ed walked to the back where he found a light still burning. He banged on the window until an old man opened it. Warm air from the room carried the odor of food into the alley. The old man was moving his jaw with quick jerks, eating.

"How about opening up?" Ed said.

The old man stared at them, looking alertly from Ed to Nick.

"Truck's broke down, we need a part," Nick said.

The parts dealer closed the window and latched it and they could hear him crossing the room. When they went back to the street, the store lights were on. Nick could read the sign on the window, *Murphy's Auto Parts*. The old man opened the door and an alarm bell began to ring. It rang with startling loudness in the quiet town, stirring up echoes against the dark buildings. They got in quickly and the ringing stopped when the parts dealer shut the door. "What do you want?" he said.

"We need a universal for a ton and a half GMC, the front one, near the transmission," Ed said.

"What year?"

"Thirty-eight."

The dealer picked up his spectacles which were lying on the counter. They were old reading glasses with one of the ear pieces missing. He put them on and disappeared among the parts bins that lined the back wall.

The room was filled with junk. Rusty engines were piled in a corner. Crankcases, connecting rods, burned out generators littered the floor. Fan belts of various lengths dangled from the ceiling. There was the copper sheen of head gaskets on the wall. The floor was crusted with grease and dirt that had dried so the boards looked paved. In the back, among the bins, the dealer was tumbling parts around. Presently he appeared with the universal in his hand. "Is that it?" he said.

"That's her," Ed said. "What's the bad news?" He brought out his wallet.

"You're sure lucky I had one," the parts dealer said. "Them things are mighty hard to get."

"If you didn't have one, we couldn't get out of town," Nick said. He saw the parts dealer listening shrewdly and knew he had made a mistake.

Ed's eyes burned with anger. "We're not so stuck we can't move," he said. He picked up the used universal and turned it in his hand. "This thing's so beat up I don't know if we can use it. How much?"

The parts dealer bent down to figure the bill, presenting the top of his head to Nick. It was a bald little head, the skin drawn tightly over the configurations of skull. One large vein throbbed and pulsed slowly. Then the head looked up and the old man said, "That'll be exactly seventy-three dollars."

"Seventy-three what?" Ed said.

"Dollars," the parts dealer said.

Ed threw the universal down to the counter. "Why, you God damned skinflint, I can buy all the universals I want for ten bucks a throw in Frisco," he said.

"That's in Frisco," the dealer said.

"Come on," Ed said. He pushed Nick roughly. They went out

and above them the alarm bell rang shrilly, and stopped suddenly, as though cut by a knife when the dealer shut the door behind them.

"You and your yap," Ed said to Nick. "Who the hell asked you to pop off?"

"I'm sorry," Nick said.

"You beg for it, you ask him to soak us, and you're sorry," Ed said.

They were standing in the light from the store and now the light went off.

"Seventy-three bucks," Ed said. "Seventy-three bucks and second hand." He started to walk blindly down the street, away from where the trucks were parked.

"Where you going?" Nick said.

"How the hell would I know where I'm going?" Ed said. They walked down the street until the sidewalk stopped. Crickets made a big noise on the edge of town. The night wind blew through the trees. The smell of tamarack came down from the woods all around. Nick offered Ed a cigarette, which he accepted, and in the light from the match he saw Ed's face, drawn and intent, worrying. He stood sucking on his cigarette, thinking. Then he brought out his wallet and Nick saw there were bills in it, several of them.

Ed counted the bills. "I've got forty-five bucks. How much have you got?" he said.

Nick counted the money in his wallet. He had eight dollars. There were fifty-three dollars between the two of them.

"We're out of the mountains. Maybe we can roll into Sacramento," Nick said.

"Sure, and maybe we could fly, if we had wings," Ed said. "Here, take my money."

Nick took the money and Ed said, "We're going to go back to that guy and you're going to talk to him. He won't listen to me because he's sore at me. But he'll listen to you."

Ed told him what to say and they went back to the store. The parts dealer opened the door and they went in. The universal was on the counter and beside it was the receipt book, filled out. The dealer had written up the sale, anticipating their return. "Make up your mind?" he said.

"Sure, we want the universal," Nick said. "My friend here got kind of excited, but I know a bargain when I see one." He brought the bills from his wallet. "How much did you say?"

"Seventy-three dollars, no more, no less," the parts dealer said.

Nick counted three tens down to the counter. "Here's thirty bucks," he said.

"It's seventy-three dollars," the parts dealer said.

"Yeah, I know, but we'll catch the rest on the trip back," Nick said. "It's all right, you can trust us. We got two loads of apples going to market and we're coming back for more. We'll pay you off for sure in a couple days."

The parts dealer shook his head. "I don't give no credit," he said.

"We've got fifty-three dollars," Nick said. "I'd give you all of it, but we need some for gas. How about forty?" He laid down another ten.

The parts dealer shook his head.

"What's the matter, can't you trust us?" Ed said.

"Sure, I trust you," the parts dealer said. "But business is business." He picked up the universal. "You need it and I've got it. Seventy-three dollars and it's yours."

"But we haven't got seventy-three bucks," Ed said.

"Then you don't get it," the parts dealer said. He started to turn away with the universal but Nick stopped him. "Now wait a minute," he said. He picked up the bills and spread them in his hand. "Suppose I give you all of it," he said. Ed tried to cut in but Nick held him off. "I just want to see what he'll say," he said; and to the parts dealer he said, "Suppose I give you all the money we've got. How about that?"

The parts dealer tried to turn away, but Nick held him. "Don't go away. I want to talk to you," he said. "It's seventy-three or nothing, is that it?"

Nick saw that the parts dealer was not listening but was trying to get away, and he held him tight. This evil little man with his hard little head and his shrewd little eyes that were never raised but managed somehow to take in everything without ever looking

up from the floor; this mean little soul who bought decrepit old
cars and trucks and took them apart very carefully in an empty
lot on the outskirts of town, hoarding all the pieces, even to the
last nut and bolt, and filling his bins with them, storing them
against the day when some unfortunate like Ed would have a break-
down and need it and he could get at him. So much like a spider
waiting in a web. Nick thought of the abandoned webs in the
packing house in which moths and flies and beetles would be
caught and struggle for days and days, becoming more tightly
wrapped in the dusty web; and where was the spider to suck them
dry of their nourishing juices? Dead and gone. Only the web
remained, steadily, pointlessly snaring its victims. But this old
man, who was a spider too in a way, would never die. He would
always be in a little web like this store, waiting for his victims.
And what patience he had. Imagine storing away a '38 GMC
universal, just one, and knowing that in the unknown future,
on such a night as this night, such a man as Ed Kennedy would
want it and all the waiting would be rewarded.

The parts dealer struggled in Nick's hands, but Nick hung on.
He felt himself stiffen in anger; he tried to control his anger, but it
mounted in him. He could feel his heart pounding and his nose
tingled. He felt that his cheek was going to twitch, the way it
does with villains in a movie, only this was real. Nick wanted to
kill the parts dealer. One blow would do it. On that scrawny neck.
One blow. Pick up the universal and cave in his head. He could
see the vein pulsing quickly now in the old man's neck. You evil
little man, Nick thought. He remembered his grandmother talking
about the devil. What a real person the devil was to her. Nick
had always doubted the existence of a real, flesh-and-blood devil,
but here he was, in this parts dealer who ate people, for it was a
kind of cannibalism to lie in wait along the dark road for the
lonely wayfarer who needed help, who needed it desperately or
he would not come to the parts dealer, knowing he would be eaten.

I'll eat you, Nick thought, and he tightened his hold on the
parts dealer. He saw that the man was frightened and he said,
"Nobody's going to hurt you. We're not a couple of crooks. If we
say we'll pay you, we'll pay you. All I want you to do is listen."

The dealer sucked in his breath to shout and Nick hit him. The blow was automatic and he regretted it the instant he gave it and he tried to undo the harm he had done by holding him but he could not reach him. The parts dealer was in the spread of Nick's arms, but when Nick tried to catch him, he cringed within himself, diminishing beneath his fingers. "Now wait a minute," Nick said. "Now take it easy, nobody's trying to hurt you."

The dealer ran around the counter to the door. He opened it and the alarm bell began to ring before Nick could reach it and slam it to silence. He tried to catch the dealer again, advancing on him as the dealer backed across the room. "Look, we're going to pay you," Nick said. "It'll only be a couple of days and you'll have your money. What the hell are you getting excited about?" But the dealer was not listening.

The dealer tried to shout, but terror locked his throat. He made another rush for the door and Nick grabbed him and hung him up against his collar and he heard Ed saying something but could not tell what it was. The old man tried to shout and Nick hit him again, had to hit him twice before he sagged to the floor and he could drag him behind the counter.

When Nick stood up, Ed was gone. The door was open and the bell was ringing. It had been ringing a long time, far away, but now, as his head cleared, the sound rushed at him.

He saw the parts dealer lying on the floor with a thin trickle of blood running from his nose. His mouth was open, exposing the small decayed teeth, the gums rotted away at the roots, looking exactly like a cannibal's mouth. I've killed him, Nick thought. He was aghast, not at what he had done, but his capacity for doing it. He had murdered in a blind rage. He's dead, he thought, I've killed him. He wanted to bring the man to life somehow, to fall on his knees and pray.

Nick was out on the street, running to the truck, before he remembered the universal. He was about to return when he thought of the parts dealer lying on the floor, his glasses splintered beside him. Dead. The thought impaled him. Not dead, not from such a mild blow. As he stood torn between the necessity of getting the part and the dread of going back to the store, two lights glared toward him down the street and a truck went by, roaring sparks from its exhaust. It was Ed heading out of town.

Nick ran to his truck. The engine was cold and he could not start it. He kept hitting the starter, but it would not start. Then it did and he was banging down the street, in a panic to be rid of the town.

8

THE road leapt out of darkness, blurred under the truck and fell back into darkness. Nick passed through Roseville and Sacramento and hit the long stretch to Stockton. It was late and the towns were dead. There were only dogs in the streets and the fog coming in from the Sacramento River. Even the highway was deserted except for an occasional dot of light that appeared dim and far in the countryside. The light wheeled back so slowly the truck felt to be standing still. The engine thrashed, the tires spun, the exhaust roared, but the truck crawled along the belly of the road until it came to a string of cars. Then it burst upon them and banged by and once more the road lay empty before him.

A marker came up and dropped back. Stockton, it said, twenty-eight miles. Beyond Stockton was Manteca and beyond Manteca was the San Joaquin River bridge and Tracy and all the gas stations and restaurants and motels, dark on the roadside. Nick tromped the foot throttle in a fit of impatience to make the truck go faster, but nothing happened. He had the gas pedal down to the floor. The truck was going as fast as it could go. How fast? He tried to check his speed, but the dashlight was burned out. He struck a match and in the flare of the light he saw the needle touching seventy-two. Instantly he hit the brakes and sat waiting for a tire to blow. He waited for it, but it did not blow and after a time he relaxed in his seat.

He felt tired and drugged. His eyes kept closing and he kept forcing them open to see the road. It had been cold in the hills and he had cranked up the windows, but now it was hot and stuffy in the cab and he cranked them down. The inrush of marshy air, wet on his face, made him dizzy. He could tell now with the

sweet air coming in how foul the interior of the cab had been.
It was sour with the smell of scorched oil. Nick alerted again. He
had not been listening to the engine, but now he began to listen to
it, expecting to hear a burned out rod. But the engine turned over
evenly, the rods were all right. He lighted a cigarette and tried
to shake the scare from his head.

A marker indicated curve ahead and as the truck made the turns,
its headlights pronged beyond the road into the bare fields that
crowded it on both sides. Alkali land. He had seen it on the trip
North in daylight, broad chalky patches of alkali wasteland stretching to the mountains in the distance.

Another light appeared, pin-pointed in the darkness. As it
drifted back, a tire blew.

Nick grabbed the wheel, expecting the truck to cramp over, but
it held to the road, the gone tire flopping on the rim, one of the
rears. He stopped the truck and when he got down, there was a
smell of burning rubber in the air. He went around kicking the
tires and found it, the right outside driver, the fabric blown out in
a puff of cotton, the tire torn half away.

Nick stood up and a wave of tiredness went over him. He wanted
to enter the cab and go to sleep, but he leaned against the truck,
knowing he would have to jack up the truck and change the tire,
but resisting it. A passenger car banged by and after it was gone,
there was not a sound. Overhead the stars shone in patches. Clouds
were sweeping in, covering the sky. The wind blasted against the
truck, making it shudder.

Nick pulled the truck off the road and set out a bomb flare. The
wind kept snapping the flame and he could not light it, but finally
he did and returned to the truck where he got his flashlight from
the tool box, but it would not work. He kept rapping it against the
heel of his hand, but it would not stay on. In the intermittent light
he saw that he had gone too far off the highway onto the sandy
shoulder of the road. The tires were sinking in the sand.

He got the block and jack and threw them under the truck and
tried to crawl to them, but the tirerack was in the way. He scooped
out the sand and crowded his chest beneath the rack and squared
the block into the sand and set the jack upon it, but found he had

forgotten the jack handle. He scuffed his ear in the process of
setting out but was so intent on changing the tire that he did not
notice his ear was bleeding. He got the jack handle and went under
again and a muscle cramped in his arm, in the bicep, tightening
every time he moved so it was a kind of medieval torture. He got
the cramp out of his arm and began to work, working and resting
in spurts until the jack took hold. The truck creaked as the load
shifted. The tires were not off the ground, but it was a beginning.
Soon the tire rack would be off his back and he could use his arms.
He kept working.

The rack was up now. He tried to move into a better position,
but his motion raised dust and he got a noseful of it, the dust stinging his nostrils so he was going to sneeze, that gasping, strangling
sensation of it, feeling it mounting in his head until he did and
got a mouthful of the dust puckery and dry so he could not breathe.
A frenzy to get out from under the truck came over him but he
gripped himself. A little more and she'll be up, he thought. Just
a little more. After I change the tires, I won't get under again.
I'll throw off the brakes and let her roll off the jack. He worked
quickly now and soon had the tires off the ground. Not high enough
yet because he could not get his hand between tire and sand, but up.
Another two or three strokes of the jack would do it, but before
he could pull down the handle, the truck began to move. He could
not see it move, but sensed it moving and he touched the jack and
knew it was moving. The truck was coming off the jack.

Nick made a quick struggle to get out from under the tire rack,
but his shoulders jammed. He ripped them through, but his head
was caught. He turned it sideways, thinking, I'll get it through, I'll
ram it through, but before he could, the truck came off the jack and
he flattened himself on the sand, waiting for the rack to come down
on his neck. I'm a goner, he thought, I'm dead, oh I'm dead. Then
the tire rack struck his neck with a stunning, crushing blow and
that was all he knew.

Nick came alive, shuddering.

He did not know how long he had been under the truck, but it
was a long time. The rack was hard on his neck. His eyes were

accustomed to the dark and he saw where the wind had piled sand against the tires. Good thing I didn't get it face down, he thought. Face down I would have choked in the sand. As it was, his face was half crushed into it. Sand covered one eye and ran into the corner of his mouth. He tried to scrape it away, but could not get down his arms. He lay thinking how lucky he was he could breathe. With every breath he inhaled dust, but he was lucky. Oh I'm lucky, he thought. After a time he decided he would try moving his head, afraid to try, but had to and finally did but could not move it. His body was without sensation from the neck down.

A car winged by and its lights whipped swiftly beneath the truck, illuminating all its underparts. The chassis and the wishbone were smeared with oil. The pan gasket was leaking or maybe it was the pan bolts, loose. When I get out I'll tighten them, he thought. He thought fervently, I'm going to get out.

Again he tried to move. He could feel the rough edge of the tire rack on his neck when he lifted his head and an odd fainting sensation came over him and as he began to spin off, he thought of sand. He was lying on sand. He would scoop out the sand and free his neck. But he could not move his arms. He could see them cramped before him, the palms upturned, the fingers slacked, but he could not get them down.

A passenger car went by, then another. After a silence a string of cars raced past the truck, one sounding its horn petulantly.

The wind was blowing sand in a restless veil along the surface of the road, making a hissing sound against the truck. Nick closed his eyes. He had broken into a sweat and dust was caked into mud on his face.

He had forgotten about Ed, but now in desperation he began to think of him. He thought how he had passed Ed a few miles out of Auburn, how he had gunned by him and watched his headlights grow smaller and smaller in the rear view mirror, becoming dim, merging into one and finally disappearing. He cursed for letting himself get so far ahead.

His thoughts were interrupted by a sound that came from the truck. He alerted instantly. The truck was settling. The discovery made him stiffen and he touched something with the tip of his hand. It was the flashlight. It went on, perversely, and in the fading light Nick could see the driver tire that supported the left rear of the truck. The terrific heat had blistered the rubber, peeled it off in strips and beneath it the scorched cotton fabric of the carcass was feathering and unravelling.

Nick listened. All his being was consumed with listening. He could hear the sand hissing along the road. The truck creaked.

Nick could not get out, he knew he could not, but terror seized him. He made a violent effort to get out from under the rack.

A car was coming up, its sound remote but beating swiftly toward the truck. The sound of its passage mounted to a frenzy, and in the brightening light Nick's legs could be seen thrashing against the sand. The car exploded by and dwindled away into darkness and silence, but the legs kept thrashing for a while longer before they fell still. One foot trembled and tried to rise. The legs stiffened, as though Nick were trying with the one last effort to throw off the truck. Then the legs relaxed and both feet lay pigeon-toed in the sand. Soon the wind had covered Nick's legs with a thin crust of sand.

A long time had passed and the wind had died down. High up the sky was covered with clouds. The air felt to be heavy and hot. The air became heavier and hotter, each moment becoming increasingly laden with something tense.

It began to rain.

9

THE slanting rain blinded Ed's windshield. The wiper was broken and would not work. He kept reaching through the window and bringing it over with his hand, but it swept back balkily and he had to stick his head out into the rain to see the road.

The rain was coming down so hard the drops were like shot on his eyes. When he could no longer blink them away, he drew his head back into the shell of the cab and mopped the water from his face with his arms, letting the truck run blind down the road.

Water was gathering in pools beside the road and where it flooded the runoffs it washed in a torrent across the highway. Ed pulled down his speed and he could hear the sound of the tires come buzzing up. The defective universal thumped beneath the load. He thought of the road ahead, miles of it, and an annoyance of the rain came over him and he cursed. He kept trying to see the road but the blurr of drops confused his eyes until they ached. The pain was as of needles in his eyes. Somewhere the cab was leaking and water began dripping on his knee.

Ed felt dizzy. It seemed that all the raindrops in the world were spinning toward him and he wanted to hit the brakes and stop the truck, but he clenched the wheel and kept driving on and on through the web of rain.

He had driven a long way and his head was nodding at the wheel when he saw a flickering point of light, sparkling and voluted in the darkness. The light held his eyes. It whorled toward him until it grew into the sooty flame of a bomb flare. Beyond it was a truck, the right side lurched down. He went by before he saw it was Nick's truck.

The odd position of the truck beside the road frightened Ed

and he slammed on the brakes but the tires began to skid. He could feel them skidding in the steering wheel, the gone feeling in his hand, and he let up on the pedal and the truck coasted a long way before it stopped.

When Ed got down, Nick's lights were small and faint down the road. He ran to the truck, but Nick was not in the cab. The rain was coming down hard against the steel cab. "Nick," Ed called out, but there was no answer. Water ran off the truck in a steady dribble that made a lonely sound. Ed walked back in the Christmas tree light from the clearance lamps. He wondered what had happened to Nick. Somebody picked him up and he's gone for help, he thought. But he wouldn't, he decided. He knew I was coming, he's got to be here. "Nick," he shouted. The sound of the rain was deafeningly loud in his ears.

Maybe he's asleep in the cab, Ed thought. He had just looked into the cab and he knew that the cab was empty, that it would be foolish to look again, but he was about to turn back when he saw Nick's legs. He crouched down and saw the water-soaked trousers, the rain running off them, the shoes pigeon-toed in the sand.

"Nick?" Ed said softly, afraid to say it because he knew he would not be answered. He touched one leg and the leg slopped over, limp under his hand.

He got under the truck, the darkness bewildering his eyes, and ran his hand along Nick's body until he felt the tire rack. Oh Christ, he thought, Oh Jesus Christ, Oh sweet Christ. He tried to get out a match but the box spilled and his hands were shaking so he could not pick them up, but at last he did and he felt sick and hollow inside when he struck the match and saw the rack pinning Nick down. He's dead, he thought, he's got to be dead. Oh, Jesus Christ. But he could not see from behind the tire rack and he got out and went under from the other side but he had lost the matches and had to touch again to see with his hands and he felt Nick's head down to his neck where the flesh was swollen tight against the rack, the rack was on him, in him, cutting into the back of his neck.

Well, get it off, he told himself. It was some inner voice screaming at him, What are you sitting here for? Get the God damned thing off. The thing to do was to jack up the truck. The jack, he thought, set the jack. He felt around until he found the jack, but the staff was bent and he could not use it. Well, get your jack, the voice said, and he crashed his head getting out. He ran back to his truck where he got the jack, but as he turned away he remembered the block. He would need it in the sand, but it was not in the tool box nor was it under the seat, nor in the back behind the load, and he looked again in the tool box where it had been all along and ran to Nick's truck. He squared the block under the axle, setting it firmly in the sand, and placed the jack upon it and began to pump. Soon the truck began to rise, but as it rose, the jack began to slip. Ed tried to compose axle and jack, but the jack slipped and the rack came down and Nick came alive, screaming and Ed lay hamstrung by the sound. Then Nick had passed out again and Ed could work.

The axle was wet and slippery with oil that had blown back from the leaking crankcase. Ed cleaned it with a handful of sand and set the jack under it once more and this time he got the truck up. It was not enough, but it was up; and at last it was enough and he dragged Nick out from under the rack.

There was only the red of the tail light to see by and Ed cursed it. He cursed the ruby glass that would not come off. He tried to kick it off but managed to smash both glass and light and ran cursing to the bomb flare that was burning on the roadside. The bomb was hot but he picked it up and ran with it, cursing the hot metal that seared his hands as he carried it to Nick.

In the flickering light Ed saw Nick's neck, the flesh laid open where the rack had been. I've got to get him to town, he thought. I've got to get him to a doctor. He cursed when he thought of all the miles he would have to go to get a doctor.

Nick's head was face down in the sand. He twisted it clear and brushed off the sand that was in his nose and mouth. In the midst of doing this, he thought, Nick's dead, and he leaned over to listen for breath.

"Nick," he said. He slapped Nick's cheek.

Nick revived in violent resurrection, his struggle beneath the truck not concluded but suspended. He clawed back as though

against the truck in furious rejection, shuddering the weight of it
up and off him. And now it was off and he was out from under it
and free.

Nick found himself holding onto the tailboard. There for a
moment he was as dead as he would ever be, but now he was
alive. He sucked in the clean night air. His neck hurt and his
mouth was filled with sand. He had swallowed some of it and he
wanted to vomit, but when he leaned over, the road tipped out
from under him and he should have fallen, but he felt himself
held firmly in two hands.

"Okay, boy, you're okay now," he heard Ed say.

Nick heard himself laughing. "I'm okay, I'm all right," he
wanted to say, but he could not stop laughing.

"Cut it out," he heard Ed say. "You heard me, stop it."

"I'm trying, what the hell do you think I'm doing," he heard
himself answer in a voice that was cold with rage. All at once he
had stopped laughing.

"That's more like it," Ed said. "How are you feeling?"

"I'm okay, I'm all right," Nick's voice shook so he could hardly
control it.

"How's your neck?"

"It's all right, I'm okay."

"Can you move it? Try moving your head."

"How many times do I have to tell you, I'm all right."

He was all right now. He pushed away Ed's hands. The back of
his neck hurt with a mounting pain. He tried to spit but sand
grated in his teeth. A bitter fluid flooded into his mouth and he
tried to vomit.

"Think you can drive?" Ed said.

"Sure I can drive."

"You're sure now. I don't want you to do it, if you can't do it."

"I said I could do it, didn't I?"

"Okay. After I change the tires, we'll stop at the next night
spot."

Nick began to vomit.

10

THE truck rounded the curve and there down the road stood the all night cafe with its lights shining and its sign flashing in the dark.

Nick parked his truck on the shoulder of the road, behind a semi loaded high with bales of hay. Trucks were jammed on both sides of the highway so the road ran between them like a death trap. A car slammed through the narrow space, the blast of its passage shaking the trucks and swirling twigs of alfalfa from the bales of hay. Nick ran across the road into the yard.

The cafe was hidden behind a jungle of trucks, semis, diesels, reefers, tankers, live stock rigs, big interstate jobs hauling all kinds of freight. Above them the neon sign said EATS, flashing its stain into the sky.

Nick passed through the forest of trucks to the restaurant on the other side. There was the faint clangor of a juke box playing a hillbilly tune. He could smell the strong smell of coffee on the sweet night air. The counter was crowded with truckers, eating, their faces hard and tired, something alien and unfriendly in their eyes.

To one side was a poultry truck, loaded with turkeys, the cages in tiers. The turkeys had their long reptile necks sticking through the slatted sides of the cages and were looking about with live bright eyes. The side of the truck was alive with their red wattled heads. They were chirping in a curious anxious chorus that sounded as though they were asking questions. Where are we going, where are we now, what are they going to do with us? they seemed to say. After a while the driver came out and got into the cab and as the truck pulled out of the yard, Nick could hear the turkeys asking questions.

He paced the yard. His neck felt stiff and sand grated in his teeth. He washed his mouth carefully at the hose and tried to drink, but it took an effort to swallow.

Behind him the singer in the juke box began to yodel.

The rain had stopped and a wind was blowing. High above, the sky was clearing. There was a cold edge to the wind, a feeling of Summer ended and Autumn here with Winter coming. It was a feeling that used to make him feel good when he was a kid. Up to now the year had been a long grind, but from here in it would be a holiday with good times ahead, Thanksgiving and Christmas and New Year coming. But he was not a kid any longer and the wind gave him a sense of depression. He thought of all the time that had passed in his life and how little he had accomplished and instantly he thought of his father. What a shriveled old man he was with a death's-head face and watering eyes, endlessly stroking his scrubby mustache. He thought of his father, first as a foetus, then as a child, a young man, then matured Yanko Garcos, fierce and sinewy with the will to make his scratch upon the world, then growing old, finished. Where was the old father he remembered, so erect of head, so bright of eye, his black mustache broad and gleaming? He was in his grave. The body had been cremated and the ashes buried in a cardboard box. He thought of his father, a soggy little lump of ashes deep in the ground.

A few drops of rain fell and after that the air grew colder. High up, the clouds were rushing swiftly in the wind. Beyond them was the clean starry sky.

Nick was about to enter the restaurant when he saw Ed's truck slip out of the darkness into the place the turkey truck had left. He watched him get down and cross the cafe yard, sloshing through puddles of water afire with the light of the neon sign. Ed did not talk to him or look at him. He kept walking to the cafe and together they went to the door.

When they entered the cafe, the sound of frying, irritating and sibilant, greeted them. The cook was scooping up hamburgers and laying them on buns and throwing on new burgers in a steady motion. He spilled eggs on the grill and laid strips of bacon beside them and stirred the hashbrowns and checked the toast in the toaster. He worked in a crouch, sweating hard, the sweat dripping onto the food, the grill, soaking his shirt. The waitress was an old woman. So many orders had come in and so many were ready at once that she could not remember whom to serve. She kept picking up the plates and looking around. Behind her the sink was filled with dirty dishes. An hour ago the restaurant had been empty, the yard deserted, but a truck had stopped and after that another, until now the place was full. But in another hour it would be empty again.

A swamper and his driver got up to go out and Nick and Ed crowded past them in the narrow aisle.

"Go down to the end," Ed said.

They went to the end and sat down beside two tanker drivers who smelled of crude oil and wore greasy overalls and shirts. The juke box had stopped playing and the room was quiet, except for the sound of frying. The men did not speak, except to order, and when they did speak to each other, they spoke quietly, their faces half turned as though not to be overheard.

"Couple of hamburgers and coffee," Ed said to the waitress.

"Nothing for me," Nick said.

"Why not?" Ed said.

"I can't swallow."

"You better try. You haven't had anything to eat since morning. You've got to eat."

"I'm not hungry."

"A single," the waitress called out.

Ed touched Nick's arm. "Get over there under the light," he said.

"What for?"

"Look, I know you can take it, but I've got to see that neck."

"I feel all right."

"Sure, I knew a guy once, walked around a whole week with his neck busted. Get up."

Nick got up and turned his back to the light. He saw the tanker drivers watching as Ed unbuttoned his coat and shirt and pulled them back.

"How does it look?" Nick said.

"It looks fine."

"Don't hand me any crap. Give it to me straight."

"I'm telling you, it looks fine. It's a little banged up, but nothing to worry about."

"You're not telling me," Nick said.

"You're nuts," Ed said. "If it looked bad, I'd tell you, wouldn't I? It looks all right."

Nick looked steadily at Ed. He had a suspicion Ed was trying to avoid being stalled on the road and he tried to read it in his face, but all he could see was irritation. "You think I'll be all right to drive?" he said.

"What do you think?" Ed said. He squared Nick again under the light and touched his neck. Nick stiffened at his touch. "Can you bend it?" Ed was saying. "Try swinging your head around." The frying sound from the grill tightened into a hiss and the room began to swim. "How does it feel?" he heard Ed say.

Nick steadied himself against the counter. "It feels all right," he heard himself answer.

"Sure, I said you felt fine," Ed said. They sat down. Somebody had dropped a nickel into the juke box and it began to play with ear-splitting loudness. The waitress brought Ed's food and he began to eat. He took several bites out of the hamburger, filling his mouth with it, took three more quick bites and finished the rest. He ordered a slice of apple pie and downed it too, swiftly, not using the fork but holding the slice in his hand and wolfing at it. He gulped his coffee in the same way and wiped his mouth on his sleeve and got up. "Okay, let's go," he said.

Their feet made hard sounds as they came out into the cafe yard. The smell of apples was sweet in the air. Already the quick rain had soaked into the dry earth and there were ovals of mud where puddles had been. There had not been a rain in several months and the valley was dry, so dry that even the lightest wind raised clouds of dust that swirled high and spread their film over vineyard and orchard until the leaf that had come green with spring was now smothered in dust. The dust coated the valley towns and the people in the towns so they looked whipped and tired in the broiling sun, but this first rain had washed them clean. There would be more rain. Nick thought of the drenching rains of Autumn wetting the

summer-parched earth and filling the vast underground rivers until
the earth was gorged. He thought of reed and cat-tail and sword-
grass growing in swamps and flocks of blackbirds swarming over
moss-crusted water that lay in great open stretches in the lowlands.

They crossed to Ed's truck.

"You go on ahead, I'll be right behind you," Ed said.

"How about the universal?" Nick said.

"Leave the universal to me." Ed walked on with Nick. "Do you
know where you're going?"

"Sure, Frisco."

Ed pulled out his watch. The time was a little after midnight,
but from the way Nick felt it should have been much later. It was
so long ago since they had left the farm that it had happened in
another life. And the affair with the parts dealer had not happened
at all. It was something he remembered from a dream. But then a
picture of the old man jumped into Nick's head, his body lying on
the floor, false teeth spilled from his mouth, blood clotting in a
pool, and he choked on his breath.

"What's the matter?" Ed said.

"Nothing," Nick said. Quickly he forced himself to see the parts
dealer again and this time there was no body on the floor, no blood,
there was just the old man rising with a bruise on his head and
running in a fury to the telephone where he found the thirty dollars Nick had left behind. He could see the old parts dealer cackling
with laughter. "By God, they tried to rob me but they got so scared
they run out without stealing a thing," Nick could hear him saying. He grinned. "I just got to thinking," he said to Ed.

Ed put back his watch. "You ought to make it by two o'clock,"
he said. "Do you know how to get to the market?"

"Sure, it's down by the Embarcadero." By now they had crossed
the highway and reached Nick's truck.

"You can't miss it," Ed said. "There's Drumm Street, Washington Street, Clay Street. It's right in there with 'em."

"Don't worry, I'll find it," Nick said. He got into his truck.

"You better watch the hills when you hit Altamount," Ed said.

"Sure, if the engine won't pull 'em, I'll throw her into low."

"Hold her in low going downhill too, or she'll race away on you."

"I'll ride the brakes."

"Brakes, hell," Ed said. "She'll get away so fast, ain't no brakes will hold her. You've got to use the engine. What's the first thing you're going to do when you get in?"

Nick slammed the door in outrage. "Sell the God damned stuff and get the hell out of there, what do you think?" he said.

Ed shook his head quietly. "No," he said. "Those guys'll take you so fast, you won't know what hit you. You're going to wait for me." He stepped clear from the cab.

Nick started the engine. He shifted into gear, but he could not go. "Ed," he said, "Look, Ed."

"What's on your mind?"

"I'd be dead, if you hadn't pulled me out from under the truck."

"Forget it."

"Forget it, hell. I guess maybe you think I'm a dummy. You've been getting in all kinds of jams ever since you hooked up with me."

Ed did not answer. He stood looking at Nick with his eyes hard and Nick said, "Maybe I am a dummy. I figured you were going to run out on me."

Ed said nothing. His silence embarrassed Nick and he laughed, "Well, I'll be seeing you in Frisco then," he said. "So long." He let out the clutch and the truck pulled away down the road. Ed stood watching the tail light dwindle into darkness. His face was like stone.

After Nick was gone, Ed returned to his truck.

There was laughter at the cafe door and two men, the tank truck drivers, stepped into the yard. They headed for a pair of Bulldog Macks parked down the road.

"So when I gets ready to go she asks me if I'll do her a favor," one of the men said. "Sure, I says, and she says she wants me to drop in on her the next time I come to Dago and I tells her, Yeah, I'll drop in. So the next load I get South, I go over, like I told her, but it ain't the same. It's never the same after that first time."

"That first time," the other said. "Nothing like it in this world." He stopped midway to the tank trucks and raised his nose, sniffing the air. "Smell it?" he said.

"Apples," the first said. "Smell mighty good." He crossed to Ed's truck and got up on the side rack and was trying to get his arm under the tarp when Ed stepped out from behind the truck.

"This your rig?" the tanker said.

"Yeah," Ed said. He kicked the tires, checking them.

"Them apples sure got one whale of a bouquet," the other said. "We got a whiff of 'em coming out. Mind if we grab a couple?"

"Help yourself."

The tanker reached under the tarp and brought out two apples and dropped down and handed one to his partner. They stood polishing the apples on their shirts and rubbing them in their hands.

"Lucky you showed up or I'd have got the whole box out of there," the tanker said. "Had it in my hand when you showed up."

"The hell you say," Ed said.

"Remember the time you put the touch on that truck load of cherries," the other tanker said. "Why this bastard swiped a couple of boxes right out from under the driver's nose, picked 'em off the middle of the load where he'd never miss 'em until he come to deliver 'em. We was eating cherries and spitting seeds all the way from Hayward to Berdoo."

"Them ain't the only cherries I ever stole," the tanker said, and the two drivers laughed, but they stopped when they saw Ed was not laughing.

"Say, that kid with the busted neck," the first tanker said. "He hauling for you?"

"He's on his own," Ed said. "I'm just breaking him in."

"I used to speculate, hauling oranges," the tanker said. "Took me three years to find out there ain't no way to get on your own."

"It'll take him three trips," Ed said. "When I get through with him, he'll wish he never saw a truck."

The two truckers looked at each other. "You're really breaking him in," the tanker said. Ed did not answer and the tanker gave his apple a final polish and held it up. "Sure a good smelling apple," he said.

The other bit into his apple and crunched it into his teeth, chewing noisily until he could speak. "Good tasting too," he said. "What

I'd give to be hauling a load of them instead of that tank of crude I got tied to my tail."

"If you had a load of apples, it'd be tied to your neck," the tanker said. "Maybe the crude smells like a dead horse, but you get your jack, regular as breath, every Friday."

They quickly munched their apples down to the core and ate the core to the seeds and started looking around for Ed, but he had disappeared. He was on the other side of the truck, checking the oil.

"Say, friend, how about another apple?" the tanker said.

"Fill your hats," Ed said.

They filled their hats and as they headed away, the tanker waved back to Ed. "Thanks, friend. Any time you need a gallon of crude, look me up."

"Thanks, hell," Ed said. "That'll cost you a buck. I ain't hauling for my health."

"A buck for ten lousy apples," the tanker said.

"If you don't like it, put 'em back," Ed said.

"Pay him," the other said. "Maybe he needs it to buy himself a square meal."

"And here's a kiss for you," Ed said. He raised one leg slightly and the tanker stood looking at him in a kind of fixed anger, but Ed turned back to the truck and he laid a dollar bill on the fender and they headed down the road to their trucks. "Say, you got more apples than I did," the tanker was saying. "Your hat's bigger than mine."

"My head's bigger than yours too," the other said.

"The hell you say," the tanker said. "Any time I can't lay mine next to yours any day in the week." And they laughed in a loud pointless way. After a while there came the sound of engines starting. The sound of the exhaust shook the air, resonating with something in Ed's chest, as though an engine were starting there too.

Ed watched the two tank trucks disappear in the dark. After they were gone, he picked up the dollar bill and put it in his pocket and resumed checking the oil. The oil had gone thick in the can from the cold and it took a long time emptying. Ed had tilted the can and was watching the heavy viscous fluid come twisting down when a shadow paused over him and stopped. Something had come between him and the light from the cafe. He turned around and saw the shape of a truck. It had come silently into the yard behind him. Ed cursed the truck as he went for his flashlight. He propped the light on the engine and picked up the can and as he continued oiling he could hear something flapping in the wind. The sound irritated him and he looked about again. It was coming from the truck. He tried not to hear it but an overwhelming curiosity crept over him and he had to know what it was. He went to the truck. The truck was loaded high with long square-ended boxes that were wrapped in butcher paper. One of the wrappings had torn loose and was flapping in the wind. Ed caught the paper and held it aside. Beneath it was a redwood box. He tore the paper and looked at the box a long time. The truck was hauling coffins. He started counting them, but stopped himself. Coffins going from a factory in some big city to an undertaker in some small town, a lot of coffins, sixty at least, for a lot of people who were still living but who would soon die. Ed thought of the people, lying in beds, sleeping, and none knowing that their coffin had been ordered and was waiting.

One for me, Ed thought. He returned to his truck and quickly finished checking the oil and cinched down the hood. He could feel the shadow of the truck, dark and oppressive upon him and he got into the cab and started the engine. A big wave of cold went through him as he shifted into gear and the truck moved from the shadow onto the road.

The universal thumped when Ed gave it the load, but after he got going, the noise stopped and he nursed the truck up to a good speed. The road blurred through the lights and passed under and back and soon he was running through Manteca and making the turns through the sweet smell of alfalfa fields and the hot ammonia stench of dairies, North toward Tracy.

The truck ran through Tracy, past Opal's joint where the rigs were lined up in the street, and on into the incline, heading steadily North, the engine laboring now.

Out of Tracy, he ran into a belt of fog that floated in a low layer on the ground. The truck looked to be running on it instead of the road. The fog deepened and an occasional rag of it caught the windshield. The way it came rushing back gave an illusion of great speed.

A mile past Foster's service station, there appeared a sudden cluster of lights in the fog. It was a traffic jam on the road. Cars were lined up on both sides of the highway and Ed could see Nick's truck among them. He stopped too and got down.

It was an accident. Three cars were turned over, one of them burning, and a big truck, a semi reefer, lay on its side, its body ripped open in a big sheet of jagged metal, the tractor cab smashed flat. The truck, seen this way, upended, looked massive and clumsy, its tires big and weighty. Upright on its wheels, it had looked agile and fleet, but broken up the way it was, it looked like a mechanical corpse.

Nick was standing in the crowd.

"What are you going to do, peddle apples right here on the road?" Ed said.

"Some accident," Nick said. "Never seen one that bad."

"Haul long enough and you'll have one that bad some day," Ed said. "Go on, pull out of here. We've got miles to roll."

Nick went to his truck, and as the truck went by slowly, his eyes were on the accident, fascinated by it.

One of the cars was a convertible. It had landed on its top and the doors had burst open. The seat was mangled into rags. Beyond it, fire was spurting with the blue flame of a blow torch from the gas tank of the burning car, a sedan. The third car stood on its wheels, but the wheels were askew.

The truck driver was walking around, continually taking off and putting on his cap. "Never got a scratch," he kept saying. "Don't see how I did it. Not a scratch." His left arm dangled crookedly and his back was bleeding. In an hour he would be stiff as a board crippled with pain, unable to move.

Ed returned to his truck. The accidents I've had, he thought. First one, way back, a long time ago, when I first started hauling, on the Ridge. Ran the truck into the side of the hill to keep from going over. Got out of it. Second one, coming out of the fog near

Turlock, hit a milk truck. Milk all over hell. Driver killed. Busted
his head like a melon. Get out of that one too. Third time, that
time in McFarland, switching tires, the bead ring flew out, ringing
like a church bell, coming over my head so I was hooped, the
split snapping together on my arm, pinching the flesh. Still carry
the scar. Could have caught my head or my throat or my body. Seen
it happen. Seen 'em cut by glass or broken up in the cab. All the
blood there is in a man wouldn't make a splash bigger than a
bucket of water. All the brains in a man's head, no bigger than a
double handful. All the guts of a man.

The truck drifted past the crowd on the highway. An ambulance
had arrived and the group had parted and in the middle of it Ed
saw a woman sitting on the pavement, her legs sticking out like
broken crutches from her dress which was bunched high on her
thighs. Blood ran in little threads down her face and there was a
mess of it on the ground.

Ed thought how long it had been since the last accident. Three
years. Too long. He was overdue. The percentage was against him,
it was piling more against him the longer he was overdue. He had
an accident coming and he wondered how it would happen, how
it would hit him. The universal was thumping and he listened to
it. If it goes out on a hill, I'll stop right there on the hill, he
thought. He checked the brakes while he was thinking about it.
But he'd seen them hold up for a long time, it wouldn't go out.
The thoughts of accidents alerted him and he sat up and watched
the road. Somewhere along here was a cutoff. He looked for it and
found it and when he went by, he saw a car waiting to turn into
the highway. He watched the car in the rear view mirror, showing
its red light as it turned away from him. He watched deliberately,
conscious of watching, but he knew that he was always watching
without knowing he was doing it, always on the alert, his eyes always on the mirror and the road ahead and the side roads. But every
once in a while, at night or in daylight, on crowded or empty highway, he would suddenly waken to danger and start grabbing for
the brake, clutching about with his eyes. Even in his sleep he would
dream of a crack-up and slam on the brakes and swing the wheel,
screaming until he wakened. That was what tired you, that being

scared, knowing you were rolling tons and every pound of it wrapped around your neck if you slipped up.

The truck was now past the wreck. Ed opened up the engine and let her go. Traffic was light, but it was the swift traffic of late night. He could see cars, the fast ones who had not seen the accident, racing toward it, unretarded by the flares, and the others, the slow ones, coming away from it, driving carefully. Drive slow, you bastards, drag ass, drive slow for about five miles, Ed said to himself. How carefully they would drive for just about five miles. Then their feet would begin to bear down on the throttle and the speedometer would creep up until after a few miles the accident would be forgotten until it was remembered suddenly, maybe a week later, and you hit the brakes and stared around to see if it's happening to you.

The truck burst out of the fog and Ed saw that he was in the hills and the stars were clear, sharp, bright, hard in the sky. Suddenly he felt wide awake and he sat up.

11

THE market was not open but already trucks were jammed on Washington Street. They were waiting, engines running, for the line to move ahead so they could pull into place and get rid of their loads. On Ceylon Street the green dealer was uncovering piles of vegetables he had stacked there the afternoon before. The smell of carrots and turnips came surging up as he rolled back the tarp and picked up a hose and wet down the green mounded bunches. All along the street men were carting out boxes of fruit and crates of lettuce and celery and sacks of potatoes and onions and laying them in rows for the buyers who would be coming soon. They were filling up the walks, crowding them with produce from the curb to a narrow space along the walls of the buildings so a man could hardly pass.

Men were coming out of the Merchant's Lunch that had been open since two o'clock. It was a cold foggy morning and it was going to be one of those days with the fog horn blowing every three minutes and the fog rolling in from the bay. It could be seen hanging like an incubus over the canyon of the street, but soon it would be coming down, soaking the market. The unloaders in their leather aprons looked angry where they stood on the curb waiting for the trucks to get in so they could unload. They kept moving about restlessly, swearing and slamming their fists into their hands in impatience, trying to keep warm while they waited for the trucks that were stalled, engines running, the drivers hitting their horns and shouting, trying to clear the traffic with their voices.

One of the produce dealers came out into the street. He was a squat, heavy set man, with a nervous irritated face. He walked quickly and energetically, looking about with swift narrow eyes.

His teeth gripped a burned-down cigar as his voice cracked like a whip in the blocked street.

"All right, you guys, let's go. What the hell's holding you up?" he said.

"Look who's sounding off," one of the truckers said.

"Come on, shake it up," the produce dealer said. "I got a load of corn parked back there. I can't sell it from a truck."

"Ah, go pull up your pants," another trucker said. "What do you want us to do, get out and push?"

The produce dealer stood looking at the trucker. He removed his cigar and spat down once, holding his eyes steadily on him.

"Get him giving me the eye," the trucker said. "Go ahead, burn a hole in me, you pecker."

The produce dealer was about to say something when a young man came from the Merchant's Lunch. He was a small man, dressed in work clothes, but his clothes were neatly pressed and he looked dapper and clean. He had a monkey's eager face and he moved with the nervous animation of a monkey as he stepped quickly across the street to the produce dealer's side.

"Did you find him?" the produce dealer said.

"He ain't nowhere's around."

"What the hell's the use of having a cop if he's not going to be around when you want him?" the produce dealer said. He went back along the line of traffic with the monkey following him.

"Hold out a cigar and he'll show up fast enough," the monkey said.

"Did you find out what's holding them up?" the produce dealer said.

"I sent Dave," the monkey said. "He hasn't come back yet."

The produce dealer stood thinking a moment. He nooded to himself. "You better go get your hand truck," he said. "We'll unload that baby right in the street."

"Okay," the monkey said briskly. He went to the produce house and the produce dealer followed the line of trucks down the block.

"Look at old Figlia," somebody shouted. "He's going to move us, by God. What're you going to do, Fig, lug us out with your lily white hands?"

The drivers shouted and blew their horns, but Mike Figlia was impervious to their jeering. He went to a reefer truck and trailer that showed Washington license plates. The driver was leaned over in the seat. A cigarette dangled from his mouth, but he was asleep. Figlia went to the tail gates, but they were locked. He returned to the cab and yanked open the door and the driver opened his eyes. He was still sleeping, with his eyes open.

"How about unlocking the back end?" Figlia said.

"What for?" The trucker's voice was low and tired.

"So I can unload. Come on." He grabbed the driver by the arm and the driver stepped down. They went to the back and unlocked the gates, but they would not swing open. The trailer was in the way. And the trailer gates would not open because the truck behind it was rammed up tight against the tire rack.

"Get in and pull her up a little," Figlia said.

"What do you want me to do, climb his tail?" the driver said. He nodded to the truck ahead.

The monkey came up with his hand cart, ready to haul out the corn. Figlia stood thinking what to do. He had an open space on his dock a quarter of a block wide waiting for the corn, and the truck and trailer were loaded with it. Within a few minutes the buyers would be streaming into the market, but it was impossible to move the trucks.

"Where the hell have you been?" Figlia said. "If you'd come in when you should have, we'd have had her unloaded by now. But you had to park your ass somewhere in some road joint, eating your head off. Just because you had to fill up your gut, I have to wait for my corn."

The driver was awake now. "I came as fast as I could," he said. "Any more cracks out of you and I'll put that corn where you won't like it." He hitched up his pants and tightened his belt.

"Hey, Fig," a voice shouted from up the street, and an unloader came running.

"It's Dave," the monkey said.

"Did you find out what's holding this line up?" Figlia said.

"Yeah. A guy's asleep in his truck right in the middle of the street."

"Well, why the hell don't you wake him up?"

"We tried. He won't wake."

Figlia squirmed in irritation. "Charles," he said to the monkey. "Go take care of it, will you?" He returned to the produce house, and Charles and the unloader, Dave, headed back along the line of trucks. One of the trucks in the line was a poultry rig full of white leghorn chickens waiting to go into the slaughterhouse on Davis. They were moulting and their feathers littered the street. The truck gave off the smell of sour droppings and chicken bodies crammed together in cages. Charles and the unloader went on down the line, past the truck.

"What's so tough about waking a guy?" Charles said.

"Wait till you see."

"All you got to do is shake him."

"You shake him," the unloader said.

"No brains," Charles said. "That's why you're an unloader."

"That's okay with me, so long as I don't have to kiss Figlia's butt," the unloader said.

Nick's truck was at the head of the line. There was a crowd beside it. Charles got a good hard smell of the apples as they passed through the crowd to the cab. The smell excited him.

"At first I thought maybe he was stalled," the unloader was saying. "But the engine was running so I know he couldn't be stalled and I looked in the cab and there he was flopped on the wheel and I gave him a shake, but he wouldn't wake up."

Charles got on the running board and reached his hands quickly under the tarp. Apples all right, he thought.

"See him?" the unloader said.

"Yeah." Charles opened the cab door. Nick was hunched over the wheel. He looked to be asleep, but when Charles shook him, he did not waken. One arm was in his lap, but the other swung down, free, the hand half open.

"Get what I mean?" the unloader said.

"He ain't asleep," Charles said. He lifted Nick's body from the wheel and pushed him back against the seat.

"What's the matter with him?" the unloader said.

Charles did not answer. He was thinking about the apples and the guy sitting in the truck, sick or dead. The apples excited him very much because he had not seen apples in the market for a long time. He got a match and lighted it, holding Nick against the seat with one hand. In the light he could see Nick's face, the eyes half open, dull and lifeless. The match went out and Charles dropped it. The unloader was leaning over his shoulder staring with wide shocked eyes. Behind him were the men waiting.

"Is he dead?" the unloader said. He spoke in a hushed frightened voice.

Charles grabbed the front of Nick's coat and held him solidly against the seat. He slapped him once across the cheek, but the head rolled with the slap, lolling over on the neck and Charles had to brace it against his arm. He slapped him again, hard, so his fingers hurt. He kept slapping first one cheek, then the other, until he felt Nick stiffen and come alive in his hands. He could hear him struggle for breath, gasping for air, his arms working as he came up for it, like a drowning man until Charles was not holding him any longer. Nick was sitting on his own, his eyes open to the light.

When Nick opened his eyes he could see the open cab door and below it the men in the street, their faces caught in the light, watching him; and the one with the monkey face, the brows thick and the eyes deep set like a monkey's, looking at him in that bright way that monkeys have. Beyond them was the stretch of the market street, narrow like an alley, with the fog snaking in over the rooftops.

Monkey face said, "You all right?"

"Sure, I'm fine," Nick said. His voice sounded far away.

Monkey face got down and Nick heard him say, "Well, if you're all right, how about pulling this heap out of the way so those guys can get past you?" And Nick said, "Let 'em get past me. I'm not holding anybody up." And monkey face stood looking at him in that bright incredulous way. "You're sure you're all right?" he heard him say.

"Yes, I am," Nick said. "I'm all right." He said it in the manner of a child trying to reassure itself, but he knew he was not all right, not at all. I'm sick, he thought, and he tried to remember how he had got here, but he could not remember. All he could remember was a vast stretch of bridge arching through darkness and below it the fog and the sleeping city bursting from it and the truck turning from the bridge and going down the silent streets past docks and warehouses, past rows of lights that were big luminous discs in the fog. He remembered the mouth of a tunnel and the truck running down into it and going and going and never coming out.

"Move over, I'll take it," Nick heard monkey face say and he moved over and he could hear the other getting in as he leaned back in the seat. The motion had made him dizzy. He felt as though he were falling and he shut his eyes. Oh, Christ, he thought. The cab was darkening now and he felt himself go unconscious in great waves of motion, as of a leaf falling, and he hung onto the seat. He was nothing now beyond one fleck of consciousness, and through it he could hear the tremendous clashing of gears. Hit the clutch, hit it hard or the gears will clash, he tried to say but before he could say it they had clashed in and he could feel himself moving. He shook his head and tried to sit up, but kept slipping down in the seat; and there it was again, the market with its lights swimming in luminous discs where the fog was coming in, but he did not know it was the fog and he kept shaking his head trying to clear it, thinking all the while, It's me. I'm sick.

12

THE corn truck had pulled into the space in front of the Crown Produce and men were unloading. The crates of corn were packed in ice and the ice was piled in the street where it was melting. The ground handler was standing in water over his shoe tops as he caught the crates from the man in the reefer and swung them to Dave, who was stacking them on the sidewalk in a solid mass of corn, eight crates deep and six high.

Figlia opened one of the crates and picked up a corn. The husk was green and the silk was fresh. He pulled back the husk and beneath it the kernels were clean and yellow, firm and ripe. The driver was standing at the rear view mirror, combing his hair, but when he saw Figlia examining the crates, he stopped combing and watched him.

Figlia dug his thumb into the kernels and the corn milk spurted out. "You call this corn?" he said.

"That's what I call it," the driver said.

They stood grinning at each other.

"How many crates do I get?" Figlia said.

The driver got the manifest book from the cab and brought it to Figlia. "Five hundred," he said. "You want to sign this now or cry later?"

"Stick around if you want to see some crying," Figlia said. He signed the manifest sheet and the driver tore out his copy and returned the book to the cab.

At this moment a buyer passed by. He was dressed in a business suit and was in a hurry. Figlia showed him the opened husk. "That's corn," he said.

"Give me twelve," the buyer said, without stopping.

"Did I hear you say twenty?" Figlia said.

"Twelve," the buyer said. He did not even look back.

"He'll take twenty," Figlia said. He folded the husk and put the corn back in the crate and closed the crate.

"You could sell a thousand, if you had 'em," the driver said.

"I can tell you one thing," Figlia said. "If I had a thousand, I wouldn't keep 'em."

Behind the cab of the truck was a door which opened into the sleeper compartment. The driver opened it and inside was a man rolled in blankets, sleeping, but all that could be seen of him were his shoes. They were tremendous shoes, worn through in the soles. An odor of unwashed feet drifted into the street. The driver grabbed the shoes and shook them. "Joe," he said softly, "come on, Joe, wake up."

The man in the sleeper awoke and sat up. He slid out, feet first, and landed on the sidewalk yawning and stretching his arms. He was a big man, fat, his face lost in the creases of it, his body distorted and bulging with the folds of glandular fat. His weight had broken his arches and he stood on broad flat feet, yawning and wiping his hands over his face, rubbing sleep from his eyes. He coughed, cleared his throat and spat into the street, and when he turned, he was smiling as though it was the natural expression of his face. "When did we get in?" he said. He had thick rubbery lips and shrewd open eyes.

"A while ago. You were sleeping," the driver said.

"Jesus Christ, why didn't you wake me?"

"I wanted to keep you out of the way," the driver said.

"Where did you get him?" Figlia said.

"That's my swamper," the driver said. "He does my sleeping for me."

"Oh, hell," the swamper said. "I got to sleep."

"Yeah, all the time," the driver said. He winked to Figlia and said to the swamper, "Are you hungry, do you want to eat?"

The swamper rubbed his hands together and the smile on his face brightened. "Sure," he said. "Where'll we go?"

"How do you like that?" the driver said. "He ate a two buck dinner not more than three hours ago and he's ready to eat again."

"Oh, hell," the swamper said, "when a man's hungry, he's got to eat."

Figlia patted the swamper's belly. "Some gut," he said. "What have you got in there anyway?"

"That's where I keep my tapeworm," the swamper said. He chuckled, shaking all over. "It's wound up all inside of me."

The driver laughed and headed across the street to the Merchant's Lunch. The swamper went to join him, but the driver waved him back. "The hell with you, Joe," he said.

"Ain't we eating?" the swamper said.

"I am, but I don't know about you."

"Well, pay me off and I'll buy my own."

"Pay you for what, sleeping?"

"Jesus Christ, I spelled you, didn't I? I took the wheel when you was tired."

"You ought to see him drive," the driver said. "Doesn't know one side of the road from the other." He went on to the Merchant's Lunch and the swamper stood with his face anxious, contorted to the point of crying. He looked around to Figlia and the dock workers, searching for sympathy, but they turned away from him. With his face puckered and his lips pouted, he resembled a clown balanced on broad flat feet.

Nick's truck pulled up behind the corn rig and Charles got down. He reached up under the tarp and got an apple and came over to Figlia, dancing the apple in his hand. It flashed golden in the light.

"What have you got there?" Figlia said. Charles tossed him the apple and he caught it and turned it in his fingers. "Where'd you get it?"

Charles nodded to Nick's truck.

Figlia broke the apple into two halves and looked at them. He had been tired a moment ago, his eyes squinted with exhaustion, but the apple wakened him. "How many has he got?" he said. His voice was excited.

"Must be around six hundred boxes."

"Who are they consigned to?"

"Nobody that I know of."

Something quivered in Mike Figlia as he sensed a killing. Nick was getting out of the truck. Figlia tossed the apple halves behind the corn crates and stepped to him. "Hey, bum," he said.

"You talking to me?" Nick said.

"Yeah. How long do you think you're going to park there?"

"Long time. Why?"

"A long time, hell. I run a business here. What do you want me to do, step all over your truck every time I sell something?"

"Don't burn your collar. I'll move it." Nick started to get into the truck, but Figlia laughed and held his arm. "Forget it," he said. "There's no hurry. Stick around until you move your load. You look like you've been rolling a long way."

"A long way is right," Nick said. "And brother, I could sure use a cup of coffee. Is there a joint in the place?"

"Yeah, across the street," Figlia said. And to Charles he said, "Keep an eye on the man's load, will you, Charles? Don't let anybody touch it."

"Yes, sir, Mister Figlia," Charles said.

Figlia touched Nick's arm and they stepped down from the curb. All along Washington men were untying ropes, pulling back tarps, taking down loads. Nick's neck felt hot and stiff. He could feel his heart pounding in it in quick throbs. A sudden sweat went over him when he moved and he stopped, waiting for the feeling to pass.

Behind him, the swamper had picked up the apple halves and was brushing them clean on his shirt.

Figlia saw the swamper with the apple and he urged Nick. "Come on, I'll take you," he said. He led the way across the street. "I've never seen you around."

"I haven't been around," Nick said.

"Hauling freight or pulling for yourself?"

"Pulling for me."

"What are you hauling?"

A strange irritation came over Nick. He felt confused and tired. His neck hurt and here was this guy pestering him with questions. He felt sick and he thought, I don't feel good at all. He felt Figlia's hand on his arm and he jerked away from it. What does he mean what am I hauling, he thought, and he said, "What the hell is it to you?"

So he's going to be one of those guys, Figlia thought. "My name's Mike Figlia," he said. "I run the Crown Produce."

"Well, why don't you go run it?" Nick said.

"What kind of talk is that?" Figlia said. "What's it going to get you, talking like that?"

"Who the hell asked you to drop in on me?"

"You wanted a cup of coffee. I was taking you to it."

"I don't need it now. I'll let you know when I do." Nick went on alone and Figlia stood in the street. He felt angry. He wanted to hit someone. Okay, brother, he thought, that's about all from you. You sold your load but you don't know it yet. He felt himself to be in complete possession of the apples. The trick was to get them off the truck. He did not know how he was going to manage that, but he knew he was. He returned to the dock where the swamper was eating the soiled halves he had cleaned on his shirt. He was not eating greedily but delicately, taking small bites and chewing slowly, sucking his teeth and wetting his lips with the rapid tip of his tongue. Figlia watched him in disgust, his anger coiling in him, seeking an objective. "Okay, sloppy, you better get going," Figlia said.

"Huh?" the swamper said.

"I said beat it. You take up too much room around here."

"You mean you want me to beat it?"

"That's right. Get out of here."

"Oh, hell, a man's got a right to stand where he wants."

Figlia took the swamper by the arm and tried to shove him but managed only to twist his body slightly. The swamper laughed wheezily. "If you want me to go, move me," he said. "Go ahead, move me." He laughed hard, his body shaking but hardly any sound coming out. "Since when did you buy up the sidewalk?" he said. "I'll stand here all night, if I want."

Charles stopped with his hand truck. "What happened to the guy?" he said. "Did you lose him?"

"Yeah," Figlia said.

"If he moves those apples, you'll lose them too."

Figlia turned to the apple truck. Six hundred boxes, he thought. Six bucks a box, thirty six hundred bucks. He could see the back tires, the rubber blistered and peeling from the overload. They had leaked air and the tires were low. Figlia smiled when he saw the tires. "He won't move 'em," he said. And to the swamper he said, "Stick around if you want, Sloppy."

13

NICK went past the Merchant's Lunch and on through the market.

Men were unloading rattlesnake melons from a truck, relaying them from hand to hand to a pile of them on the produce house floor. Cantaloupes were being unloaded from a semi, crates of them, big and yellow, and rich with the smell of ripeness. A potato rig had come in along the line and the sacks were being tumbled down and carted into storage bins. There were loads of celery and lettuce from Salinas and Thompson seedless grapes from Reedley, and loads of nectarines and peaches and pears. The market was a medley of smells that somehow separated and identified themselves when Nick looked at the different crops. Across the way from Levi-Zetner's a truck load of turnips and green onions had come in and the unloaders were stacking the bunches in a neat high mound around the lamp post. By now grocery trucks were beginning to appear in the market and the early buyers were prowling the streets, looking over the morning's wares, picking what they wanted. A man leaned out of a new red truck that had the sign San Mateo Market Basket on its sides. "Got any persimmons, Sam?" he shouted. No, there were no persimmons. Nor were there any apples. In all the market there was not a single fancy eating apple. Just a few boxes of cooking pippins that were mottled and shrunk from being held in cold storage. Nick began to feel better as he walked along the street, looking for apples and not finding any. The load of apples he had brought in had frightened him, but now he was not frightened any longer. He knew he would sell them for good money. How much money, he could not say, but it would be good; that he knew.

Where Washington ran into Front Street was the waterfront.

119

The Embarcadero was dark and empty. The few trucks that came through ran fast, not stopping. The fog horn was blasting somewhere out at the end of a wharf, guiding ships that passed in the harbor. The air was wet with fog. Water glistened on the web of railroad tracks that ran along the waterfront. The air was cold. Nick began to feel lonely and sick again and he headed back toward the little cluster of lights that was the market. He tried to make himself think of all the produce houses without any apples, of the markets and the grocery stores that did not have any, of the people in the city waking in the morning with a hunger for apples and himself with the only load in town. He tried to make himself think of the apples being sold and of the money lining his pockets. He tried to make himself feel good, thinking of money, but somehow he had forgotten about Ed and now he remembered him and began to think of him, where he was, what he was doing, if the truck had broken down and if he was stalled. He'll be all right, he thought, he'll come in.

Back at the Crown Produce a man stepped fiercely along the dock. The handlers were still unloading corn and the crates filled a quarter of the block. Figlia was waving a cob at the man who was red with anger. His eyes flashed as he walked off with quick stiff steps. "Eight dollars," he was saying. "Eight dollars a crate. What the hell do you think you're selling, gold?"

"Sure, Golden Bantam," Figlia said. "You need it and I've got it. Come on back. Maybe you can talk me down."

"Sure, you'll come down a nickel, you big-hearted bastard," the buyer said. "You know what you can do with your God damned corn." He got into his truck and drove off.

The driver of the corn reefer stood nearby and Figlia said to him, "He's crying, but he'll be back."

"You ought to give away a free handkerchief with every crate," the driver said.

"That's an idea," Figlia said. "Nothing but the best for my customers." He saw Nick and winked at him. "What do you know, bum?"

Nick nodded to the buyer's truck. "Nothing like keeping 'em happy, is there?" he said.

"The trouble with him is he don't know how to lean back," Figlia said. "Had your coffee?"

"I've been walking through the market."

"How does it look?"

"It looks pretty good."

"You found that out in one quick walk?"

"If there isn't any and you've got some what does that make it?"

"It all depends," Figlia said. "Come on, let's get some of that coffee and we'll talk about it."

"I'll have the coffee, but I don't feel like talking," Nick said. He started away, but Figlia caught his arm. "Wait a minute," he said. "Let's cut out moving in circles. How about your load?"

"What about it?"

"Are you taking it on a tour or are you going to peddle it?"

"Oh, I'll sell it. No hurry, is there?"

"No, not at all, only get your truck the hell out of the way. it's blocking my dock."

"I thought you had something tough on your mind," Nick said. He went to his truck, ready to move it, but before he got in he saw that the left front wheel was down. He went around to see what had happened. Figlia was saying, "Get your rig out of the way. That corn truck'll have to pull up pretty soon." The tire was flat.

"Come on, come on, we haven't got all night," Figlia said.

"My tire's flat," Nick said.

"Well, switch it and get going."

"I haven't got an extra."

"The hell you say? What do you want me to do, buy you one?" Figlia said. He shouted so men up and down the block heard him. Charles was watching from the corn truck. He came over and stood behind Figlia, his monkey face tight and stubborn, not looking at Nick but through him.

Nick bent down to the tire. The valve had been tampered with so the air would leak. "What do you think we're running here, a parking lot?" Figlia was saying. "I've got stuff moving in and out all the time. Shake it up."

Nick came around to the walk again. There was a little crowd standing on the sidewalk, waiting to see what would happen.

"I'll move it as soon as I get my tire up," Nick said.

"You'll move it now."

"I can't do that. It'll cut my tire."

"The hell with your tire. I want my dock cleared." Figlia turned to Charles. "Go to the Ace garage and get them to send out a tow car. We'll pull him out into the street," he said.

"Okay, Mister Figlia," Charles said.

"You touch my truck and you'll have me in your hair," Nick said. "I'll get it up in five minutes. All it needs is a little air."

Charles stood blinking his eyes, waiting to go.

"All right, you've got five minutes," Figlia said.

Nick screwed in the valve and got the pump from the tool box and began pumping the tire. Figlia stood beside him, suddenly tractable. "How is it going?" he said.

Nick kept pumping the tire. He wondered who had loosened the valve. Someone had done it. Valves didn't come out by themselves. But why do a thing like that? He could not figure it out.

"Hey, Dave," Figlia shouted to the freight handler who was working at the corn truck. "Come over and give this guy a hand."

"He's doing all right," Dave said.

"Sure, but you're going to make a buck doing it."

Dave came over, but Nick would not give up the pump. He kept working at it. The tire was beginning to rise.

"You heard him," Dave said. "He told me to take over."

"He can go take a flying frig at himself," Nick said.

"Sure, but how about me? You're gypping me out of a buck." The handler took the pump from Nick and began to work at it. Nick stood up, straightening the kinks out of his back. Figlia was smiling at him.

"You're a hot-head," Figlia said.

Nick returned to the sidewalk. "Somebody let the air out of my tire," he said.

"You're not only a hot-head," Figlia said. "You're nuts. Who the hell would want to let the air out of your tire?"

The swamper who was leaning against the wall, watching everything with his shrewd eyes, laughed in that strange wheeze that sounded like crying. The sound startled Figlia and he looked sharply at the swamper. To Nick he said, "What you need is that cup of coffee, maybe with a shot in it. You're so dead you're dreaming."

"Oh, hell," the swamper said. "Good hell, that ain't a dream, that's a nightmare." He went on laughing, helplessly, the sound mirthless and painful.

Figlia went to the truck. He stood looking up at it. "Why don't you tell me what you're hauling?" he said. "What's the big secret anyway? Maybe it's something I can use. Maybe I'll take it off your hands and you won't have to chase around all over the market looking for a buyer. You can unload right here."

"Don't hand me that crap," Nick said. "You know what I'm hauling."

"Now how would I know that?" Figlia said.

"Maybe you smelled it," Charles said.

"Not me," Figlia said. "My smeller ain't so good. All I can smell is cigars."

"And dames," one of the handlers said. "If a dame passes within a block of here, he points her like a setter."

"He gets his nose right in there," a buyer said. "He can smell a dame almost as good as he can smell a buck. Walk past here with a dollar in your pocket and you're a dead wop."

"That's me," Figlia said. He got on the running board and reached under the tarp for an apple and dropped down with it in his hand. "Well, what do you know!" he said. "Look at that, Charles. Think we might be able to use them?" He tossed the apple to Charles.

Charles looked at it. "I don't know," he said. "I'd have to see the whole load before I'd say."

"That's Charles for you," Figlia said to Nick. "He never wants to take a chance, he's always wanting to see the whole load. But I'm willing."

"Aren't you afraid you'll lose your shirt?" Nick said.

"I don't mind," Figlia said. "I've got a lot of shirts. How much do you want for the whole load?"

Nick tilted back his head and watched Figlia.

"I'll take them as is, cash on the line. What do you say?" Figlia said.

Nick did not know what to say. Two dollars a box was the cost, but there was the cost of hauling and the intangible costs of his neck under the rack and the worry that fretted him about the old man in the parts shop and all those hours on the road and Ed nursing his truck somewhere in the dark, trying to make it to market without breaking down, and it amounted to something beyond dollars and cents. He wanted to state four dollars as a price, but he knew that it would be wrong because it would only be a beginning. The real price would come only after bargaining.

"Help him out, Charles," Figlia said.

"It's hard to say, Mister Figlia," Charles said. "Now if they're all like this." He tossed the apple back to Figlia who caught it, polished it in his hands, took a bite out of it and spat the bite out quickly. "You call that an apple?" he said to Nick .

The way Figlia said it frightened Nick. Maybe he got a bad one, he thought, the one rotten out of the whole load. "What's the matter with it?" he said.

"It's pulpy, that's what's the matter with it." Figlia threw the apple into the street.

The handler named Dave came from behind Nick's truck. "She won't pump up," he said. "I keep pumping but she won't come up."

"She was doing all right when I had it," Nick said.

"Maybe so but look at her now," Dave said. "She's way down flat. I been pumping my back off."

Nick went to the tire and felt around it until his hand came to a deep cut along the side. It had been slashed with a knife. Or an axe, he thought.

"What's the matter with it?" Figlia said.

"How would I know?" the handler said. "All I know is she wouldn't come up."

Nick came around the truck. He saw that the handler had an axe in his belt, the blade flat against his side.

"Too bad, all that pumping for nothing," Figlia said. "You must have run over some glass or something." He brought out his wallet and removed from it a dollar and held it out to the handler.

"Thanks, Mister Figlia," the handler said. He had his hand out for the dollar when Nick hit him. The handler went back against the truck and Nick hit him again. The handler got out his axe, but Nick kicked it from his hand and clubbed him down. He picked him up and slugged him and the handler's eyes rolled back showing white and his jaw went slack. Figlia tried to separate them, but Nick would not allow himself to be separated. He hit the handler in the belly and he could hear the breath go out of him and he went to hit him again but Charles and Figlia got him and the handler was lying on the sidewalk.

"Let me go," Nick said.

"Now take it easy," Figlia said.

"He cut my tire. Let me go."

"Don't be nuts," Figlia said. "You don't think he'd stand there pumping his butt off if he cut it."

"If he didn't cut it, then you did," Nick said. "Is that the way you want it?"

"Now what do you do with a guy like that?" Figlia said to Charles. And he said to Nick, "Where do you get those ideas? Whoever cut it, it looks like you're stuck here for a while anyway. Why don't you let me handle your load? I'll make you any kind of a deal you say, consignment, cash sale. All you've got to do is name it."

"Nothing doing," Nick said.

"What are you afraid of? I'm not going to ream you. You'll get a fair price. All I'm trying to do is give you a hand."

"Whose idea of a fair price?" Nick said.

"Yours and mine, we'll work it out together and make a deal. What do you say?"

It sounded fair enough to Nick, but he felt befuddled and tired. Waiting for Ed made a big lump of confusion in his head and he could not think. He wanted to sell the load and get rid of it, but he did not like Figlia. Something in the man's face worried him, something he saw behind his eyes. Without knowing how, he knew that there would not be anything fair in any deal he made with Figlia.

"There's no use talking about it," he said. "I can't sell."

"The hell you can't. They're your apples. If you can't sell them, who the hell can?"

"I bought it with another guy. He's coming in with another load. You talk to him when he gets in."

Figlia's face tightened in exasperation. "You can sell if you want."

"But I don't want," Nick said. "You'll have to talk to my partner."

"I'm talking to you. What's the matter with you?"

Nick shook his head. "Nothing's the matter with me. He told me to wait."

"This guy you bought the load with, when will he get in?"

"I don't know," Nick said. The struggle with the handler had made him dizzy again and he shut his eyes and braced himself against the truck. The smell of apples was nauseating in his head. Now he wanted the coffee, he needed the coffee. He wanted to get away to the joint and sit down.

"This guy, your friend," Figlia said. "I buy from a lot of truckers. Maybe I know him."

"His name is Ed Kennedy," Nick said. "You talk to him when he comes in." He left the truck and went to the Merchant's Lunch across the street.

Charles said to Figlia, "If that's the guy I think it is, your name's mud."

"My name's Mike Figlia and nobody is changing it that I know of," Figlia said.

"He wouldn't give you the sweat off his balls," Charles said.

"He isn't here yet," Figlia said. He went into the produce house, removed his smock, put on his coat and came out. The handler had got up and he was leaning over, shaking his head. "That's the toughest buck I ever made," he said to Figlia.

"And all for nothing," Charles said. "You might as well kiss them apples goodbye. You haven't got a chance in hell of getting that load."

"You wouldn't like to make a little bet?" Figlia said. He went down Washington toward Drumm Street.

14

A light burned in Shorty's Grill, but the door was locked. Figlia pressed against the glass and he could see someone behind the bar. He knocked on the pane and rattled the knob. The street in the market was warm, but here on the Embarcadero it was cold, and the aspect of the street was colder still. Something frigid and silent drifted from the open docks across the way, beyond the wide expanse of pavement. Far out on the harbor a tug gave two short blasts on its horn, sounding lonely and lost in the night. An empty truck and trailer rattled toward Mission, the sounds ringing out. The fog horn was very loud and something in Figlia's head shuddered, as though his brain were cringing from a blow. Before it could recover, the blast came again.

"All right," Figlia shouted, banging the door. "Shake it up in there. I'm freezing my tail out here."

The figure at the bar disappeared and after a time two figures appeared, one of them short and wide and toddling from side to side as it walked. He was a small man, no higher than the knob on the door, normal from the chest up, big-headed and broad-shouldered, but deformed and dwarfed from the waist down. He toddled to the door on his bandied legs. "We're closed," he said in the voice of a child.

"In a pig's eye you're closed," Figlia said. He shook the door again and the dwarf named Shorty opened it. "Honest to God we are," he said in the pleasant voice that was so much like a boy's. "What do you want?"

"I want to come in. What do you think I want?" Figlia said. He went in. The dwarf shut the door and they crossed the dining room. The other figure, an old man in a soiled white apron was scatter-

ing sawdust from a bucket, fisting it up in his hand and sowing it
to the floor. There was a beery, scorched-grease smell in the room,
the smell of bodies and smoke and foul breath, but the place was
empty except for the old man, but empty with him in it too. He
had no more presence in the room than did the juke box or the
walls or the tables with the chairs up-ended upon them.

"What's the idea of giving me that stuff about being closed?"
Figlia said.

"Honest to God, I didn't know it was you," Shorty said.

"You and God," Figlia said. "Who's in back? Anybody I
know?"

"Same old crowd. Who else would be here this time of the
night?"

Then it's all right, Figlia thought. If it's the same crowd, she'll
be there. If she isn't, one of the others will do, but they've got
guys tagging after them. It's this one calls herself Tex that I want.
It'll be clean with her, no guys, nothing. She's the one, if she'll
do it.

They passed through the dark cafe into the hallway that stretched
back like a cave in the dark. Behind them the old man had begun
to sweep, rolling the sawdust and the night's debris in a wave before him with the broom. There were the charred crushed stubs
of dead cigarettes in the mess, some of them red-tipped as though
the mouths that smoked them had bled. The room was silent except
for the whisking of the old man's broom. Beneath this sound, so
low as to be nearly inaudible, could be heard the faint bouncing of
a band. The sound swelled out of figment when Shorty opened
the door at the end of the hallway and they crossed another room.
And now there was laughter mingled with the tinkling of the
band, the sound growing until it blasted into full volume when
Shorty opened still another door, loosing a dazzling flood of light.

The room was crowded with men and women, dancing in
drunken embrace on the floor and sitting at the bar and at tables.
A haze of tobacco smoke filled the room. The band turned out to
be a juke box playing so loudly that the music was distorted. Someone in the back shouted, "Figlia!" and a naked hairy arm was
raised, showing a stiffly erected forefinger.

"Hey Brooks, what do you know?" Figlia said.

"Come on over, I'll buy you a drink," the voice said.

"Not now," Figlia said. "I got business." He looked down to Shorty. "Where's Mitch?"

"Over in the corner," Shorty said. "Honest to God, Fig, you must think you're something special. Why don't you come in the back way, like everybody does?"

"Because I don't like the back way," Figlia said. They passed through the noisy room.

"What do you want to see Mitch about?" Shorty said.

"Just a friendly call," Figlia said.

"You said you came over on business, you old throat cutter."

"Yeah, but it's got nothing to do with you," Figlia said.

"Well, pardon me if my nose is long," Shorty said.

They came to a table that was occupied by five girls and two men. The girls were all of a kind, too much red on the lips, too much dye in the hair, calculating rapacious eyes that were as cold and hard as ice. The men were of a kind too, with similar soiled pimp faces. They were both slight and tense with a kind of animal nervousness that gave them a constant look of anger. One of the men, Mitch, had washed-out gray eyes that looked as though someone had spit them there. He was sandy haired and had a long narrow head. He had let his hair grow and combed it back in a pompadour that kept falling over his ear. He kept touching it with the heel of his hand. In his arms he held a toy dog, a Mexican hairless. The dog was brown with a chocolate brown nose. Even the inside of its mouth was brown. It had brown protruding eyes set in a delicate miniature head. Mitch held the dog snugly in his arms, and the dog was not cold, but it shivered endlessly.

The other man, Frenchy, was dark and French looking, though he was an Italian. He had a hard predatory glint in his eye. Both men had soft pasty complexions that came from avoiding the sun, and though they were wirey and strong, they looked to be weak with only certain muscles, the muscles of eating and rising and sitting and lighting cigarettes, well developed. They did not move, but something in their manner changed as Figlia and Shorty stood beside them.

"Look at 'em with their ears up," Figlia said to Shorty. "What's the matter, Mitch? Did you think I was a cop?" He looked down at the two men.

The washed-out one laid his arm across the shoulder of one of the girls and began talking to her quietly. The dark one was saying, "Tomorrow night we better meet at the other place I was telling you about. This one is getting too crowded."

"Is that right?" Figlia said. "Now what do you know about that?" He pulled up a chair and sat down. He touched the dark one. "What's the matter, Frenchy, am I crowding you out?"

Frenchy removed Figlia's hand and said to the girl beside him, "It's a good idea to change places every once in a while so nobody'll get a line on us. They're always watching these joints."

"That's where you're right," Figlia said. "I know one guy who's got his eyes on you for sure, and that's fact." A silence fell on the table and the two men stiffened. The five girls turned to Figlia and one of them said, "Who's got his eye on us?"

"Don't let him scare you," Frenchy said. "If they had anything on us, they'd move in. They can't do a thing, if we keep moving around."

"Don't kid yourself about that," Figlia said. "This guy has got his eye on you all the time and there's no moving out from under it."

The girls and Mitch looked at each other, but Frenchy turned briefly to scan the door.

"Cut out the crap. What do you want?" Mitch said.

"I want to tell you about the guy who's got his eye on you," Figlia said.

"Sure. And what else?"

"Nothing else. All I want to do is tip you off." Figlia got up. "Where's Tex?" he said. "I haven't seen her around lately."

"What's it to you?"

"I don't like the way you talk," Figlia said. He roughed Mitch's hair. "I don't like the way you keep picking up your hair either. In fact, I don't like you." Mitch started to resist, but Figlia stiffened his hand and drew it back to slap him. Shorty said, "She's sleeping in back."

"Get her," Figlia said.

Shorty went to the back and Figlia said to Mitch, "Okay, you can put up your hair now. I'm not going to hit you."

Mitch put up his hair. The drunk girl said, "I've got to know who's got his eye on us. I've got to know it."

"Oh, he's spoofing, honey," one of the girls said. "He's just a great kidder."

"Are you?" the drunk girl said.

Shorty came in with the girl, Tex. She was young, not more than twenty, except for the eyes which had the hardness of glass, and her mouth, which was thin and tight. She had been sleeping in her clothes and she twisted her skirt around and hitched it up. The light in the room blinded her and she squinted, trying to see.

"Oh, it's you," she said to Figlia. She went to the table and got a cigarette from a pack lying there. "You don't want to stand too close to these two," she said. "They've got lice." She lighted the cigarette. "What's on your mind?"

"I was going to have something to eat," Figlia said. "I thought maybe you'd like a bite."

"I don't know. I don't feel like a bite. What time is it, anyway?"

Figlia showed his wrist watch.

Tex shook her head, trying to clear it. "I don't feel hungry," she said. "All I feel is a cup of coffee."

"They serve a pretty good cup right here," Mitch said.

"Why don't you drop dead?" Tex said. She and Figlia started out.

"When will you get back?" Mitch said.

"Don't wait up for me in case I'm not," Tex said. They went out and Shorty went with them to the door. He laughed in boyish laughter as he opened the door. "Fig's some kidder," he said to Tex.

"I've pulled a leg or two in my time," Figlia said.

"I mean that stuff about someone watching. You sure got them scared."

"What's the matter, don't you believe me?" Figlia said.

"Oh, cut it out," Shorty said in that laughing voice. "You know me better than that, Fig."

"Okay, only don't say I didn't warn you," Figlia said.

"No kidding, are you on the level?" Shorty said.

"Of course I'm on the level." Figlia touched Tex's arm and prompted her into the street. "Oh, my God," Shorty said. He shut the door and bolted it quickly and they could see his face, the eyes wide and frightened, pressed to the glass, searching the street.

Figlia laughed. "What'll you bet he shuts down the joint and goes home and hides under the bed," Figlia said.

They went along the Embarcadero. The fog was coming in thick now. It made a wall right up to a space near the buildings. They walked through patches of it to Drumm Street and went along Drumm toward Washington. The fog horn sounded to be in the middle of the Embarcadero, blowing at them instead of ships in the harbor.

"Where did they pick you up?" Figlia said.

"L.A."

"You haven't been working lately."

"So I haven't been working. What about it?"

"Nothing about it. I just said you haven't been working. That's kind of funny for a good-looking girl like you."

"You can drop the build up. You didn't come over to buy me a cup of coffee."

"You're mighty right, sister. How would you like to make a couple of easy bucks? I didn't want to ask you in there. They'd cut it to pieces."

"Thanks for nothing. You're not doing me any favors."

"Why not? I thought you could use a little money."

"How much?"

"Fifty."

"What's doing?"

"Pick up a guy and keep him off the street for about an hour."

"What's in it for you?"

"Never mind about me. Get him out of the way and you'll get your fifty."

"Where'll I find him?"

"He's having coffee at the Merchant's Lunch."

"How will I know him?"

"You'll know him. He's a big guy, wears a leather jacket with the collar up, walks like he had a stiff neck, needs a shave. You can't miss."

They were on Washington now. Fog was coming down over the lights, smidging them.

"Suppose I can't hold him for an hour," Tex said.

"You've got tricks. Use them," Figlia said.

They went along the wet street, toward the market.

15

NICK felt someone staring at him and he turned, wondering who it could be. The men in the Merchant's Lunch were eating along the counter, and the waiter was busy at the urn. The dishwasher clattered dishes at the sink. The cook was scraping the soiled surface of the grill with a brick. The feeling pressed on him as though some force were reaching across space and touching him and he turned to the window where buyers who crowded the market at this hour struggled by in an endless stream. The feeling chilled him. It was like frost in his hair and he was about to go out when he looked up and saw high on the wall behind the counter a gaudily colored poster of a glaring eye, above and around which were captioned the words THE EYES OF THE WORLD ARE ON YOU, BUY BONDS. The poster was covered with cobwebs and grease and though the message was no longer potent, the eye was. Nick could feel it looking sharply at him and he turned away. It's only a picture on a wall, he thought. I can look at it and it doesn't mean a thing. But in spite of this, the eye troubled him. It gave him a sense of being watched by some aloof and impersonal being who knew everything that was going to happen to him. What can happen to me? he thought. Nothing, not a thing, nothing can happen to me. But he began to go through all his fears and doubts. His neck, he could die? I'm not going to die, he thought. Not me. Then it was the load? He was going to lose it or sell it badly. I'll wait for Ed, he thought, and that will take care of that. But what about Ed? Nothing about Ed, he decided. He could take care of himself. Nothing could happen to him. But how about the old man in Auburn? He dispelled any thoughts of the old man quickly, before any picture of him could come into his mind, but for some reason a tremendous feeling of guilt came over him and he looked up again to see what he could read in the eye, but he could read nothing and he turned away feeling intimidated and troubled in his conscience.

Down the counter were two men playing dice poker. "Caballo-caballo," one of them shouted as he raised the leather dice cup and slammed it down upon the counter and raised it in the furtive manner of a card player opening his hand. "Arrive," he said in a confident whisper. He had thrown three aces. They kept up a constant slamming of the cups upon the counter.

The narrow space along the counter expanded into a wide room at the back where men played cards at the rummy tables. They played silently, their eyes intent on their hands, hardly watching each other, seeming more to be playing alone than together. Beyond them was a door marked GENTS. Men went into it and came out buttoning their flies or fastening their belts as they spat on the floor. Or they leaned over and blew their noses, first one nostril then the other, into a corner of the room.

The dishwasher, who had a lean sensitive face, came balancing a high stack of plates in his hands. He looked very intelligent with his fine gray hair, his high forehead, thin narrow nose and deepset thoughtful eyes. He piled the dishes beneath the counter and returned to the sink where he lighted a cigarette and stood smoking it. He was tired. After he had finished smoking the cigarette, he resumed washing the endless mound of soiled dishes that appeared at his elbow. He carefully wiped each plate on both sides and methodically thumbed out the crust of sugar that had settled into the bottoms of the cups.

The waiter was a middle-aged man with a dark pleasant face. There was a wart on his cheek that made him look like a potato. His eyelids dropped over his eyes as though he were having difficulty keeping them open. He came over to Nick and stood before him.

"Sleepy?" Nick said.

The waiter nodded. "Sleepy," he answered, shrugging, "I come two o'clock," he said. "Market don't open till three, but I come at two. Why? Don't ask. All they drink is coffee. One cup, two cups, three cups. I can make no money selling just the coffee, but all the same, I come." He held out his hands in a gesture of help-lessness.

Behind him on a shelf were three plates of raised doughnuts piled in high mounds, as many as the plates would hold. A fourth plate was piled with snails that were crusted with icing flecked with raisins. Beside them, near the cash register, were boxes of cigars, one atop the other, Corina Larks, Optimo, Diligencia, AAPetri-Toscanelli. The flag on the register showed ten cents.

A man rose from the counter. He was a short, round-faced Italian with sad brown eyes and thick hairy hands. He was dressed in a cheap imitation tweed suit that was tight across the shoulders and "high-water" at the shoes. The suit was new with sharp creases still in the trousers. As he headed out, one of the dice players paused at his game. "Hey, Barbusso, where you goin', hey?" he said. He blocked Barbusso's path and the other dice player got behind him so he was hemmed in.

Barbusso shrugged. "I go to work," he said.

"You goin' to work, hey?" the dice player said. He pulled Barbusso's tie from his vest and pulled his shirt out of his pants.

"You look like monkey in that suit," the other dice player said.

The card players had come up from the back and one of them, a long headed gentleman with a delicate underjaw, said, "Ever since he own his own produce house, he is gentleman."

"Are you gentleman, Barbusso?" the dice player said.

Barbusso shrugged. The men here were having a joke at his expense, and he had infinite patience. After all, a month ago, he had been one of them. He had known the bitterness of working for others, making money for others, and taking home his pittance. Now he was one of the others, on his own. "When you are boss, you have to dress up," he said.

"Yah, you hear that, he's boss," the dice player said. The men laughed and punched each other enthusiastically, as though at some great joke. "Hey, Barbusso! Barbusso, you tell me, hey?" the dice player said. "Before you was boss, you get up at three o'clock in the morning, hey?"

Barbusso nodded, doubtfully, wondering what the point was. "Yes."

"But now you get up one o'clock. And some day, Barbusso, when you get to be real big boss, you don't bother to go to sleep at all."

The men laughed all down the counter as Barbusso went out, holding his hands up to his ears and waving them.

A worker came in. He was bright-eyed and pink-cheeked. The kinky black hair on his chest sprouted out of his open shirt. He had the quick happy movement of a character in an animated cartoon as he sat down and slapped his open hands on the counter.

Arena, you son of a bitch, where's my coffee, where's my doughnuts?" he shouted.

"Ah, shut up, you big bastard," the waiter said. "You make too much noise. All the time, too much noise."

"Ah, you big stiff. You been dead all your life, you don't know it. Somebody forget to bury you out at Lawnpark. You got to make noise around here so somebody wake up."

The waiter placed two doughnuts on a plate, filled a cup with steaming coffee from the urn and brought them to the worker.

"What's the matter with you, Arena?" the worker shouted. "I want four doughnuts, four. This is a man what is hungry."

"If you sell produce like you talk, you be so rich you own the whole market," the waiter said.

"Who wants to own the whole market?" the worker said. "Is enough I own my pants." He broke a doughnut and slopped it into the coffee which was strong and black as ink.

"Hey, Giordano, what you hear about Pete?" the worker shouted down the counter.

"He's comin' pretty good, but they don't take off the bandages yet," said Giordano.

"They say he's all right? The doctor say is nothing broken? He gonna come through all okay?" said the waiter.

The worker shook his head. "They take off them bandages no telling what they find," he said. "Nobody knows what's under them bandages."

As Nick sat listening to the talk he felt a sudden painful concern for the man, whoever he was, lying somewhere in a bed, strait-jacketed from head to toe in bandages. Perhaps he was burned, or hurt in an accident, surely hurt with hidden bones broken. He felt sick for the man and knew he was only feeling sick for himself.

He did not know how badly hurt he was either. What would the
men in the restaurant do, he wondered, if he folded down his
collar and showed them his wound? He was afraid to look at it
and several times he had slipped his hand to the back of his neck
to touch it, but something stopped him, he could not say why.
His occasional moments of dizziness puzzled him, but he laid it to
sleepiness. I'm just sleepy, he told himself. A little shut-eye and
I'll be okay. He could hardly hold up his head and his eyes burned.
A sound rumbled endlessly in his ears as though they were
fastened to a sea shell. It was the sound of a truck in his head,
running all those miles from the apple farm.

He finished his coffee and stood up, balancing himself beside the
counter, one hand on a stool, and beckoned to the waiter. "How
much do I owe you?" he said.

The waiter smiled. "You no different from the others," he said.
He wrote on a bill and pushed it across. Nick laid down ten cents.
The effort to get up had made him dizzy. He was waiting for it to
pass when a girl came in. The restaurant was narrow and he had
to sit down again to let her go by. After she had passed, he got
up and went out. It was only when he was outside that he remembered how quiet the room had become when the girl had
come in. He looked through the window and saw the men sitting
arrested in their seats, suddenly quieted, their eyes on her. In the
back the men playing at the rummy tables had stopped playing. The
cook stood with the brick raised in his hand. Even he, Nick
thought, even that old cocker with the rooster-look stiffening his
face at sight of the girl.

Across the street Figlia was watching intently. He went into the
produce house when Nick turned away from the window. The
corn truck had departed and already half the row of corn was
sold and gone. The buyers moved about in an agitated crowd on
the sidewalk. People sure like corn, Nick thought. They'll like
apples too, when Ed comes in. The corn is nothing to what the
apples will be. From somewhere among the crowd came the wheezy
laughter of the swamper. Nick went walking along Washington,
looking into the produce stalls.

The floorman at Levi-Zetner's was counting tomatoes. He had

sold all his boxes of ones and was checking on the seconds. If he pushed the seconds, he would sell them too, but you can't move twos when the floor is covered with ones.

"Can you use some tomatoes?" he said to Nick. He had mistaken him for a buyer.

"No," Nick said. "But how about apples. You got any apples?"

"Not an apple in the place," the floorman said. He was busy stamping the lot number up and down a stack of boxes.

"That's too bad," Nick said. "I could use some apples. People keep asking for 'em. I could use about twenty boxes."

"Come in about next week," the floorman said. "It's a little early for apples right now."

"They'd be kind of high, wouldn't they, with apples short?" Nick said.

"Sure, a million bucks a box, if you haven't got any."

"How much would they be if you had any?"

"If I had any, they'd be a little less."

"Sure, but how much?"

"Beat it, will you?" the floorman said. "Can't you see I'm busy?" The floorman walked to the back.

"What's the matter, Bill?" one of the clerks said.

"The son of a bitch is apple crazy," Nick heard the floorman say. "He wants to know how much they are if you haven't got any."

Nick went on toward Davis Street. The market was thick with buyers, buying their needs for the next day and hauling them back to their stores to lay out on counters for the housewives who were sleeping with their husbands now, but who would soon be awake and making out shopping lists. Nick thought of them in their homes and apartments, the families, husbands, wives and children, living in the big city, all the lives in the city, all of them tied to this shabby little street. When he had first walked through it, it had seemed blocks long, but now he could see how small it was, active and teeming in the sleeping city, an island in the dark.

Now that the produce trucks were gone from Washington, the street was crowded with men pushing two-wheeled hand carts, jockeying them with curses and shouts. One of these was Charles, his simian figure runted behind the high stack of corn crates he was hauling. He walked fast, steering his truck with a touch of the hand or a kick of the foot, the hard muscles of his backside lumping alternately with each stride.

"Watch your legs," he shouted.

A hand truck loaded high with sacks of potatoes moved toward him, coming fast. "Watch *your* legs," the handler shouted.

"They're your legs," Charles called out. He was running hard, blinded by the crates he was pushing, not seeing the way or trying to see it.

"They're your legs," the handler answered.

The two hand trucks smashed together, splintering the crates and spilling the potatoes into the street.

"Why the hell don't you watch where you're going?" Charles said and the handler said, "Why, you prick, if you weren't rolling that thing like you owned the God damned street, it wouldn't have happened."

Charles tried to hit the handler, but the handler spun him around. He went in to hit him, but Charles slipped his hand to his back and when he brought it out his hatchet was in it. Before he could use it, men stepped in and held him.

"All right, what do you think you're doing, opening a box?" one of the men said.

"Let him use it, it'll make him feel big," the handler said. "How big does it make you feel, you prick?"

"Ah, shut up," a buyer said. "What are you getting so hot about? It was just an accident."

Charles slipped the hatchet back into his belt and righted his truck. He stacked the crates of corn and hooked the truck under them, tilted it back, started it with a kick and off he went, shouting, "All right, you guys, watch your legs, they're your legs." The men scattered.

"Look at him go," the buyer said.

"That Charley can sure handle a truck."

"He runs that thing like somebody had built a fire under his butt," a handler said.

The crowd drifted back to their buying and selling. The traffic resumed its flux in the street. A poultry truck turned down Davis.

It was loaded with turkeys. Their heads stuck out of the cages, erect and bright-eyed, looking about like tourists passing through the market.

Nick followed the truck around the corner to a slaughterhouse. A sign above the double doors said, FINE DRESSED POULTRY. The truck had gone in and was parked in the center of a large room. In a corner of the room were a number of garbage cans. The cans were blood stained and full of feathers. There was an odor of wet feathers in the air. Along a wall ran a conveyor chain from which dangled many sharp hooks. The chain disappeared around a corner of the wall, but beyond it reappeared, passing through a steam bath, a plucking machine and on between two rows of naked-armed, white-dressed women. Their hands were raw from handling the dressed poultry, plucking the pin feathers. The last of a run of white leghorns was passing through the line and the women stood ankle deep in white feathers.

The turkey trucker got down from the cab and called out, "Hey, George."

A beefy man in a blood stained apron came from around the corner. "Well, here's that turkey man," he said. "How many you got?"

"I don't know," the trucker said. "It's down in the book. Two more trucks coming in. Is this where you want 'em?"

"That's fine," the manager said. "Hey Earl," he called back to the line of women. A young man came from behind the plucking machine. Feathers were in his hair and he kept brushing them off, the feathers clinging to his arms and hands.

"Earl, you want to start unloading them birds?" the manager said.

"Hell no. But I will," Earl said. He went to the truck and opened one of the cages. The turkeys were alert and suspicious. They began to chirp in loud frightened voices, crowding to the far end of the cage. They put up a fight as the man Earl grabbed them and fastened them head down on the conveyor hooks. He emptied cage after cage until the chain was heavy with the live turkeys. They beat their wings and struggled against the hook, their heads erected somehow on all that long neck in that inverted position, knowing they were moving, but where?—trying to see where they were going.

Nick watched the birds disappear around the wall. Something must be going on back there I can't see, he thought, for the turkeys did not reappear at once. He could see the empty chain clattering through the steam bath and the plucking machine. The last of the white leghorns had been picked and the women were resting on boxes, waiting for the turkeys. Soon Nick saw them coming along the chain. They still struggled, but now it was not against the hooks. This struggle was terrific and aimless, futile and violent. They shuddered and jumped in convulsions, tightening all their muscles and loosening them, beating their wings and going through the motions of running as though trying to crowd all the life they might have lived into one desperate moment. Now and then a bird squawked, the sound human in its terror, and at the cry all the turkeys that remained in the truck became agitated and began to throw themselves against the walls of the cages as though the voice had screamed murder.

The turkeys began to pass through the steam bath and the women stood up, waiting for the first of them to come through the plucking machine. Soon the line was moving toward the women. The manager walked with the first turkey, feeling its breast. It had been stripped of its feathers and it hung naked and white from the hook.

"Good birds," the manager said.

"Beauties," one of the women said. She was short and squat with flabby flesh and loose pendulous breasts. Her neck was as broad as her face and she had the florid complexion of a butcher. She grabbed the turkey and swiftly cleaned it of its pin feathers. "They're doves," she said. "Aren't they doves, though, nice and broad through the breast?"

"That's the way we want 'em," the manager said. He stepped to the space hidden behind the wall and Nick heard him say to someone, "How do they look?"

"They look fine," a voice answered, and without seeing the source of it, Nick knew that whoever it was, was old. He followed the chain to the corner where it turned and he saw that he was right.

Seated high on a stool was an old man. He caught the turkeys as they came up and wiped his fist casually across their necks and when they moved away their necks were slit. Blood spurted to the floor. Back along the moving chain the turkeys kept looking around with that fatal curiosity, wanting to see. Nick could feel the assault of their eyes as they saw and their struggle against the hook became more violent as they neared the old man, who was sticking them as quickly as they came to him, which was very quickly. Occasionally a live turkey would get past him and he would walk with the chain until he had caught up. Blood soaked his shoes and coated the floor and there was the warm suffocating smell of it in the air.

The sticker saw Nick and winked at him. He waved toward the women and Nick could see the glittering point of the knife in his fist. "Now if we could get 'em with breast like that," he said.

"We're working on it," the manager said. "That's what we want. Lots of breast with plenty of white meat."

"You said it, kid," the sticker said. When he smiled, he showed yellowed teeth, just the fronts. They had been pulled out along the sides and the empty gums showed when he smiled.

"Something you want?" the manager said to Nick.

"Just looking," Nick said. "He sure knocks 'em off, doesn't he?"

"He sure does," the attendant said. "Anything comes down that chain, gets stuck. He don't even look to see what it is."

Nick followed the manager to the truck.

16

TEX was about to go into the street when she saw Mitch go past the restaurant window. Wouldn't you know it? she thought. She went back and sat down. After a while Mitch returned, still looking for her. He saw her at the counter and came in.

"I've been looking for you," he said.

"Why don't you go look for yourself?" Tex said. "Maybe you'd be surprised what you'd find."

"Very funny," Mitch said. "What did that guy want?"

"What guy?"

"You know who I mean. That produce dealer, what was he after?"

"You know what he was after," Tex said.

Mitch stood looking at Tex and she said, "All right, you don't have to like it, but your end of nothing is nothing."

"I can't talk to you in here," Mitch said. "Come on, let's go."

"Can't you see I'm having my coffee?" Tex said. "You wouldn't want me to go away and leave my coffee." She started to drink, but Mitch took the cup from her hand and put it down. He paid the cashier and led her out.

"Now suppose you tell me," Mitch said.

"What's there to tell?" Tex said. She looked across the street to see if Figlia had seen them. The men with the hand trucks kept booming by.

"That's what I'm asking you," Mitch said.

Figlia stepped out from behind Nick's truck and crossed the street. "I don't know how it looks from there," he said, "but from here it looks like he was bothering you."

"He's not bothering me," Tex said. "We were just saying goodbye."

"Say goodbye to the girl," Figlia said to Mitch.

"Goodbye, Mitch," Tex said.

"Too bad you're not going his way," Figlia said. "You're breaking his heart."

Tex went along Washington, dodging the hand trucks as they came off the street into the produce houses. She turned down Davis, wondering where Nick had gone. There goes that fifty bucks, she thought. Even if Nick was handy, Mitch would queer it. She knew Figlia could not hold him long. She went past the alley, past the slaughter house. That was him in the slaughter house, she thought after she had passed it, and she went back and there he was talking to a man in a white coat. I'm going to catch a big one this time, she thought. She opened her purse and got a cigarette out of it and decided to pretend to be looking for a match. She started walking to the slaughter house entrance, looking for a match, timing it so Nick and his friend were at the door when she reached it. "How about a light?" she said.

She turned to Nick, but Nick did not move. The man in the white coat brought out a lighter and flashed it. "Here you go," he said and he held the lighter to her. Tex leaned to it, getting the light, and she heard Nick, say, "I'll be seeing you," his steps going away.

The slaughter house manager extinguished the lighter and returned it to his pocket. "What are you doing, working overtime?" he said.

"Yeah," Tex said. She had her eye on Nick. She saw him turn down Washington.

"What do you make for overtime, time and a half?" the manager said.

Tex did not answer. I let him get away, she thought. Right in my lap and I let him get away, but how do you nail a guy if he doesn't look at you? She went after Nick, down Washington.

Behind her, the driver of the poultry truck had joined the manager. "How would you like to cut yourself a piece of that?" the manager said.

"That's what I'd like," the driver said. "Boy, wouldn't I like that, a good big slice and I'm the little boy who's got the knife to cut it." He clapped his hands and rubbed them together briskly.

Figlia still had Mitch cornered when Tex came up. He tilted his head and she knew that Nick had gone on down the street. She nodded as she took Mitch's arm. "Well, honey, would you like to go home?" she said. "All right," she said to Figlia, "I'll take him home now."

"What's the matter, can't he go home alone?" Figlia said.

"Oh, but I need him," Tex said. "I get lonely when he's not around. Come on, Mitch honey." She urged his arm and they went down Washington. She could see Figlia looking worried, trying to figure it out.

The only way he could go is down, she thought. He wouldn't go up a side street because he already did that. He's got to go down.

She walked quickly, her mind on Nick.

"What's that honey stuff?" Mitch said.

"Don't you like for me to call you honey?" Tex said. "You're my honey, don't you know that? I've been crazy about you a long time, honey."

"You said it, you've been crazy a long time," Mitch said. "Where do you think you're going?"

"Why, I'm taking you home, honey. I just can't wait to get you home."

"The hell you say. What do you think you're pulling?" Mitch tried to free his arm, but Tex held it tightly. "Oh, take it easy," she said, "Can't you take a little kidding? Hasn't anybody ever called you honey?"

"The hell with you," Mitch said.

They had reached the Embarcadero, but Tex could not see Nick. The fog was down low and thick but back in the market it would not come down. The heat from the bodies of the men working in the street kept it off the ground. He must be somewhere near the corner, she thought.

"Why don't you stop bothering me," she said to Mitch. She said it loudly. "Who do you think you are, anyway? Leave me alone." She released his arm and pushed him off.

"Now wait a minute," Mitch said. "Now take it easy. Who do you think you're shoving around?"

"Go away, just go away," Tex said. Mitch tried to hold her arm, but she knocked him off balance so he nearly fell. He came at her, maddened, his mouth drawn over his teeth, and she screamed. She fought him off, screaming, and she saw Nick running toward her. He slugged Mitch once and then she caught Nick's hand and they were running from the corner into the darkness that blinded the Embarcadero.

17

THEY ran along the Embarcadero to Pacific Street and up Pacific to Front and crossed Front, walking.

"Did he hurt you?" Nick said.

"No, thanks to you. Lucky for me you were there," Tex said. "Do you think he's following us?"

"Not a chance. His head hit the sidewalk."

"That's too bad for the sidewalk," Tex said. She thought, exultantly, I've got him. All I've got to do is get him to my room. The running made her breathe hard, her mouth open. It made her look frightened. She held Nick's arm and looked quickly over her shoulder.

"Take it easy, you're all right now," Nick said.

"I keep thinking he's back there," Tex said. If I can get him to come in, that'll fix it, she thought. This way he'll beat it the minute he gets me home. "He knows where I live," she said.

"He won't bother you," Nick said. "If he does, lock the door."

"Sure, and if he kicks it in, I can scream," Tex said. "I like to scream." She released his arm. I can pick up any bum in town for two bucks, she thought. But when it's for fifty, he's got to be hard to get. "I don't think I better go home just yet."

"Sure, walk around. Maybe you can pick up another bum," Nick said. "What are you doing out this time of the night anyway?"

"I work over at the Ferry Building," Tex said. "This is the time I get off."

"Why don't you ride a cab? Or maybe you like being grabbed at," Nick said. He thought, if Ed gets in, he'll see the truck. He can't miss it, not where it's parked. Maybe he'll have the load sold by

148

the time I get back. "Where do you live?" he said. "I'll take you home."

"I hate to put you out."

"That's okay. Glad to do it."

He's in, Tex thought. All I've got to do is get him there. "It's down Merchant," she said. He thinks I'm a nice girl, she thought, and she took his arm again. Somehow it made her feel nice, holding his arm and letting him take her home. There he would tip his hat, if he had a hat, and say a pleasant good night. Might even give me some advice and warn me about men, she thought. She laughed, thinking about it.

"What's so funny?" Nick said.

"I'm scared," Tex said. "When I'm scared, I laugh." He's a nice guy, she thought. The thought was not a sarcasm but an appraisal.

They started across Merchant. A car passed and Tex stopped in the middle of the intersection.

"What's the matter now?" Nick said.

"I can't say for sure, but that looked like his car," Tex said. ·

"You're seeing things. He's still back there holding down the sidewalk," Nick said. They went along a walk that was paved with bricks, along Merchant in a direction opposite to that of the car. Tex freed her arm and turned to take a look down the street where the tail light was disappearing in the fog.

"If that's his car, he'd have stopped," Nick said.

"Sure, he's dying to get some more of that treatment," Tex said. She led Nick quickly down Merchant toward a light that grew bigger as they approached it. "I know it was his car," she said. She pushed Nick into the doorway, and they stood in the darkness out of reach of the street light, listening. There was the sound of fog dripping down the walls of the building and the fog horn far off. Nick started to say something, but Tex silenced him with the pressure of her arm. They stood tightly together in the narrow hallway. The second floor landing light was burned out and the stairs went up in darkness.

Nick struck a match and looked up. The stairs went up in a cave of high wooden walls that were water streaked from the fog that came in from the bay every night. There was the sweet mouldy smell of rotting wood. Nick turned to Tex. Pressed against each other the way they were, she knew he could feel the come and go of her breath.

"Okay, go on up," Nick said. He flattened himself to let her pass and she felt his body, hard and muscular through his clothes, as she went by him up the stairs.

He struck another match as she fumbled in her purse for the key. She tangled the key in the lock and Nick caught her hand, to take it from her. "It's all right," she said, "it's in, I've got it in."

She unlocked the door and swung it wide. She thought, if he comes in, I've got him. She crossed to the light and turned it on. Behind her, Nick had entered the room and was looking about, inspecting it. She closed the door and leaned against it, wondering what he thought of home. The bed was one of those push up contraptions that disappeared into a wall. It was down, the covers tussled but not slept in. There was a hollow where a body had lain.

"Not much, is it?" Tex said.

Nick bounced the bed. "It's better than a truck," he said. "Ever try sleeping on a steering wheel?"

"No, but I've slept in a train," Tex said. "It beats sleeping in a train."

Nick nodded. "Well, I guess you're okay now," he said. He went to the door.

"Thanks for bringing me home," Tex said. "I don't know what I was scared of, but thanks."

"Who was that guy?" Nick said.

"Just a guy. Can I fix you a drink?"

"No, I've got to get going. He acted like he might be an old boy friend."

"Some of 'em don't know when they're dead. Let me fix you a drink."

"Okay, if it's a short one. I've got a load sitting in the market and I don't like to be away too long."

"A short one it is," Tex said. "One drink and you can be on your way." Over my body you'll be on your way, she thought. What's your hurry, you big lug? He was big. His jeans, faded and shrunk, showed the lean tapered lines of his legs. And those big shoes. She removed her coat and threw it on the sofa. Her skirt had twisted again and she straightened it with Nick watching her.

Well, why don't you go? she thought to herself. You were in such a rush a minute ago. Why don't you open the door and beat it? I'm in my room and your end of it is finished, so get out and go. I'm supposed to hold you here for an hour, but you can go.

She thought, if I can get him to bed, that'll tear it. Suck your thumb and go to sleep, little boy. There was a strange immature boylike quality in his face for all his size. I'll rock him to sleep, she thought, that's what I'll do, and when he wakes up he'll be in one hell of a hurry to get out of here, but it'll be too late.

"Will you light the heater?" she said. "It's cold in here."

While Nick was lighting the heater, she went into the bathroom. There was a sharp antiseptic smell in the room and another smell that was like unwashed feet, but was not. When she shut the door, there was a douche bag hanging on the back of it. She removed the bag, coiled the tube, stuffed it into the bag and hid bag and tube in the towel cabinet. There was a cigarette on the washbasin. Where it had burned down it had left a yellow stain on the porcelain. She threw the cigarette into the toilet and flushed it down and tried to remove the stain, but it would not come off. She put away a big bottle of mouth wash and box of douche powder that were on the water closet.

What am I doing that for? she thought. He's not coming in here. She took a quick hard look at herself in the mirror. A calculating critical face confronted her. Not good, but not bad either. It would do. She looked down at herself where her skirt went in at the waist and flared out at the hips. She rubbed the palm of her hand lightly on her hip and something shivered at the base of her spine. It'll do until something better comes along, she thought. It'll do for him. They can't see you for anything, if they don't want to, but when they do it's for one thing.

The glasses tasted of mouth wash. She rinsed them out and as she dried them she continued to observe herself in the mirror, her face pliant and speculative. I wonder how he'll be? she thought. The young ones aren't very good. They get too excited and he's young. But he's got a tough face. And he's big. I like 'em big. And that beard too. She could feel it rasping against her cheek. But he was so young.

She carried the cups into the living room. Nick was sitting on the bed, looking at the perfume and lotion bottles on the dresser. "That's some bar you've got," he said.

"I'm saving it for when I'm hard up," Tex said. "Right now, I'm in the money." She brought out a fifth of bourbon from the dresser and poured some into each glass. She poured it straight, not cutting it with water, a stiff one for Nick and a short one for her. She handed him his glass and raised hers.

"How are we doing?" she said.

"It looks like we're doing fine," Nick said.

"Here's to friendship."

"Yeah, here's to it, short and sweet," Nick emptied his glass and got up from the bed.

"I wish you wouldn't go," Tex said. "Do you have to go?"

Nick reached into his pocket and brought out a handful of change. "See that, sister, that's all the money I've got in the world," he said.

"Who said anything about money? I just want you to stay," Tex said. She surprised herself. She really wanted him to stay, not for the fifty dollars Figlia had promised, but for himself. She saw him watching her critically, his face wise and alert, but not cold and cynical the way the old ones were. She saw him trying to make himself look tough, but he was soft. The softness was in his eyes that had not seen too much and in his full gentle mouth. I'll bet he doesn't even know how to kiss, she thought. He doesn't know anything. The thought pleased her. He looked clean standing before her and somehow being in the same room with him made her feel clean too. A curious longing came over her, as of lost youth and first love, and she ached when she thought of him going away.

Something of her thoughts must have come into her face, for she saw he was puzzled. He looked at her as though seeing her for the first time. She laughed and took his arm and led him to the chair. "Sit down," she said. She made him sit down. "I'm going to make some coffee," she said, "and we're going to drink it and talk. You'll stay?"

"If you really want me to," Nick said.

She looked at him and her eyes suddenly burned. "I want you to," she said.

"Okay."

"Swell. I'll go put the coffee on. Make yourself at home." Tex started to go, but Nick stopped her. "A minute ago you looked like chipped glass," he said, "but now you're different."

Tex drew away her hand and went to the kitchen. She got the pot and filled it with water and coffee and as she set it on the stove, she discovered that an old feeling had come on her, a feeling of innocence and adventure. She had not had it in a long time, but now it was on her and she returned to Nick feeling excited.

He was standing by the window. The room was hot and the window was misted with the vapor of their breaths. Nick tried to open it, but it would not move. He hit the sill with the heel of his hand, but it refused to move. He hit it several times and suddenly it opened and the ringing, echoing, far-off, empty sounds of night surged into the room. The wind carried on it the briny smell of the sea. The fog horn sounded loud now. There was a screeching cry beyond the window.

"Seagulls," Tex said. "They fly over all the time." She leaned to the window and she could hear them in the fog. They sounded above the building. The fog came wet and cold into the room. She stood looking into the darkness, listening to the gulls. "I hear them in my sleep," she said. "They make me think of drowning." The fog horn sounded and a quiet lonely feeling crept into the room. She kept looking at Nick, holding him with her eyes. He had said he would stay, but she knew soon he would have to go. Don't go, she thought. I don't want you to go. She thought it very hard. Don't go, you don't have to go. I want you to stay. Please don't go. The gulls screeched outside, very near the window.

Nick touched her shoulder, to turn her around, but she pushed away his hand. It was done with a fierce gesture, as though his touch had revolted her. The rejection sent a flood of panic through Nick. He felt sharply cut in some vital place that was the core of himself. He felt unwanted and worthless and he said to himself All right, you can go now. Pick up your hat and go, but he

lingered on, long after his dismissal, waiting for a word of for-
giveness and acceptance. Why couldn't he go? She had told him
to go.

The gulls were screeching near the window, sounding loud now,
as though they were about to soar into the room. "I don't know
why I did that," Tex said. "I want you to hold me. Please hold me."

Nick did not move. He had wanted very much to hold her, but
her words had the effect of turning him away. When she did not
want, he wanted and when she wanted, he did not want. God
damn it, he thought. He forced himself to take her in his arms
and when she felt his arms around her, she clasped him with her
body, letting her breath go. At once she had a feeling of clothes
being superfluous and she wanted to tear them off. She stroked his
back with her hands, feeling the cleft of his spine, and she moved
her mouth on his cheek, lightly so it felt electric, the beard bristly
on her lips. Fumbling, she unbuttoned his shirt and got her arms
under it and around him. That naked strong body. Hard as a rock.
She stroked his back fiercely, circling the palms of her hands in a
gesture of sharpening desire, and when it was sharp, very sharp so
it balled in a lump and hurt hard, ready to burst and pour, she
brought her arms out from under his shirt and coiled them around
his neck, bringing him down as she yearned herself upward, mouth
parted and tongue hard. Suddenly she heard a cry of pain and felt
herself thrown off. Nick was standing with his head bent far back
and his face gritted with pain.

"What's the matter?" Tex said.

"My coat, take it off." Nick spoke in a hiss, hardly to be understood.

Tex removed the coat and saw beneath it the bloodstained shirt
clotted into the wound; and the wound festering and raw on his
neck. Nick buckled and she caught him and half carried him to
the bed and he fell upon it, face down, and lay holding it as though
he were falling, the bed, the room, all of it spinning and falling.
The wound had broken open and blood oozed in a startling red
through the shirt. She wanted to call to him, but she did not know
his name and she said, "Are you all right? Answer me!" shaking
and trying to waken him.

The gulls screeched outside. The fog horn came into the room. Nick released his grip on the bed and one arm hung loose over the side, the hand slack.

Of course he's all right, he's got to be all right, Tex thought. She tried to turn him over, but he was heavy. In the effort to move him, she bent close to the wound and she could smell the sweet nauseating odor of it. She thought, This guy in my room. I don't even know his name.

She got her coat and put it on, tangling herself in the sleeves. Oh, Christ, she thought, what a mess I'm in. I've got to get him out. Without any knowledge of what she would do, she went to the door. She had forgotten the light and she returned to the bed and turned it off. Beyond the window were the market lights making a big glow in the fog. Figlia, she thought, he'll get him out. But now that she knew what to do, her movements became even more frantic.

She went out, shutting the door and her feet rattled quickly on the steps as she went down.

18

SHE ran from the room, but when she got into the street, she thought of him lying on the bed with that neck and she thought, I ought to go back. It might not look so bad after the second look. I ought to take care of him. She could see herself with towels and a pan full of hot water, taking care of him and she tightened herself. The hell with him, she decided, who the hell does he think he is anyway? All they ever want is taking care of, in bed or in the house or out in the world, always coming home for that stiffening of the chin that trembles so easily when the going is tough. All right, dear, things aren't as bad as they look. You can face life again. You stiffen them and what do you get? The hell with him, let him die. I'm not going back.

And he will, she thought, nobody with a cut like that, nobody; but she wanted to go back. It was like a rope tied to him that grew tighter the farther away she got from the room.

On Davis the slaughter house manager and the driver of the poultry truck were still standing in the doorway. "Hey, if you got a minute, I got a minute," the manager said.

"A minute's about your size," Tex said.

The driver laughed. Behind them the clerks were unloading the last of the turkeys. The choking smell of feathers, like the smell of rain on ground that has gone dusty from the long summer, drifted into the street.

Tex went on to Washington. All the big trucks were gone now and there were only the small trucks that belonged to buyers who came from the grocery stores in all the little towns along the Peninsula. The street was beginning to unload. Where there had been solid stacks of boxes, crates, sacks, now were open spaces where

the buyers had bought and hauled away. The fresh greens that
had been piled around lamp posts and upon the weathered brick
walks had wilted into a few scattered leaves and broken carrots.
The ice that packed the corn and lettuce and celery that had been
brought into market by reefer trucks early the night before had
melted and water ran in a dirty stream along the gutter.

Tex went down Washington feeling as though she were stretching herself, pulling away from Nick. Why don't I just go back and
get it over with? she thought. This won't help at all. She could not
get the smell of him out of her face. The smell of sweat and
pure male, the way they do when they come in from work. She could
feel his beard, not stubby and sharp the way it is a day after being
shaved, but silken like the growth of three or four days. She could
feel his hands on her shoulders, the fingers wooden hard, and his
back when she held him, like a board. You're one of these sick
female cats, she thought. Why don't you go back and fill up on
him and get sick of him and throw him out? She tried to remind
herself of the revulsion that came on her when she was with men,
but it did not work. All she wanted was to go back.

The sidewalk was empty in front of Figlia's produce house.
The long row of corn had disappeared. There was only a truck
with the load still on it, covered with a tarpaulin that was tied
down with a criss-cross of ropes. Beside the truck stood a small knot
of men. Over at the end of the stall were a number of crates of
broccoli, one of them opened, showing the neatly tied bunches of
green. The swamper who had lost his trip back and was waiting for
a ride North out of town, kept picking up one of the bunches of
broccoli and throwing it down. "What do you call this stuff?"
he said. "What do you do with it?"

"They're vegetables," the handler named Dave said. "You order
'em with a side of steaks."

"What do you do with 'em after you order 'em?" the swamper
said.

"You eat 'em, you ass hole," the handler said.

"Yeah, you folks in the city," the swamper said. "You'd eat shit
if somebody was to tell you it was good. You know what'll happen
if you eat that stuff?" He picked up a bunch of the broccoli and

threw it down. "You'll get a rabbit nose. You got rabbit brains already and you'll get a nose to match."

Tex went to Figlia. "Mike," she said.

"Sure, kid, just a minute," Figlia said. To the swamper he said, "What's the matter, don't you like broccoli?"

"Grass," the swamper said, "nothing but grass. Back home I feed it to my rabbits. I ain't dumb like you jokers. I eat the rabbits."

"Where did you say you came from?" Figlia said.

"From up Washington State, where they raise men," the swamper said. "Where I come from we grow hair on our ears. I'm no God damned hay eater. I eat meat. Any of you guys know what meat is?"

"Sure, it costs a dollar a pound," the handler named Dave said. He was breaking up an empty crate and piling the pieces on the sidewalk. "Two lamb chops, two bucks."

"Hell, I can get a whole woman for that. Ain't that so, lady?" the swamper said.

"Your kind of woman," Tex said. "Please, Mike, I've got to talk to you."

"In a minute, kid," Figlia said. The market cop came up, eating a pear. It was a juicy pear and he had to lean over to keep it from dripping on his uniform. "You ought to stick around, Riley," Figlia said. "This guy is a regular three ring circus."

"The racket I'd get in, if I had any brains," the swamper said, "I'd be a butcher or get in the produce business. I'd get crummy rich."

"What the hell do you want to get rich for?" Figlia said.

"I'd eat twelve meals a day, I'd never go hungry," the swamper said.

"Hell, you'd have to be richer than I am to feed the gut you carry around," Figlia said. "There's no money in this game."

"Ho-ho," the swamper said. "Next thing he's gonna tell us he made a million bucks but the government got it all. Guys like that got everybody by the balls. You pinch the farmer and you pinch the eater."

"You know what Figlia's motto is," the handler said. "It's *soak 'em!"* He was pushing a piece of paper under the pile of sticks.

"Sure, folks kick about it, but what the hell can they do?" the swamper said. "They gotta live, they gotta eat."

The handler lighted the paper and the broken crate began to burn. The men crowded around it, holding out their hands, waiting for the fire to grow so they could get the heat.

"All right, you guys," Figlia said. He kicked the pile of sticks into the gutter.

"Hey, what's the big idea?" the handler said.

"He's scared to death you'll burn a hole in the sidewalk," the handler said. "Don't you know he owns it?"

"Why don't you guys scatter around?" Figlia said. "What do you think this is out here, the Masonic Temple?"

"We like it here," the swamper said. He rubbed his big hands together and shuffled his outsize feet. "What's the matter with you, what're you getting so hot about? Don't you know, if we had half a chance, we'd be right in there doing the same as you?"

The waitress who reported for work at the Merchant's Lunch at three thirty in the morning went past Tex. Her hair was thrown up into a knot and her eyes were swollen from lack of sleep.

"Hey, Lucy," Charles said.

Lucy was crossing the street, but she stopped. "What do you want?" she said.

"You know what I want," Charles said.

The swamper began to laugh in that wheezy laugh. "Lucy Bowles," he said.

"Ah, shut up," Lucy said.

"Look at her," Figlia said. "Don't she look like warmed over death? It's that day life getting her. What's the matter, Lucy, don't you sleep days?"

The swamper laughed again, his eyes on Lucy. "Ah, go to hell," she said. She crossed to the Merchant's Lunch.

Figlia turned to Tex. "What's on your mind?" he said.

"That fellow you told me to pick up," Tex said.

"Is he in your room?"

"Yes."

"Then I suppose it's all right for me to take an apple," Figlia said. He went to the truck and got several apples from under the tarp and dropped down. He tossed one to the buyer. "Have an apple," he said.

"For Christ sake," the buyer said. "Where did you get that?"

"Load just came in," Figlia said. "Want an apple?" he said to Tex.

"What's the matter with the apples she's got?" the swamper said. He went again into that irritating wheezy laugh.

"Why, they're almost as big as yours, huh, Fatty," Tex said. And to Figlia she said, "I've got to talk to you, Mike."

"Sure, kid," Figlia said. He squeezed her arm and winked to the men. "If you'll excuse me a minute, boys."

They went into the produce house. Figlia's office was on a mezzanine. Half way up Figlia said, "What's biting you?"

"That fellow I got in my room."

"What about him?"

"Do you know why he holds his neck out like it was stiff?"

"Maybe he's got a stiff neck. How would I know?"

"He's got a hole in it as big as your head. He's half dead. He's going to die."

"You're crazy. He wouldn't be walking around."

"He is. You can't see it until he takes off his coat. He's on my bed."

"I'm glad it's your bed and not mine."

"I've got to get rid of him and you've got to help me, Mike." Figlia shook his head. "Not me, sister. I like 'em alive."

"I wouldn't have picked him up if it wasn't for you."

"Why drag me into it?"

"Because you are in it, you louse."

"Don't call me a louse, you bitch."

"You're a dirty louse."

"That makes you one up on me. Why don't you call a cop? He'll get rid of him for you."

"He'll put it on me, the way you're trying to do, you louse."

"All right, you bitch." Figlia held out his hand as though he were trying to lead a stubborn child. She refused it, but they went down the stairs.

"You get him out of my room," Tex said. "You put him there and you've got to get him out." She was screaming and the men in the street could hear her. Charles came up.

"That's enough of that," Figlia said. "Here's your fifty bucks. Beat it!"

"I don't want your lousy money," Tex said. "Just get him out of my room, that's all I want from you."

Figlia replaced the money in his wallet. "What's the lady talking about?" Charles said.

"The lady says there's a gentleman on her bed," Figlia said.

"You louse," Tex said.

"You bitch," Figlia said. "Charles, will you help the bitch out to the street?"

"Beat it," Charles said.

"You've got to get him out of my room," Tex said.

"I'm surprised, Mister Figlia," Charles said. "Just one gentleman? A girl like her ought to have three or four gentlemen in her room."

"All right," Figlia said. "I'm losing my patience."

"You heard him," Charles said. "The man's losing his patience." He held Tex by the elbow and rushed her to the street.

Behind her Tex could hear one of the buyers saying, "What's the matter with her?" and Figlia saying, "She tried to put the touch on me," and the swamper saying, "Why doesn't she touch me? I don't mind being touched," and the beefy laughter of the men.

Why does he want him out of the way? Tex thought. Fifty dollars for it. He didn't pay, but he offered and for him that's reckless. On Davis she crossed to the other side of Washington and doubled back to the Merchant's Lunch where the waitress was in her place behind the counter and the market men were playing their interminable dice poker, making the dishes jump every time they pounded the leather cup onto the counter.

"This time I get you, Romano," a voice gloated. "Hah!" followed by the slam of the cup and the clatter of dice. "How you like that, hey Romano?" the voice shouted and a deeper voice said, "I show you how I like," and again the slam of the cup

and the rolling of dice and the hard rattle of Italian accompanied
by the coarse laughter of men. The smell of cigars, stale and
fumigant, surged from the door as she passed it on her way to a
mound of potato sacks. The earthy odor of the potatoes came up
to her as she hid behind them.

Across the way Figlia was talking to the market cop. "Who the
hell named you Riley, anyway?" he said. "You move that truck
out of the way or I'll move it."

"What do you want me to do, push it?" the cop said. "I can't
move it without a key."

"Tow it then," Figlia said. "I don't care how you do it, just
so you get it off my dock. All night I've been stumbling over that
pile of junk."

"You can't tow that thing with a flat tire, loaded the way she
is," the cop said.

"Then unload it," Figlia said. "Or maybe you want me to unload
it. Is that it?"

"Where's the driver?" the cop said. "He must be somewheres.
He'd move it, if somebody'd tell him."

"How the hell would I know where he is?" Figlia said. "All I
know is his truck's getting in my hair."

"I seen him go up the street with a girl," Charles said.

"Sure, he's laying up with some dame while his truck blocks up
my dock," Figlia said. "What do you want me to do, roust him
out of bed? Are you going to move that truck or will I have to
move it?"

"Jesus Christ, I'll be glad to move it, but I can't with that load,"
the cop said.

"The hell with the load, we'll get it off," Figlia said. He shouted
to the handlers, "Here you guys, get in there and knock off them
side racks and unload them apples so Mister Riley here can tow
this heap away."

"Who's going to pay us?" one of the handlers said.

"I'll pay you," Figlia said. "Get in there and unload her."

"What's going to happen to the load?" the cop said.

"What do you mean what's going to happen?" Figlia said. I'll

sell it for the best price I can get and knock off my commission.
It'd serve the son of a bitch right if I gave it away."

"We can't have all them boxes cluttering up the sidewalk,"
Charles said.

"All right, you guys, get going, what do you think I'm paying
you for?" Figlia shouted to the handlers.

The men started to take down the side racks. The buyers stood in
a group waiting for the apples. One of them came along the sidewalk, an ugly man with a pink face and a protruding underjaw.
"Hey, Mike," he said, "I think I can use about four of them corn."

"Think again, Menasco," Figlia said.

"You mean you can't spare me four?"

"Brother, I can't spare you none."

"What's the matter, you're not sold out already?"

"Sold out half an hour ago. What did you think we were going
to do with that stuff, hold it for seed?"

"No, but I thought. My goodness, you had a half a block of it.
You sure moved it in a hurry."

"Yes, it did move kind of fast," Figlia said.

The side racks were down now and the handlers unloaded the
first box of apples. Figlia picked one out of it and twirled it under
Menasco's nose. "Haven't got any corn, but how about an apple?"
he said.

"Apples?" Menasco said.

Figlia winked at the buyers standing around him. "Get old
Menasco waking up," he said. "You don't want any now, Menasco.
You'd better wait until they're all gone."

Menasco bent to the box and went through it. He was methodi-
cal and business like. "How much a box?" he said.

"Six fifty," Figlia said. Menasco whistled and Figlia said, "How
many do you want?" and he held up ten fingers. Menasco shook
his head and held up four. Figlia turned to Charles and said, "Get
out your book, Charles. It begins to look like the boys are going
to soak up the apples."

"Hold fifteen for me," one of the buyers said.

"Stand in line, boys," Figlia said.

Tex saw the buyers crowding Figlia, shouting their orders faster than Charles could get them down. It's his load, she thought. Mike's swiping it.

She went back up Washington. This'll get him out, she thought. This'll get him, this'll do it. He'll wake up fast enough when I tell him they're swiping his load. He'll come down and catch Figlia at it and make him pay. A whole truck load like that, the way they're buying it, it'll add up to a lot more than fifty dollars. She thought of all the money Nick would be getting and she began to run up Washington, eager to get back.

19

ED'S TRUCK came out of the hills and headed North
through the Livermore Valley, along the long stretch of road that
fled through Dublin and on beyond it to the hills, running fast,
making great speed. The highway fell back in a blur under the
headlights and the engine sang. Running fast, the universal made
no noise at all. Ed could hear the tire sounds coming up from beneath the truck, growing louder on the turns as the weight of the
load bore down. Hold it, he thought. He was tired. He was so tired
he could hardly keep open his eyes and his head fell forward to
the wheel. Just for a second he thought, I'll sleep for a second. I
know this road.

He could see it reaching out before him, going past the wreck-
ing yard piled high with the rusting rotting carcasses of old cars
and trucks, past the stock farm, past the abandoned Naval base
that was overgrown with weeds, on through a patch of eucalyptus
trees that grew in a clump just before Dublin, on past the gas stations and stores and houses of the small town, past Walnut Creek
Junction, on into the hills again. The road had changed in all the
years he had been trucking. It had been widened and divided and
straightened, but this stretch of it was the same as it had been long
ago when he started trucking and it made him think of the old
days, the days when he expected so much from a trip. The loads
he had hauled, apricot and cantaloupe and tomato, Thompson
Seedless grapes and Elberta peaches and cherries from Castro
Valley. Asparagus from Stockton and Calymyrna figs from Minkler. All the loads he had bought and sold, buying and trading, the
wicked vicious way you had to trade, as though every man were an
enemy and there was no price that could not be cut down. He
remembered a load of oranges and a wop named Figlia. *I'll give*

you a nickel more than the Los Angeles price, he says, and I says,
What do you know about the Los Angeles price? And he says, I
make it my business to know, and I says, Then you know you
aren't giving me a break, and he says, What do you mean, break?
I'm doing you a favor. I'm giving you a day's wages. The thought
aroused an ancient rage in Ed and made him sit erect in the seat.
You know what you can do with your favor, he thought. Right up
Mike's, that's what you can do. What a sucker I used to be. Just
like that kid, Nick. I used to think you buy a load and sell it and
make a lot of jack, then you buy another load and make some more
jack and you keep that up until you got a pile. What a cinch.
They're standing around to hand it to you, all the honest Johns.
Work hard and treat 'em right and they'll treat you right. What a
sucker you have to be to believe it. You start out thinking it's a
straight cinch. But it isn't straight and it's no cinch. All the tricks
you have to know in this game. Nothing's on the level, it's all up
and down crooked, everything figured out backward. Ain't no
Johns standing around to hand it out. You've got to pull tricks and
take it. Take the loads. Not every load sells. Just the loads in the
beginning or at the end of a season. The first loads of melons, or
grapes or tomatoes or apples, two or three hauls. You've got to
know where to find 'em, and after you find 'em, you've got to cut
'em down, like that farmer. Six hundred bucks right in my hand if
it wasn't for that Nick. You've got to know where the crops come
ripe early and buy 'em up and haul 'em in fast and get out quick
and even then you've got to keep your eyes peeled because they're
all after the gravy. That chiseling, that screwing. The less I pay
out, the more there is for me. That *for me,* that thinking of *me,* all
the time *me.* Nothing straight about it. All crooked. All angles. A
dirty, filthy, rotten game. If you've got something, they eat out of
your hands, but if you haven't you're like the rotting produce in
the gutters. Nobody wants you but the beggars and the dogs. Ed
thought of himself as he used to be long ago, a young man with
ideals about work and honesty and all the rewards. Sold down the
river long ago, sold out for rottenness and cheating and double
dealing. The crap I've pulled, he thought. I'm going to pull it on
Nick. I'm going to take him. I'm going to cool him. I'm going

to send him back to his piddling job, to his piddling life. That Nick
Whosis or Stugotz or whatever his God damned name is, he thinks
he's going to go right out and find himself a lot of fat hauls and
make some fast money and buy himself a bigger rig and haul
bigger loads, expanding all the time until he owns a regular freight
line with diesel jobs stacked in the yard, twenty, thirty, maybe
forty of them, all painted red with the sign STUGOTZ FREIGHT
LINES on the side racks and Nick Stugotz or whatever his name
sitting on his pratt in the office, smoking six bit cigars and ordering
the drivers and the swampers around. Some dream. Ed knew all
about that dream. You believed it when you were a kid, like that
Nick. He won't know enough to be glad when I stand him on his
ear, he thought. He'd be glad if he knew, but he don't know, he'll
never know until it's too late, like I know it now, like I could have
known it any time if I had listened to Mabel. I wish I could go
back. I could have if I had listened to her. Why didn't I listen to
her?

Ed checked the road and shut his eyes again for that split second
that was like an eternity. He knew this road from Seattle down to
Tia Juana and East to Denver. Wish I had a buck for every mile,
he thought. Be a rich man, richer than a son of a bitch. All the
miles from hell to breakfast and back again, wrap them twenty
times around the world, stretch them out to hell and gone, to
nowhere, to nothing, not a God damned thing.

He opened his eyes to check the road. The truck was rambling
over the small bridge at the end of the long curve that straightened
for the run through Dublin. He sat up and tried to shake the
sleepiness from his head. Christ, I'm sleepy, he thought. The truck
was running past open fields, through the Eucalyptus grove. The
thick muscular trunks of trees rushed back as the truck went swiftly
through the sleeping town, its exhaust rattling in the quiet streets.
The headlights reflected from the dark windows of stores and
houses, making them come alive like eyes. Then the truck was out
on the other side.

The truck had topped the hill and was running into the downgrade when the universal snapped. The engine began to race, running wild under the hood and Ed could hear the broken drive shaft

thrashing around under the truck and he hit the brakes but the pedal slammed down to the floor. There were no brakes.

Oh, Jesus, he thought. The road fell away into darkness. How the hell am I going to stop her? he thought.

There was a loud metallic ping as the flopping drive shaft broke off and the pounding under the truck ceased. The truck was free wheeling down the hill. The speedometer went past fifty and Ed thought quickly, I'd better bail out, but when he went to open the door, the rush of wind tore at him and drove him back. The truck began to leave the road and he caught the wheel and brought it around. He could not see the road in the darkness, but he knew that it fell straight away across a narrow valley, mounted a hill, made a slow turn and dropped again in a series of turns.

Ed refused to think of the turns. The hill will pull me down long before I get to them, he thought. I'll never get into the turns. He sat riding the wheel, holding it hard. He had become deafened in the excitement, but suddenly he began to hear again, and the sound of the engine racing wildly blasted upon him and he cut it and now in the silence there was only the mounting sound of tires. A chill stroked through him as the speedometer drifted past seventy and the steering wheel felt light in his hands.

Ahead, the red glow of a tail light sprang from the darkness and rushed back on him in a mounting glare and he hit the horn, kept hitting it until he was on the light and around it and the road was clear before him. Suddenly he knew that the hill could not begin to slow him down, he knew it could not and the chill stroked through him again, like a knife. But it is, he thought, I know it is. She's going to slow me down and the truck's going to stop and I'm going to get out and shake the scare from my head.

The speedometer reached its limit at ninety, but the truck kept gaining speed as it crossed the base of the narrow valley and began to mount the hill on the other side. For half the space of the hill, the needle did not drift back, but just as he reached the crest of the hill it ebbed through ninety and down toward eighty. When it gets to sixty, I'll jump, Ed thought. I won't wait to think about it, I'll just yank open the door and jump.

The needle was still above seventy when the truck topped the hill and swung into the long descending turn. Now what do I do Ed thought. He tried swiftly to plan the descent. In a minute I'll be in the curves, he thought. What the hell do I do then? The road was open on both sides. There wasn't an embankment to run the truck against like that time in the Ridge. There was only the naked road. Now what the hell do I do? he thought. I'll run her off the road down the hillside. Maybe I can hold her on wheels. It'll be better than rolling over.

Every now and then the truck gave a little bound and after that it seemed to soar. The headlights swung over the side of the first curve and Ed braced himself. I'm going to come out of it, he thought. I'll hit the curves wide and if she starts rolling, I'll hit the floor. Nothing's going to happen to me, I'm going to make it.

He hit the first curve going wide and he made it. The second curve was on him before he was ready, but he swung hard with the load lunging over and the tires squealing and he made it. He made two more turns, but finally he could not, and the truck turned as though to follow the curve, but went on straight, rolling side over side over the edge of the curve and down the hill with a sound like the kicking of cans, spilling its load all the way until it slammed to a stop against a boulder.

Ed opened his eyes. He was all right. He could move and nothing was broken. He could breathe. He could even stand up if he wanted. He was fine. The back cushion had fallen over and it made a soft weight on his chest. his head began to ring. The shock had numbed him. Soon it would wear off and he would hurt all over, but he was going to be all right. Wet began to soak into his shoulders and he smelled gasoline. Tanks must have burst, he thought, but the motor's cut off. It's all right. In a minute, after my head clears, I'll get up and kick open the door and get out. If it's jammed I'll kick in the windshield. I'm going to be fine. He wondered how long Nick would wait for him in the market. He had told him to wait and Nick would wait, yes he will, he'll wait. I'll get out and hitch a ride North and Nick'll be waiting. I'll go to Frisco and meet Nick and we'll sell the load and split the money and I'll buy another truck, a good rig, one of those cab-over-engine jobs, maybe a semi with a trailer so I can haul a good big load. All right then, what are you sitting around for, he told himself. Get off your butt and get going, let's go, let's get going. He shut his eyes.

A stinging urge to piss himself came over him and he let it go and it went on a long time, flooding warm down his leg. Now what do I want to do that for? he thought. Because I'm scared, I'm yellow scared. He could see the darkness pressing in on the truck and he had a sensation of someone out there in the dark watching and waiting. Well wait, you bastard, he thought. You'll wait a long time.

Rubber was burning. Ed could smell it. He opened his eyes and saw the battery was shorted. The cables were red hot. He lay watching the snake glow of the cables. All I have to do is kick them off, he thought. If it starts a fire I'll step on it, I'll piss on it if it burns.

The cable started to burn with the small flame at the end where it was oil soaked, but Ed had shut his eyes. He was breathing loudly. I've got out of tougher ones than this and I'll get out of this, he was thinking. I'm going to get out of it, I've got to get out of it, I don't want to die, I'm not going to die.

The flame crept along the length of cable. When it reached the gasoline it sputtered and went out. Suddenly it exploded and Ed felt himself engulfed in flame.

Lights stopped on the road ledge, the lights of a big truck that was hauling tomatoes. A sign on the cab door said *Ernie Blankenship, Produce*. The man in it was driving alone. He got out and came running down the hill. He ran across the field. He was running to the truck when he heard one hoarse encompassing scream and he stopped, transfixed by the sound. The tanks were exploding and the truck was a tremendous pyre in the middle of the field. The fire illuminated the whole hillside. It was reflected in little points all down the hill. One of them was in the grass at the driver's feet and he picked it up. It was an apple. It smelled ripe and sweet in his hand. The hillside was covered with the golden apples that sparkled and glittered in the light of the fire from Ed's truck.

20

TEX went up the stairs. She listened at the door, afraid Nick would not be in the room. But he was, she could hear him breathing. She opened the door quietly and went in. The big hulk of him lay on the bed. He mumbled something as she went to the bed. He had rolled over and was lying on his back. "Hey," she said and she shook his shoulder. He was big and inert as a clod. His shoulder was moist from sweat, where he had lain on it. A heavy sweaty odor came up from him as from a child. He twisted his head in irritation and she shook him again. "Hey," she said and Nick wakened and rose swiftly to his elbows, his face aghast and anxious. "Ed?" he shouted. "Is that you, Ed?"

Tex drew back but Nick caught her arm. His hand was tight on it, viselike. "It's not Ed, it's me, Tex," she said. She jerked free her arm and switched on the light. Nick was sitting on the bed, his mouth open, breathing the slow breath of sleep. "Huh?" he said.

"It's me," Tex said. "Wake up."

"Where's Ed? Is he in, did he come in?"

"Who?"

"Ed. He ought to be in by now. Is he waiting?"

"Is who waiting? Who are you talking about?"

"Ed," Nick said. He said it in exasperation. He rose to his feet and Tex could see him staring with the focusless intensity of the blind, his face still aghast and anxious. She shook him again, firmly this time.

"You're dreaming," she said. "You're all right now. It was just a dream." She pushed him down to the bed. "You sit here," she said. "I'm going to get you some coffee. Remember, I said I'd make you some? Will you drink it?"

171

Nick did not answer and Tex shut the door that opened into the hallway and went to the kitchen. The fire was still going, but the coffee had boiled away. She threw out the contents and was making a fresh pot, when she heard the swinging door open and when she turned she saw Nick, his face awake now and smiling. She opened the oven and lighted it so the room would warm. "That must have been some dream you were having," she said. "Could you eat some toast?"

"Sure. What did I say?"

"I don't know. It sounded like a name."

"What name?"

"I couldn't make it out. Something like Ed."

Nick came to the stove and stood warming his hands. His face was disturbed and puzzled. "I had a dream about him," he said, "but I can't remember what it was."

"Who's Ed?" she said.

"Guy I'm hauling with."

"What were you dreaming? Try and remember."

Nick shook his head. "I wish I could," he said, "but it won't come back."

The coffee began to make and Tex got the cups and set them on the table and brought out the toast from the oven. Nick sat down and she saw his neck when she passed behind him to get a small can of milk from the icebox. "Small cow," she said as she placed it on the table, and a bowl of sugar and spoons. She poured the coffee and sat down and watched him stirring his coffee. He is a nice guy, she thought, funny how you can see it in his face. Now take Mitch, take Figlia, take Frenchy, take any of them, take him. He's sweet.

"What are you thinking about?" Nick said.

"How do you know I was thinking anything?"

"Your face."

She wondered what he could read in her face. "You must be worried about Ed to make you dream like that," she said.

"I am," Nick said. "I wish he'd come in."

"Oh, he'll come in," Tex said. She buttered toast and they sat drinking the coffee and eating the toast. "How is your neck?" she

said. She had not meant to say it. She had meant to drop it on
him about his load, but there it was.

"It's all right," Nick said. "Why?"

"No reason, just asking."

"Does it look bad? Look at it and tell me."

Tex stood behind him. He had been monkeying with it and got
it to bleeding again, but having it opened to the air was making it
look all right.

"Where did you get to in such a hurry?" Nick said.

"You scared the daylights out of me," Tex said. "I went to get a
doctor, but I couldn't find one, so I came back to fix it."

"That's some arm you've got," Nick said. "You just about tore
my head off."

"That's what I'm going to do," she said. "I'm going to tear off
your head after I fix up your neck." Nick tried to turn, but she
did not let him. She tugged the shirt from the wound and he
leaned back with it.

"How is it?" he said.

"Not bad. A little swollen, but not bad."

"Don't kid me, tell me."

"I'm telling you." Nick turned around and she could see him
watching her.

"Maybe it'll give you a laugh," he said, "but I can't see it, I
don't know what it looks like. I keep thinking I'm going to die."

"It's just a bruise," Tex said. "It's a bad one, but you aren't
going to die." She decided to dress it. "What do you say we clean
it up?" she said. She ran some water into a pan and set it on the
stove and got cloths from a drawer. "You'd better take off that
shirt," she said as she went to the bathroom. When she returned
he had removed his shirt. He was hairy. He had a hard muscular
body, white where it had not been exposed to the sun. The hair was
on the tips of his shoulders and on his arms and across his back and
matted on his chest.

"Sit down," she said.

Nick sat down and Tex began to clean his wound. She wiped
the dried blood off its fringes and soaked alcohol into a wad of
cotton. Nick tightened his arms, his muscles going hard as the

alcohol bit into the wound. She worked quickly, cleaning off the wound with the alcohol, dried it and treated it with antiseptic powder, wadded dry cotton over it in a flat pad and wrapped a gauze bandage around his neck so it made a scarf. "I guess that dudes you up," she said. "What's your name? I don't even know your name."

"Nick."

"You're not a Nick," she said. Nick tried to turn to her, but she was taping the bandage. "You're a Paul or a David or a Jim. You're not tough enough to be a Nick."

"Is that so?" Nick said.

"Don't be insulted. You know it's so. What are you doing in the market? They're all crooks. They'll take you so fast, you won't know what hit you."

"You can tell that just from my name?"

"That's right," Tex was finished and she let Nick get up. He was tall. Her eyes were on a level with his mouth. Those thick lips, tightly set, but soft. There was a place on his shoulder where the skin was hairless. She rubbed lightly the palm of her hand upon it. He was warm.

"You look like a Hazel," Nick said. "You fit your name all right."

Tex looked up and Nick said, "There's a letter in your purse. I was looking for a mirror so I could see my neck."

Tex could feel the warmth of Nick's body radiating toward her. She touched the hair on his arms and chest. The hairs were black and curly. "What makes you so hairy?" she said.

"Don't ask me," Nick said. "Nobody in my family is. I used to worry about it. Thought I was turning into an ape."

"It's awful," Tex said. "I'll bet you shed."

"A little on the left shoulder," Nick said. "I think I'm getting bald there."

"Maybe you can wear a toupee," Tex said. "Don't ever go out without any clothes on. Somebody might take you for a bear and shoot you." She clutched his chest hairs in her fist and pulled them so it hurt and when he came forward, she held him around the chest, her face to it. "God, you're warm," she said. "You feel like you've got a stove in you." She laid herself against his chest and she could feel the hair springy against her, his heart thumping, feeling to grow bigger as she listened. She felt him forcing up her face and she hardened her mouth. "Is that your truck with the apples?" she said. He raised her face and she tried to keep her mouth hard but she could feel it parting and wetting and she said, "Is it?" Nick picked her up and was carrying her from the kitchen into the bedroom and Tex said, "The one that looks like an army job, the one with the apples." Nick laid her on the bed. She did not want him to get up. She wanted him to stay. She held him down. "Figlia's stealing them," she said.

"Stealing what?"

"Your apples. He's selling them from the truck. That is your truck, isn't it?"

Nick got out of Tex's arms and picked up his shirt. It was soiled at the neck and he threw it down and picked up his coat.

"He's getting six and a half a box," Tex said.

Nick put on his coat. Tex lay on the bed watching him. She felt congested and hot. Nick went from the room and his steps sounded down the stairs. She listened to them going away down the street. She made herself believe he was still in the room and her heart pounded. She raised her hips from the bed and let them down again into the softness. He's here, she thought, and she unfastened her skirt and inserted her hand beneath the belt. The insides of her legs felt flabby and tired. She clasped them together and parted them and held herself tightly with her hands. She made herself believe it. She believed it, was believing it and she felt plunged into ice, the ice over and through her, and she felt chilled and began to shiver.

After a while she got up and went to the stove and stood over it. She thought of Mitch beating her. "Don't, Mitch, please, Mitch," she heard herself say. "Please don't, Mitch. I was supposed to get him out of the way for fifty bucks, but I've got something better. He's going to collect for his load, a lot of money, plenty for all of us. We can take it from him. I'll help you, so help me I will; please, Mitch."

Now what made me think of that, Tex thought. The heat came off the stove, but it could not warm her.

21

NOW when Ed comes in, Figlia thought, there won't be any truck. There won't be any load. There might not even be any jerk. All there will be is the money and I'll have it. There'll be the kid's rights, but they won't be in anything but words and you can't collect on words. All there will be is a say-so between Ed and the kid, with Ed only in on the hearing of it. So they'll sue. Let 'em sue. I'll claim blockage of my frontage. How can you run a business with your frontage blocked? How can you run a business with junk piled in the streets? They won't get a cent and if they do they'll only get peanuts.

He saw the big semi come in. Ernie Blankenship's rig with the tomatoes that were now so many hours late they would wind up in tomorrow's market.

"Back it up, get it back," Charles waved the truck in until it jarred to a stop against the curb when he held up his hand. "Okay, hold it." Ernie stepped down and came around to the walk. He had a bruised looking face with scarred lips and the mouth of a deaf mute. When he spoke it was with an impediment hardly to be understood.

"Where the hell you been?" Figlia said.

"What can I say after I say I'm sorry?" Ernie said. He spoke in short snuffling grunts.

"You're sorry. Don't you know what time we open?"

"Didn't know you closed."

"Okay. How about the tomatoes, how many did you get?"

"About four hundred. Couldn't get no more. Diaz was sold out. You ain't the only guy after Mexican tomatoes."

"You didn't roll back half empty?"

176

"Hell no. I filled up on oranges."

"The hell with the oranges," Figlia said. "I ordered tomatoes."

"You don't know it, but you ordered oranges too," Ernie said. He untied the ropes and folded back the tarp. The tart smell of oranges surged into the market.

"Well, get the tomatoes down," Figlia said.

"No oranges, no tomatoes," Ernie said. "I ain't going to let you skim off the cream."

"Okay, unload 'em," Figlia said.

"Tomatoes and all?"

"The works. I won't have any trouble getting rid of the oranges for you."

"Not for me, brother! The oranges are your grief."

"All right, for me then. Get 'em down."

"You're buying the whole load?"

"That's right, that's what I said, isn't it? How many times do I have to say it?"

"With you I don't hear so good the first time," Ernie said. He coiled the ropes and hung them on the cab hooks. He folded the tarp and dropped in on the walk. He pried up the tail rack and got it down. The unloaders were waiting and he waved them in and they began to work at the wall of boxes that were belly packed with oranges stacked on their sides so the fruit would not be crushed.

Down the walk the buyers were grabbing up the last of the apples. A tow car was parked in the street and the driver was fastening a chain to the front axle of Nick's truck.

"There must have been two loads of them apples," Ernie said.

"All I got was one," Figlia said. "Come in about an hour ago. Six hundred boxes. Just about sold out."

Ernie went over and picked up an apple. "They're the same apples," he said.

"That's what I call hot stuff," Figlia said. "They're so hot I can't keep 'em on the floor. A week from now apples will rot in the market, but right now they're sizzling. Like those Mexican tomatoes. Move 'em quick, unload 'em fast, sell 'em out before they can make a loss."

"I seen a load like this back up the road," Ernie said.

"What road?"

"Altamont. That's why I was late. Truck hauling 'em went over the side."

"What kind of truck?"

"GMC."

"What happened to the driver?"

"Dead."

"What did he look like? Was he a—" Figlia tried to assemble in his mind a picture of Ed that he could describe, but Ernie said, "Listen, brother, nobody'll ever know what that cookie looked like. He was burned."

So it's just the kid, Figlia thought. No Ed. It's just between me and the kid. "What happened to the load?" he said.

"Spilled."

"Apples weren't hurt, were they? They weren't burned?"

"Not a scratch. Funny how that is, the truck smashed the way it was and them apples all over hell and not even scratched."

Figlia looked at Ernie. "Ernie," he said, "how would you like to make yourself some quick change?"

"What doing?"

"Go back to that wreck and pick up them apples. I'll give you a couple of boys to help out. Won't take more than half a day."

"How would you like to kiss my ass?"

"What's the matter, don't you want to turn a quick buck?"

"Sure, but I'm no God damned grave robber."

"What do you mean, grave robber? Nobody's going to let them apples rot. Somebody's going to get 'em and it might as well be you."

"You get 'em. I seen that guy cook," Ernie said. He tore the manifest sheet from his book. "You better go up and practice writing big numbers because that's how much money I want when I get back," he said. He handed the sheet to Figlia and went across the street to the Merchant's Lunch.

Figlia stood thinking about the load of apples that were scattered on the hill. Maybe get three, even four hundred boxes out of six, he thought. Just pick 'em, like minting money.

"Charles," he said.

Charles alerted instantly, his pencil hanging over the order pad.

"Charles, I want you to take two of the boys and go on up to Altamont when you wind up what you're doing. Use the Reo. You can pull off the road onto the hill. It must be right there in Altamont, you can't miss it. Must be off the road. Just get out and get 'em and if anybody asks what you're doing, tell 'em they're yours. Tell 'em they were on order. But nobody'll bother you."

"You want I should go now or later, Mister Figlia?" Charles said. "I'm pretty near done here. I could go right now."

Figlia did not answer and Charles saw him looking up the street. "When do you want me to go, Mister Figlia?" he said.

"Soon as you finish with them tomatoes," Figlia said.

The swamper sucked his teeth noisily, his tongue moving in a bulge beneath his cheek. "There's that guy who pushes that apple rig," he said to Figlia. Figlia said nothing and the swamper said, "I'll bet that was his partner cracked up in Altamount. I'll bet he don't know nothing about what happened to him. I'll bet something else, Mister Figlia."

Charles turned and saw Nick coming.

"I'll bet you ain't going to tell him," the swamper said. He laughed wheezily. "I'll lay you ten to one you don't tell him, Mister Figlia."

Nick stepped up.

"Well, if it ain't Buster," Figlia said. "What do you know, Bus?"

"The name's Nick and I don't know a thing," Nick said. "I hear you're selling apples."

"Oh, we're moving a few," Figlia said. "Semi was coming in with a load of tomatoes and we needed the space your job was taking up, but we couldn't move it with the load, so we took it down. Folks see them apples, they want to buy 'em, so I let 'em. Only forty boxes left."

"That means five hundred and sixty sold."

"Something like that, but I'll move the rest in no time. Make it six hundred."

"Okay, six hundred then, at six and a half bucks a box."

"What do you mean six and a half?"

"That's what you sold 'em for, isn't it? Or maybe I got it wrong. How much would you say it was?"

"It's six and a half," the swamper said, and Figlia said, "Sure it's six and a half, but how about my end of it?"

"Who said anything about your end?" Nick said.

Figlia caught him by the arm. "Come on, we'll work this out in my office," he said, and Nick said, "What's the matter with working it out right here? At six and a half dollars a box for six hundred boxes, that makes thirty-nine hundred dollars. Right?"

"Right," Figlia said. "Let's go up and I'll make out a check." He led Nick back through the produce house and up the stairs to the office. He sat at his desk and lighted a cigar. "Sit down," he said, "take it easy."

"You make out that check," Nick said. "Let's get it over with."

"Sure, sure, we'll get it over with. I'm not going to run you out of your load. Sit down." When Figlia saw that Nick was not going to sit down, he waved the cigar at him. "Let's say you just rolled in with a load of apples," he said. "I see 'em and I want to buy 'em and you want to sell 'em. What would you say was a fair price?"

"Suppose I'm not selling?" Nick said.

"Sure, but let's say you are. How much do you want?"

"Six and a half."

"Six and a half is what I got. I'm talking about your end."

"I want all of it, six and a half."

"You're crazy. I've got something coming for selling them."

"Who told you to sell 'em?" Nick said. "I don't remember telling you. If somebody told you, I'd like to know about it."

"Somebody was going to sell them, so I did," Figlia said. "And I'm ready to settle, if you'll stop blowing through your hat."

"But I didn't tell you," Nick said.

"All right, so you didn't," Figlia said, "but I did and they're sold and I got six fifty, so what do you say we split? Three and a quarter, how is that?"

"I want six fifty," Nick said.

"Why you son of a bitch, I know what you paid for that load. Two bucks a box and I'm giving you three and a quarter and you're overpaid. All you got coming is maybe six bits for the haul, and you're making seven fifty."

"How do you figure that's all I got coming?"

"A day's wages, that's all any of you bastards got coming. So it took you three days to find that load and haul it in. Three days at twenty five bucks a day, truck and all figures seventy five dollars, but I'm willing to let you play big shot and give you three and a quarter."

"I want all of it. I want six and a half bucks a box. I want every cent of it. I want thirty nine hundred dollars."

"You know what you're going to get, don't you? Right in your hand, a whole shovel full."

"Six fifty, that's what I'm going to get."

"How about four? That's more than you'd get anywhere."

"Nothing doing. You tried to short-arm me and if you'd got away with it, you'd have got the load for nothing, so now I think it's fair you pay off. There's no cut back for losing."

Figlia got up. He walked around, biting on the cigar and thinking about it. "Look," he said, "somebody's been steering you wrong. Where did you get the idea I was short-arming you?"

"Who cares where I got the idea?" Nick said. "Just so you pay me."

"Was it Tex? I'll bet it was Tex."

"Who's Tex?"

"She's the trick that picked you up. Was it her?"

"You mean Hazel Wexley? She picked me up?"

"That's right. I'll tell you the kind of dame she is. I paid her a hundred bucks to get you off the street."

Nick looked at Figlia, but he saw Tex, moving about with her hips swinging, the way she had. The angry look in her face. Not being able to touch her. One hundred bucks, and hard to get, he thought. "You're a God damned liar," he said.

"I can prove it," Figlia said.

"Then why did she tell me you were swiping my load?"

"Because she's going to make more. She's going to make all you get. You watch out for her. She's a tough nut. She didn't tell you for nothing."

Nick grabbed Figlia. "You're trying to ball me up," he said. "Cut out trying to ball me up."

"I'm trying to straighten you out," Figlia said.

"I don't know about that. All I know is I want three thousand nine hundred dollars."

"You don't know who your friends are and I'm trying to tell you," Figlia said. "I'm a friend of yours."

Nick pushed Figlia toward the desk. "Go on, lay it on the line," he said. "I don't want to talk to you. I want to get out of here."

"Okay, okay, but why don't you give me a couple of days until my accounts come in?"

"I want it now."

"I haven't got that much cash."

"Then give me what you've got and I'll take a chance on the paper."

Figlia opened the safe and counted out five hundred dollars in bills. Then he sat at the desk and made out a check.

"What's your name?" he said.

Nick told his name.

He wrote out Nick's name on the check. "Look, Nick," he said, "you're not giving me a fair shake. I can do you a lot of good around here. Maybe I did take you for a sucker, but now that we understand each other, I can give you some breaks. You're going to need 'em because you're new at this game."

"Sign it," Nick said.

Figlia signed and blotted the check. "How long do you think you're going to hang onto this money?" he said. "So you hit it this time. Why don't you stop and think how it's going to be all the times you miss?"

Nick picked up the check. It was made out for thirty four hundred dollars. "Don't get any idea you're going to stop this," he said.

"Now how would I do that?"

"You'll be at the bank first thing in the morning."

"A lot of good that's going to do me, with you standing there ahead of me in the line."

"Yeah, and it better not bounce."

"It won't bounce," Figlia said, "I promise you it won't bounce." The produce dealer sounded frightened. "But I'm telling you, you're making a mistake."

"That's okay with me, as long as I can keep making them like this," Nick said. He laid the check on the bills and placed bills and check in his wallet. It was an old wallet with a picture of Polly in the window. The money made such a wad in it that he could not fold it. Well, what do you think of that, he said silently to Polly's picture. How do you like that? His hand shook. Thirty-nine hundred bucks, he thought. More money than we paid out for the two loads. Wish it was all cash; but don't worry, it will be. First thing in the morning, before he can pull anything, I'll be at the bank. I'll get it all in bills, a roll big enough to choke a hippo. Let's see Ed top that. Not a chance. Suddenly Nick stopped being angry with Figlia. He could see him standing there, biting on the cigar. He held out the wallet.

"Does that make you sore?" he said.

"Hell," Figlia said, "I like to see a kid make a killing."

"The hell you do,". Nick said. He shoved the wallet into the front pocket of his jeans.

"Sure I do," Figlia said. "You took me, but that's okay. Maybe next time I'll take you."

"Not if I see you coming first," Nick said.

Figlia laughed and punched Nick lightly on the shoulder. "That's the boy," he said. "Go ahead, get sharp on me."

"Well, Christ, you made me sore," Nick said.

"Stay sore, it'll make you rich," Figlia said.

"I'll tell you what I'll do," Nick said. "You can have the next load cheap. I'll tell Ed to give you a break, when he comes in."

Figlia stood mouthing the cigar and watching Nick. "You think he's coming in?" he said.

"Sure he's coming in," Nick said. "Hell, yes, he's coming in."

"You don't get any feelings about where he is?"

"No, I don't get any feelings. I just know he's coming in."

"Okay," Figlia said.

They went from the office, down the stairs, but Nick was troubled. "Tell me something," he said. "On the level."

"Sure, what's on your mind?"

"Did you really give that girl a hundred bucks?"

"Sure, but that's okay. That's a horse on me."

Nick went out to the street, thinking about it. The hell with it, he thought. It turned out all right, didn't it? I've got the money and nobody's going to take it away from me.

The tow car driver had the front wheels of the truck raised off the ground. "You don't have to tow her," Nick said. "Just fix the tire so I can roll. If she won't fix, put on a new one." He brought out his wallet and peeled a fifty from it and held it out to the driver, but the driver turned to Figlia, who nodded. "Sure, fix him up," he said.

The swamper's eyes were on the fat wallet. "Boy, did he shell out?" he said.

"You know he did," Nick said.

"How much did he pay?"

"The whole six and a half, what do you think?"

"Well, push my face," the swamper said.

"You mean you paid him six and a half?" one of the buyers said to Figlia.

"Look, boys, if this gets around, they'll laugh me out of the market," Figlia said. "Kid like him taking an old timer like me."

"Brother, this is what we been waiting for," the buyer said to Nick.

"You said it," another buyer said. "We knew it was coming, but we didn't know when."

"He must be getting old to let it slip through his fingers like that," the first buyer said.

"Oh, hell," the swamper said. "A man don't get old that quick. The kid did him in. Let's see it again, Jack."

Nick grinned as he opened the wallet and flashed it around.

"Well, push my face and call me Susie," the swamper said. "Look at it, fit and full and fat as a pig. It took some doing to pork up a wallet like that."

"Most of it's check," Nick said.

The swamper whistled and one of the buyers said, "You don't

know what this means, boy. You took Fig. Old Fig makes his own prices around here."

"Not this time," the swamper said. "This time *he* was made."

"He made me and broke it off," Figlia said. He laid his arm across Nick's shoulder. "And get this," he said to the others. After I gave him all that money he asks me, how do I feel. How did you expect me to feel, happy?"

"I didn't expect you to sing," Nick said.

The men laughed and Figlia said, "Seeing how that's about the first time anybody ever shook down the Fig, how about letting me buy the drinks?"

"Listen to him," the swamper said. "He's even going to pay for his own wake."

"We've got to bury the body," Figlia said. "What do you say?" He touched Nick's arm.

"I'd sure like to," Nick said, "but I don't think I can. Ed ought to be in pretty soon and I want to be here when he gets in." He shoved the wallet into his pocket.

The swamper stopped smiling. His big face had been creased in smiles, but suddenly he sobered and looked nervously to the others.

"Don't worry about Ed," Figlia said.

"He's going to wonder where I am."

"Leave it to Charles. You'll tell him, won't you, Charles."

"Sure," Charles said.

"You've got to go," the buyer said. "Any time anybody makes a killing around here, the dead man's got to set up drinks."

"Sure, I'm dead and I'm buying," Figlia said.

"Go ahead, get your drink," Charles said. "You don't have to worry about a thing."

The swamper began to smile again. "Hell, no," he said, "you don't have a thing to worry about," and he began to laugh in the way that sounded like crying. He kept looking around and laughing as Figlia took Nick's arm and they led the men across the street.

Figlia pounded the counter in the Merchant's Lunch. "Joseph," he shouted to the waiter, "bring out the bottle. Here's a dead man buying drinks."

Joseph brought up the bottle from beneath the counter and stood it on the table. He set out shot glasses and poured water chasers. "Who die?" he said.

"I did," Figlia said.

The workers and produce dealers looked up from where they were eating at the counter and men stopped playing at the card table in the back.

"Who give it to you?" the waiter said.

Figlia pointed to Nick.

"Him?" the waiter said. He shook his head sadly. "I don't believe it."

"Show him," Figlia said to Nick. "Go ahead, show him."

Nick brought out his wallet again and the men crowded around. The bulging wallet looked to be full of money.

"Show 'em the check too," Figlia said.

Nick removed the check and handed it around.

The waiter made a cutting gesture across his neck. "You cut his throat, eh?" he said to Nick.

"Sliced it like salami," Nick said.

"Well, you watch out, he don't slice you," the waiter said. He poured the drinks, and the swamper and the two buyers and Figlia and Nick picked up their glasses.

"You mean we better watch out he don't slice us," the buyer said. "Here's to tomorrow's prices."

"Here's to the kid," Figlia said.

The swamper caught Figlia's eye and winked. "Here's to Ed," he said.

"Sure, here's to him," Nick said. He raised his glass and for a moment he and the swamper were drinking alone. The others joined and the glasses were emptied.

Figlia put down his glass, suddenly in a hurry. He held Nick's arm. "All right, kid," he said, "let's get going."

"Where are we going?" Nick said.

"Shorty's," Figlia said.

"Ah, Shorty's," the waiter said. He gave a quick excited grunt.

"What's there?" Nick said.

"Get him, he wants to know what's there," one of the buyers said. The waiter kissed the bunched fingers of his hand.

"Dames," Figlia said. "I'm going to get your ashes hauled."

"Boy his age is all fire, no ashes," the waiter said.

"We're going to put out some of that fire," Figlia said.

"Brother, I wish I was young, I go with you," the waiter said. "Here, you better have another drink." He poured a stiff shot for Nick and the men stood around grinning as he downed it.

Tex watched from the window. When Nick and Figlia came out, she stepped into a produce stall. "Hello, Tootsie," the produce dealer said. "You want to buy something? I got potatoes, tomatoes, onions, yams. I got some nice yams. You like to candy some yams?"

Tex paid no attention and the produce dealer shouted down the line. "Hey, Jake, look who I got for a customer."

"Oh my," Jake said, "that's the kind of customers I like, Georgie. You better trade with me, lady. I keep my customers satisfied."

Tex stepped into the walk. Figlia and Nick had disappeared. As she started away, Jake came to Georgie. She heard him grunt, the same sound that Joseph the waiter had made in the restaurant, and she knew that he had his hand up to his shoulder and was showing off the length of his arm.

22

SHORTY opened the door for them and Figlia said, "Shorty, I want you to meet a friend of mine, Nick."

"Hello, Nick," Shorty said. He held out his hand and Nick held it for a moment, feeling it blunt and mittlike in his fingers.

"Come on in and close the door," Shorty said. "We don't want the light to get out, do we?"

Nick shut the door, his eyes on the room before him. It was like a room in hell, with smoke coiling in a low cloud against the ceiling and men and girls crowded at the tables and the bar, their voices raised in a kind of hysterical gibberish from which emerged precise and shotlike words of profanity. He could see the leggy, breasty, toothy, blonde, brunette, redhead, thin, fat, comely, homely figures of the girls sitting with legs crossed or parted, or walking with mincing steps across the room. As they went into the room, he heard the gelded tittering of the girls.

Men played poker at a row of tables against the wall. One of the players looked up and said, "Why, hello there, Fig."

"How are you, Pop, you old bastard?" Figlia said. "How you doing?"

"Oh, I guess I can't kick," Pop said. He spoke in a whining snivelling voice and he had a mean, small-eyed, tight-mouthed face. There was a small stack of chips before him on the table. "Maybe I'm gittin' too old to kick," he said.

"You still hiding your chips in your pocket?" Figlia said.

"Hell, no, I'm losers," Pop whined in that snot-nosed voice of his. "I been having plenty of luck lately, but it's all bad."

"Don't let him give you none of that crap," one of the players said. "He's got half the chips on the table in his pocket right now. He's murdering us."

"Why, whatever give you such a notion, son?" Pop said. "You know you won the last hand yourself."

"Christ, yes," the player said. "I drew a pat flush and everybody dropped out so I won the ante. But he wins all the big hands."

"Hell, I wouldn't complain about the ante," Pop said. "It's four bucks every time you win. A man can get mighty rich, just winning the ante."

"All right," the dealer said. "The hell with all this wind. Are you in or out?"

"Christ, I don't know," Pop said. "I ain't even looked at my hand." He rippled the chips through his fingers and picked up a stack. "Hell, let's say I'm in." He shoved the stack into the pot.

Figlia touched Nick's arm and they moved off into the room. "Pop Fox," he said. "He'll drive 'em nuts and have all their money before he's through."

They passed among the tables to one at the far end of the room and Nick saw five girls seated with a small dark man with black hair. He could see the man's hatchet face turn and suddenly become unfriendly when it saw Figlia.

"Hello, you pimp," Figlia said.

"Who you calling a pimp?" the man said.

"I'm calling you a pimp, you pimp," Figlia said. He pulled up a chair from one of the other tables. "Sit down," he said to Nick.

"Look, there are plenty of other tables," the man said.

"We like it here," Figlia said. He found another chair and brought it over and sat down. "Frenchy, this is Nick," he said.

Frenchy looked briefly at Nick. "All right, it's Nick," he said. "So what?"

"What do you mean, so what," Figlia said. "I could go to any table in the place, but I come to you because I'm trying to be friendly. Where's Mitch?"

"He's getting his face fixed," one of the girls said.

"What's the matter with his face?"

"Somebody stepped on it," the girl said.

Figlia nodded to Frenchy. "Somebody ought to step on your face too," he said. "How about some drinks?" He thumped the table and shouted to the bar. "Shake it up over there, we want some drinks."

Nick looked at the girls and their faces alerted as his eyes went over them. Three were young and common looking. The fourth was dark, brunette, attractive in a hard glittering way. The fifth was an older woman with glassy eyes, porous leathery skin and a thin muscular neck broken out with wrinkles. She resembled a milk-wagon horse that would know every stop on the street.

"Take your pick," Figlia said.

Nick liked the fourth, but he did not know how to assert his choice without hurting the feelings of the others. The waiter came. He looked more like a bouncer than a waiter. "Where's the guy that's in such a big hurry?" he said.

"Here I am," Figlia said. "What about it?"

"You're in such a hurry you're looking to get the bottle in the teeth," the waiter said.

"I'll try it that way next time," Figlia said. "Tonight I'll have it in a glass. Name it, girls."

The girls ordered drinks, the fourth abstaining. She kept looking at Nick in a quiet amused way as Figlia ordered a double shot for him.

"Well, here's a man who'd like to bury the body," Figlia said. "Who is it going to be?" He broke out a pack of cigarettes and handed it around. The fourth did not drink or smoke. Just like Polly, Nick thought.

"Is she the one?" Figlia said. "Go on, kid, talk up, you can't hurt anybody's feelings. They don't care."

Nick killed his drink and stood up. He felt a faint swimming sensation. The girl stood up too and came to him and they stood together, the girl big and bosomy against him.

"You be nice to this guy, he's a good friend of mine," Figlia said.

"Dance?" she said.

"I'm not very good at it."

"Let's take a whirl."

"Sure, let's go," Figlia said.

They began to dance and she felt good in his arms, breasty. He could feel them cushioning against his chest, and the roundness of her thighs pressing through her clothes. Her face tilted up and he could see her mouth, laughing, the way it had of going from ear to ear when she laughed.

"You'll need a new pair of feet after I get through with you," he said.

"You're doing fine," the girl said. "What are you afraid of?"

"I'm not afraid of anything."

"Sure you are. You're afraid."

"The hell I am."

"Then why don't you hold me tighter? There, tighter, that's it, tighter, there." She held him tightly.

The drink began to take effect and Nick felt a ring of cold numbing his mouth. The girl was heavy and bosomy in his arms. His hand was in the small of her back, down where it began to curve out, smack against it, and he could feel the smooth struggle of her body as they danced.

"What's your name?" he said.

"Nadine."

It was an ordinary name but for some reason it made him think of a sexually precocious girl he once knew. At eight she was playing with the boys in the empty piano boxes in Cliff Smith's back yard. He remembered her throaty giggling as though she were being tickled in some secret place. The dignified cocky way she stepped out of the boxes, the snickering self-conscious boy behind her. "Well, who's next?" she would say. "Step up, boys." She had learned it from her mother who was a whore.

Something made Nick look over her shoulder and he saw Tex standing against the wall, watching him over the heads of the crowd. When she saw he had seen her, she went along the wall past the gambling tables. Nick stopped dancing. The girl saw him observing Tex and she touched his arm lightly, stroking his biceps with her finger tips in a way that suggested she was feeling more sex than strength.

"What do you say we go to the bar for another drink?"

"Sure." Nick wanted to look back, but he let the girl lead him to the bar.

Tex walked past the poker table where Pop Fox was playing and went to the table where Figlia was sitting with Rocky and the others.

Figlia was leaning to Frenchy, talking, when he saw Tex. Frenchy had not seen her and he said, "Well, what about that guy." Figlia nudged him to shut up and said to Tex, "Well, if it isn't Rosey. How are tricks, Rosey?"

"Tricks are okay," Tex said. She pulled out Nick's chair.

"All the seats are taken," Frenchy said.

"That makes this one taken twice," Tex said. She sat down. "Where's Mitch?"

"He's fixing his face," one of the girls said.

"He can fix his face, but how is he going to put back all those teeth?" Tex said.

"Maybe he'll get him some new ones," Frenchy said. "Girl's teeth, a whole mouthful of 'em."

"On him they look good."

"Not half as good as the girl is going to look."

"I'll have to stick around to see."

"Sure, you'd better do that little thing."

Figlia nodded across the room. "Looks like your boy friend kind of threw you down," he said to Tex.

"Sure, he got himself a real piece," Frenchy said.

Tex saw Nick standing with the girl at the bar. "Here's to my friend," she said. She drank the drink down.

There was a sudden burst of cursing at the poker table and Pop Fox stood up laughing.

One of the players was pounding the table. "I never saw such luck," he was saying. "I never saw such crazy God damned luck. One straight, one full house, one flush after another."

"Sure, it's all luck. I never could play worth a damn," Pop said as he gathered the chips from the table and poured them into his pockets. His coat bulged with chips, the weight of them drawing it tight across his chest. "Well, I guess I made me a day's wages in fifteen minutes. Guess I'll drop out and give one of the boys a chance. I'm no pig."

"A hell of a chance with him walking off with all our money," a player said.

Pop Fox laughed in that screeching senile laughter of his as he stepped away from the table. "Hey Bebby," he shouted to Tex, "you comin' with me, or do I have to come over and get you?"

"You'd better save it, Pop; you're going to need it."

Pop came to the table. "What's the matter, don't you think I got the money? Why hell, if that's what's worrying you, I got plenty of jack." He brought out a handful of chips from his pocket. "Not bad for a penny ante poker player, huh?"

Tex looked toward the bar and saw Nick watching her. "Well, come on then, let's spend 'em," she said.

"Why hell, what are we waiting for?" Pop said.

Tex stood up. "I don't know, what *are* we waiting for?" she said. "You Daddy Fox, you're always keeping me waiting." She locked arms with the old man and they left the table. She felt Nick's eyes on her as they went to cash in the chips. "Oh you Daddy Fox, are you going to give me all that money?" she said.

"You bet, Bebby. Treat me right and she's all yours," Pop said.

"Are you going to buy me a drink, Daddy?" she said.

"You bet, anything you say, Bebby girl," Pop said. They pushed past Nick and Nadine to the bar and the old man slapped his hand on the bar top. "Hi there, the little girl here wants a big drink," he shouted.

"Give me a double shot of bourbon with a water chaser," Tex said. "What are you going to have, Daddy?"

"Why, nothin'," Pop said. "I don't smoke nor drink. All I got is but one habit." He burst into a cackle of laughter that stopped as suddenly as it began. The bartender poured the bourbon into a double shot glass.

"Are you going to buy me the bottle too, Daddy?" Tex said.

"Anything you want, Bebby. All you got to do is name it."

"Oh, you're a sweet Daddy." Tex downed her drink in one gulp and crushed the old man to her and kissed him full on the thin withered mouth. "Take me home, Daddy," she said quietly, pleading, as though she could not wait to get him to her room.

"Yes, siree, Bebby," Pop said. He paid the bartender and grabbed the bottle from the bar and they headed toward the door. On the way out he could not contain himself and he stopped Tex and buried his face into her neck. He did something to her neck that made her laugh throatily, her face upraised.

"Look at the old bastard," somebody said. "He's eating her."

"Why not?" somebody else said. "What else can he do but eat?"

Tex felt Nick's eyes on her as they went out.

Figlia saw Nick leave the girl, Nadine, and press through the crowd toward the door, the girl bewildered heading back to the table.

"What's the matter with you?" Figlia said. "Why did you let him get away?"

"What did you want me to do, tie a rope around him?" Nadine said. "He walked out on me."

"You call yourself a woman? You're a dog. You're not even a dog. Where's Mitch?"

"I told you, he was getting his face fixed," Frenchy said.

"He could get himself a new face by now. Where is he?"

"He ought to be here any minute. Relax."

"She's getting away with the kid and you want me to relax."

"She don't want him. She's got the old man. Take it easy."

Figlia grabbed Frenchy by the coat and jerked him to his feet. "I want Mitch," he said.

"Okay, okay, okay," Frenchy said.

Mitch was in a room with a willowy blonde. She was winding a bandage around his head. He had a black eye and a cut chin.

"What do you want?" Mitch said.

"I've got a job for you," Figlia said.

Mitch bent his head down to his hands. The girl was fastening the bandage with adhesive tape. "Not interested," he said.

"The hell you're not. There's five hundred bucks in it."

"I don't care if it's five grand, the way I feel."

"He feels pretty bad," the girl said. "Some guy with Tex slapped the Jesus out of him and he feels something awful."

"Now you don't say?" Figlia said.

The girl smiled. She had a smooth round face that was as soft and white as whipped cream. When she smiled it was a loosening of the face and a falling open of the mouth, revealing small pearly teeth evenly spaced in pink gums.

"How long has this little number been in town?" Figlia said to Frenchy.

"Oh, a couple of days," the girl said.

"Couple of days and we haven't met? What's your name?"

"June O'Day."

"Yeah, I know, but what's your real name?"

"June O'Day."

"Her name is Margaret Burcham," Frenchy said.

"Oh, Frenchy," the girl protested delicately, and she said to Figlia, "June O'Day is my professional name. I used to work in Burlesque."

"You ought to see her do the bumps," Frenchy said. "She can throw it right in your eye."

"Well, June, it's too bad you weren't in there a minute ago," Figlia said. "You could have picked up the guy who shellacked Mitch."

Mitch raised his head.

"Yeah," Figlia said. "He's lousy with money. You could have made yourself a nice piece of change."

"Is he still out there?" Mitch said.

"No. Tex got him. They're out in the street somewhere, but you can pick 'em up easy. They haven't been gone long."

"What about the five hundred?"

"He's got it in his wallet, and my check for thirty-four hundred."

Mitch looked quietly to Frenchy and Frenchy shook his head.

"Hell, the two of you can take him," Figlia said. "They must be on the Embarcadero. If they're not there, you'll find them in her room. If you don't get it, she will. I'd like to see you boys do yourselves some good."

Mitch stood up and straightened back his hair.

"The two of you together, it'll be a cinch to roll him," Figlia
said.

"What do you get out of it?"

"The check."

"And we get the cash?"

"The cleanest five hundred you ever made," Figlia said.

23

"WHERE are we going?" Frenchy said.

"Over to her room," Mitch said.

"Do you think she'll be there?"

"Sure she'll be there. Where the hell do you think she's going to be?"

"I don't know, but I don't think they'll be up there yet. She's got to shake that old gunser."

"Hell, she's shaken him already and she's got that other guy up in her room. She ain't going to waltz him around no docks so somebody else can roll him for all that dough."

"I wouldn't go to her room if I was him," Frenchy said.

"Of course you wouldn't," Mitch said. "You ain't him."

"Okay, have it your way," Frenchy said. It was cold and his clothes felt soggy in the fog. He felt somehow that the job would not be worth the five hundred dollars they were supposed to collect. When you split it two ways what do you get? he thought. And how you have to get it. It's going to be a tough five hundred any way you look at it. The thing to do, really do I mean, is kiss the two hundred bucks we're out on Tex goodbye and kiss her goodbye and don't never pick 'em up like her no more. Sisters like her are poison, what I mean. Not when they come like that new one, that June. Dumb, make ten bucks and give you ten, really dumb. Any time one like her gets out of line, smack her up and she's back in. But that Tex!

"So she's got him in her room. How do we work it?" he said.

"We'll walk in, quick, before he knows what hit him," Mitch said.

"I don't know about that."

197

"What's the matter, you ain't scared?"

"That's not what I said. All I said was I don't know."

"What don't you know?"

"I don't know about walking in, quick, before he knows what hit him," Frenchy said.

"You're scared," Mitch said.

"I don't like fooling with Tex," he said.

"When we get through with her, she's not going to like it either," Mitch said.

"You know what I mean. She's always fouling us up."

"I'm going to pay her back for what that guy did to me. And I'm going to collect my two hundred bucks," Mitch said.

"You might collect something you don't like," Frenchy said. "If you ask me, I'd drop her. We should have dropped her a long time ago."

"She was into me a hundred bucks by then," Mitch said. "I ain't going to let no chippy do me out of no hundred bucks."

"Okay, it's your funeral," Frenchy said. What the hell am I saying, he thought. It's mine too. The next time one comes up like her, it's no deal. He remembered the morning Mitch brought her to the room. We were getting ready to pull out, he thought, and he comes up with this dame. It turns out she ain't got a dime to her name, no clothes, nothing, just the rags on her back, a fuzzy sweater that looks like she must have slept in some gutter and her skirt that she keeps twisting around and shoes run down at the heels so her feet keep caving in. Them raw legs of hers without no stockings. That burned-up look in her face. New member of the firm, Mitch says. Sure, I says, what I like is the class that oozes out of her. What are we going to do, run a bed for bums? What do you mean, bums? Mitch says and I says, Who else is going to want that? and Mitch says, Maybe you will, when I get some duds on her. So first thing he gets some grub in her. She's hungry, what I mean. And afterwards he takes her to town and when they get back, she's dressed in exactly the same clothes, sweater, skirt and shoes, but new. He's taken her to a beauty parlor and she's got her hair up. Looks clean. But she's still got that poison look in the eye. That's poison, I think, I don't want none of that poison. I don't want

none of her. Not the way she looks at Mitch. Not the way she
don't mix with the kids. Too good for us, that's how it is. Mitch
lays out a hundred bucks and that makes him think he's got his
hooks into her, but I got a feeling he hasn't got a thing, not a
thing. The kids are talking, having a good time on the way North,
but she just sits there, looking poison. Too God damned good for
all of us. We stop to eat at Tiny's in Fresno and first thing you
know she runs out on us. She hides in the john and won't come out
and Babe has to go in after her. A mile North out of town a tire
begins to pound and we pull up to one of them hick beer joints
because Mitch sees a car with tires we can use. So we go in and
we're playing the juke and buying drinks while Mitch is collecting
us a tire and what do you know, she holes up in the john again.
Mitch is ready to go, but she won't come out, so Babe goes in after
her and it turns out she don't want none of us. When Mitch picked
her up she was so crummy, about all she could pick up was fleas, but
now he's fixed her so the boys will give her the eye, she wants to
be on her own. She don't go for cutting us in. I'm all for dropping
her. So she wants to get on her own. So to hell with her. When they
get ideas like that, you might as well drop 'em, but Mitch is hot
after his hundred bucks. So Babe and Susie go after her and when
they bring her out, her face is burning, the slapping around they
give her. One of them beer joint Romeos gets the idea he's going
to help her, but he can't make up his mind because Mitch has that
shiv look in his eye and we get in the car and we're moving out
when this guy decides to chase us, but it turns out it's his car
Mitch jacked the tire off of. The front end piles on the ground, but
it's a close one there for a minute, brother, what I mean. Suppose it
wasn't his car? She's been nothing but trouble, all the time trouble,
and it ain't stopped yet, not by a long shot, not the way I feel.

Frenchy felt Mitch's hand on his arm. "Do you see her?" he said.

"No, but we're almost there."

They had come to the building where Tex lived. Mitch led the
way to the entrance. A window was lighted high up in the face of
the wall. "What did I tell you?" he said. He stepped into the
darkness of the stair well and was swallowed by the darkness.
Frenchy followed him. "Take it easy," Mitch whispered, his

voice disembodied in the dark. "Let's take our time about getting up. Just follow me and take it easy. It'll be a cinch if we take it easy."

"Okay, just so we take it," Frenchy said, the whisper fierce and impatient in the dark.

They went slowly up the steps. There was a slit of light under the door and it swept across their faces as they rose to the second floor landing. Frenchy stepped to the door and stood listening.

"Hear anything?" Mitch said.

Frenchy did not answer. He could hear his heart pumping, he could hear himself breathe.

"What are you waiting for?" Mitch said.

Frenchy pressed quietly against the door, then lunged against it and the door sprung open.

The room was empty.

"What did I tell you?" Frenchy said.

"Okay, so she's down on the Embarcadero," Mitch said.

"That was twenty minutes ago. Christ knows where she is by now."

"Anyway, they'll end up here. That's for sure."

"You want to bet on it?"

"Hell, no, what would I want to bet for? I know they'll be here."

"Yeah, all we got to do is sit it out until they come back."

"We'll take a walk and if they ain't on the Embarcadero they've got to be here."

"You're sure of that now? That's what I like about you, the way you're so sure. No matter what it is, you're always so God damned sure."

"Well, how do you figure it? The bed's here, they've got to end up here."

"Okay, have it your way," Frenchy said.

When they got to the Embarcadero, a freight train was switching box cars up and down the waterfront. In the ruddy glow of the switchman's light Frenchy saw someone on hands and knees, crawling on the other side of the track. It was Pop Fox.

"What are you looking for, Pop?" Frenchy said.

"Muh teeth, muh teeth, I'm looking for muh teeth." The old

man spoke through his gums, his voice sounding as though his mouth were full of mush. "Crumby little bitch, she was just usin' me for a come on. Her and that feller."

"Which way did they go? Maybe we can catch up with 'em."

"The hell with 'em. All I want is muh teeth." Pop resumed his crawling, rubbing his hands on the ground.

Frenchy came across a short length of pipe lying beside the tracks and picked it up. Big guy like that is going to take some cooling, he thought. I'll have to lay him out first crack. The pipe felt hefty in his hands.

They kept walking in short spurts, stopping to listen. After a while they thought they saw something ahead, unreal because it was too far away, looking like nothing in the world but a swirl of fog. After a time they saw Tex and Nick walking together, not clearly but unreal and distant, more like ghosts than living flesh and blood.

24

TEX walked on ahead. Every time she turned, Nick pushed her shoulder and made her face about, away from him. She kept trying to turn and he kept pushing her away. She did not have on her coat and she held herself with her arms.

"Listen, lover, I don't mind your pushing me around," she said. "But it's cold. I'm cold." She had turned again and she stumbled when Nick pushed her around.

"You were hot enough a minute ago," he said.

"Yes, but I'm cold now. If you were a gentleman you'd let me wear your coat."

"The hell with you. Who cares if you're cold?"

"I do. I'm freezing. Let me hold that arm of yours to warm me up, just your arm. Or take me home. How far are we going to walk anyway?"

"What's the matter, don't you like walking? Or is it the company you don't like? Maybe I'm not old enough, is that it? You like 'em plenty old."

"If you're talking about Daddy, he's not so old," Tex said. "He can't be a day over sixty."

"Sure, he's just a kid," Nick said. "Get in bed with him and you can think about it all night."

"What can you do that's any different, lover?"

"That's all right about what I can do. What made you pick up an old cocker like that?"

"What made you pick up that girl?"

"I don't know. Maybe it was because nobody gave her a hundred bucks."

Tex tried to turn, but Nick pushed her again. "Go on, keep walking," he said.

"Who gave who a hundred bucks?" Tex said. "Get it off your chest."

"I thought your name was Hazel," Nick said.

"It is."

"Then why does Figlia call you Tex?"

"That's my name too."

"He told me he paid you a hundred dollars to pick me up."

"I'd pick you up anytime for free, you know that, lover."

"Did he pay you or didn't he?"

"I told you he was swiping your load, didn't I?"

"You did it so you could roll me for all I've got."

"Did he tell you that too, or did you think that one up all by yourself?"

"He told me, but it's true, isn't it?"

"Sure it's true. You're a cinch to roll. All I've got to do is knock you down and get my hand in your pocket." Tex stopped again and this time Nick did not push her. "You know how easy that's going to be." She pressed her hand against his chest. "All I have to do is give you a shove and over you go on those big flat feet."

Nick tried to take her in his arms, but she laughed and stepped beside him. She took his arm and they began to walk again. "Oh my, but you're warm," she said. "Just like you've got a fire in you."

"Don't kid yourself you started it," Nick said. "If Figlia paid you to pick me up, that must have been a fake fight I had with that guy."

"It was."

"Then that makes him a friend of yours."

"I guess you can call him a friend."

"Nice friends you have. Did he get a cut out of the hundred?"

"Now what would you say?"

"I'd say he did. He sure earned it, and so did you; but Figlia's going to want his money back."

"Is he?" Tex said.

Nick stopped and looked intently at Tex. "You had me nailed a while ago but you let me go. I'd like to know why."

"Maybe Figlia is right, maybe a hundred isn't enough."

"Is thirty-nine hundred enough?"

Tex caught Nick's arm again. "Maybe it's you I'm after," she said. "After all, love is better than money. You can always get rich, but you can't always find love, wouldn't you say?"

"Hell, no, not with thirty-nine hundred dollars in his pocket," Nick said.

"You know something? I wouldn't worry about money, if I was you," Tex said. "If you're going to worry about it, why don't you get in your truck and beat it?"

"Do you want me to?"

"Sure, why not? That's why I picked up that old jerk and waltzed him past the bar, wasn't it? So you could get in your truck and beat it out of town?"

"Serve you right, if I did," Nick said, "but I can't. I have to wait for my partner. He's coming in with another load."

"I haven't got a thing to do with it?"

"Hell, no. We went in on two loads together and I've got to be here when he gets in. I'm new at this game and he thinks he's got to steer me around or I'll get gypped."

"You almost did."

"You mean Figlia? I'd have beat his ears down if he hadn't come across. You know what I'm going to do when Ed gets in?" Nick removed the wallet from his front pocket and opened it, showing the sheaf of bills. " 'You know that load of apples?' I'm going to say. 'You know how scared you were I'd get gypped? Well, guess what? I peddled the whole batch, six hundred boxes, and you know how much I got? Six and a half bucks a box, thirty-nine hundred berries.' "

"That ought to kill him," Tex said.

"Sure it'll kill him," Nick said. "We only paid two. His eyes'll stick out a foot when I flash this wad."

"My, aren't we excited!" Tex said.

"I guess you can call it excited," he said.

"Don't let it throw you," Tex said. "It isn't all the money in the world."

Maybe it isn't, Nick thought. Some people could blow it in in one night, they could lose it on one roll of dice, they could drop it on one horse, they could lay it on one blonde, this money that meant so much to him.

The surf smashed through the pilings and washed back. The surface of the water, oily and luminous, looped and freed the reflections of light that came from a lamp. After Nick had watched the water rising and falling, the street became unsteady, like the bank moving when you watch rivers, or earth moving when you watch clouds.

Tex stopped walking and Nick saw her look back into the darkness. "Looking for something?" he said.

"I thought I heard someone."

"The old man looking for his teeth."

"No, something else."

They listened together but there was nothing beyond the seagulls flying, lost in the dark, doomed to fly until the morning winds cleared the sky of fog.

"I don't hear a thing," Nick said.

"Don't you hear steps?"

"Not a thing."

"It sounded like someone walking."

"Let 'em walk," Nick said. They went on along the waterfront. Above them the seagulls screeched, calling to each other, trying to find their way. Ahead a light glowed in the milky fog and when they came to it, the light turned out to be many lights along a slip where men were loading cargo into nets that were hoisted into a ship.

Nick began to think of Ed driving the limping truck, engine pounding, universal thumping, trying to get to the market. He had forgotten his dream but something in the back of his head remembered and he sucked in his breath, his hackles rising. A wave of worry went over him like a fever but he thought, He'll come in. If he's broke down, he'll fix her; if he needs a part, he'll get it. He'll have her rolling; he'll get in.

They started away from the lighted slip and Nick saw Tex turn back again, the look swift and furtive, and if he had not been so tired, he would have worried about it; but he was too tired. Something burned and ached behind his eyes and he felt feverish and sick. When he listened, he could hear a faint nagging hum as of telegraph wires in the wind, the sound in his head. The muscles along the front of his thighs felt tight and strung. His head kept nodding forward and he kept tilting it back, trying to keep awake. He could hear the slow come and go of his breath. He could never hear it when he was awake, but now he could, inhaling and exhaling, as though deep within himself, in spite of himself, he had fallen asleep. He could feel the girl's hand on his arm and it was like some strange girl's hand on some strange fellow's arm. He could hear his steps mingling with hers, far away, like the steps of some strange couple going to some far off room. He thought of an open window and the sounds of the harbor carried in on the wind, with himself in bed, listening, and the sounds dying until he had fallen asleep. And Tex, where was Tex? A moment ago he had wanted her. I want her, he had thought, but now he felt a coldness toward her. He reached over to remove her hand from his arm and send her away, but she misunderstood his gesture for one of affection and opened her hand to his. How warm was her hand. The fog had wet his clothes and he felt soaked to the marrow, frozen.

They walked past buildings and dark spaces where slips opened to the harbor. Men lay on loading docks, huddled against bulkheads and piles, waiting for daylight, hours away. Some walked with their collars up and their arms clasped tightly to their bodies. The fog horn made a great sound and in the spasms of silence Nick could hear the smashing and washing of the surf against pilings. Waves rolling in, carrying on them the scum and sewage of the harbor, and when the wind shifted, a smell rose from it, the giant bad breath of the city.

Nick wanted to sleep, but I can't, he thought. If I sleep now I'll never wake up, I'll never be there to cash Figlia's check in the morning.

He felt someone shake his arm. Tex. She said, "How about a cup of coffee?" and when he looked up he saw they had come to a greasy-spoon restaurant built into a corner of one of the warehouses, its lights smothered in the fog.

"Doesn't all this walking make you hungry?" Tex said. "All of a sudden I'm hungry."

They went into the restaurant and sat down. After the waiter had gone, Tex had a sudden quiet compulsion to look over her shoulder. She knew someone was standing outside, beyond the window, watching her and all she had to do was turn swiftly and she would catch him, but not yet, she told herself, not now. Then instantly she thought, Now, and she turned and saw Frenchy. He was an apparition, gone the instant she turned, but she had seen him, she knew she had, it did not surprise her that she had.

Nick was observing her with narrowed eyes.

"You really ought to eat something," Tex said.

Nick turned to the window too. The juke box had stopped playing and the sound of surf came up, smashing against the pilings beneath the restaurant so the floor shook. Fog pressed against the windows and the room was like a ship at sea. The ham and eggs sizzled on the grill. The waiter was leaning over the counter, talking soundlessly in pantomime, with one of the men. The juke box played again, the same tune.

"What's on your mind?" Tex said.

"For two bits I'd go back to the truck," Nick said.

"Good idea," Tex said. "If you're tired, you could get some sleep."

She could see Nick going angry and she removed a cigarette from her purse and pretended to look for a match. "Got a light?" she said.

"You're nothing but a two buck whore," Nick said.

"Five bucks," Tex said. "The cost of loving's gone up."

"You God damned whore."

"Go ahead, honey, give it to me, tell me what a bad girl I am."

"I don't have to tell you, you know what you are. You're a rotten whore."

"Oh, yes, I've led a wicked life and I'm going straight to hell, that's for sure now, unless you step in and save me. Save me, lover."

"Save yourself, you whore."

"Don't get any idea you're calling me any names, brother. Sure

I'm a whore. I could be a secretary or a sales girl or a file clerk or a soda jerk, but I'm a whore. I like being a whore."

"That's because you don't know any better."

"I know where I stand. That's more than you'll ever know."

"What's wrong with where I stand? I'm on my own. I've got a truck. I just sold a hot load and I'm going to sell a lot more. With a little luck, I'll buy me a couple more rigs and I'm on my way, but you'll still be a whore."

"The difference between you and me is we're both flat on our backs, but you don't know it."

"Jesus, what ever soured you up that way? Did you ever try getting a job and doing something decent for a living?"

"Sure, I got me a job once punching a typewriter, took dictation, made eighteen a week. Couldn't begin to keep myself in nylons. The boss tried to get me to go out nights. Wasn't he being nice to me, letting me work? If I'd be nice to him, I could work steady, extra money if I would, but I wouldn't. So I got me a job working counter in a store, sold ties and shirts. Employment agent wanted a commission for finding me the position and the manager wanted a commission because he gave it. So I got me a job working as a file clerk in an insurance office. Three hundred women doing nothing but make files on a lot of folks who were dead or going to die, twenty two fifty a week, work thirty years and you get a pension. We used to call it the big lay. So I got me a job jerking sodas, sixteen a week, the boss kept all the tips, but I got to drink all the malts I could hold and wrestle with the comptometer jockeys on the make."

"Maybe you weren't cut out to work," Nick said. "Maybe what you need is somebody to take care of you. Why don't you get married?"

"I tried that too," Tex said.

Nick looked at Tex and Tex said, "Well, aren't you going to ask me about marriage? Marriage is so nice. You fall in love with a fine upstanding young man and you marry him. After two weeks in bed, you come to."

Nick looked away and Tex said, "Aren't you going to ask me about my baby?" She opened her purse and brought out a picture of a young man holding a child and handed it to Nick. "Paul writes to me about her all the time. Shirley is four years old today, he writes, and she wants to know when she's going to see her mama. When are we going to see you, Hazel?"

"She looks like you," Nick said.

"Sure, she looks like me. Wish her luck."

"What made you walk out on them?"

"I got sick of being broke in this land of plenty. I couldn't take it no more. I wouldn't mind if there was nothing and you with plenty of nothing, but when they dangle plenty in your face and say this is yours if you'll pay, I couldn't take it. None of that ten percent down and untie the knots in your head the rest of your life for little old Tex, none of that *for richer, for poorer* stuff for her. I couldn't go for the long hard life."

"You walked out because he was broke," Nick said. "You were born a whore."

"Sure, and you were born a sucker. You're the one I feel sorry for. You still think you're going to pay your way with nickels."

"Don't kid yourself, I know how tough it is."

"It's tougher on you than it is on me," Tex said. "I've got something to peddle. They beat a path to my bed. I don't have to lay up with no bald-headed pot-bellied slob to hold down my job or trade a free piece now and then to get a square meal. I don't have to kiss nobody's pratt. You're trying to get on your own, but you never will, but I am. I'm strictly on my own."

Nick shook his head. "You sound so bad, I don't believe it. You're just talking."

Tex smiled. "You'd better drink your coffee before it gets cold."

"I wish I hadn't met you," Nick said. "I wish I hadn't come out after you. Why did I come out after you?"

"I don't know, why did you?" Tex said.

Nick stood up ready to go and Tex raised the cup to her lip again. She could feel Frenchy watching her. It sang in her, knowing he was out there watching.

They had been walking along the docks for a long distance and when Nick looked at Tex, he could see her attention was on something ahead in the fog, far away. I know why I came out, he thought. I want her. He remembered himself with her in the room, the way everything in her jumped when he touched her and he knew he had to come out. I had to, he thought.

What the hell are we doing out here when we could be in the room? he thought. A while ago I was carrying her to bed and nothing happened and now here we are, wasting time. Pretty soon it'll be daylight and it'll be too late. Why don't we go up now, while there's time? He looked again at Tex and again he felt the crippling pain of longing. He wanted to open her dress and run his hands over the rounds of her shoulders and into the warmth of her neck. He wanted to remove her clothes and make her stand freezing in the wind that carried on it all the sounds of the harbor. When he kissed her, her lips would be cold and behind them he would feel her teeth chattering. How light and strong she would be in his arms, when he carried her to bed. He would lay her down and look at her, his eyes hooded with longing. But there was no time, scarcely an hour until daybreak, and here he was tormenting himself with waiting. Why don't we go to your room, he wanted to say, but a shyness came over him and he could hardly look at her. She must know how I feel, he thought.

Tex stopped walking. Behind them the freight train had finished switching its cars and was returning, its lantern swinging. The tracks which crossed and crisscrossed the smooth belly of the pavement glistened in the red light. The train bore down upon them and Nick held Tex's arm and led her onto a dock. She shivered and drew against Nick, her face against his chest.

Nick turned Tex in his arms. He saw her glance past him, the look swift and furtive. Behind him, beyond the sound of the scummy surf that smashed through barnacled piles and spilled itself in a yeasty foam onto the mucky shore beneath the dock, he heard the stealthy scuffle of a step. He had to see, but when he tried to turn, Tex's arms were like steel around his neck.

"Nick!" he heard her say, and he tore himself free but before he could turn, something cracked into his skull and he went numb and blind. He felt himself go; I'm going, he thought, and he tried to hold himself. He felt a hand forcing his pocket where

the wallet was and he tried to seize it, but he sensed another
blow coming and he clawed out, encountering face, eyes and mouth,
and far off he heard someone screaming and he clutched the face
until he felt an arm encircle and tighten against his neck, garroting
him, and he tried to squirm free, but he was caught, his arms were
caught, and he felt himself reeling; but he twisted and with all his
remaining strength he bit the arm just above the wrist, hard. But
there was another blow, after which there was nothing.

Frenchy rolled Nick over and went through him, but did not
find the wallet. He hasn't got it on him, he thought, and he stood
up. He could hear Tex's feet rapping on the pier, going away and
he thought, She's got it! and ran to the end of the pier. The train
was still passing, going slowly along the tracks. She'll try to get
around the short end of it, he thought, and he ran against the
passage of the train but she was not there. He ran in the other
direction, with the cars now, but he could not find her. The cars
were running close to the buildings and there were boxes of
freight piled on the pavement blocking the way. She's got to be
here, he thought, and he stood looking for her when he saw her
cramped between boxes and train. She stepped out when she saw
him coming, but he had her cornered.
"All right, gimme," he said.
"Get out of my way."
"Hand it over."
Tex tried to get by and Frenchy grabbed her. She turned in his
arms, presenting her back to him and he could not reach her hand.
He slammed her around, but she held her arm high and he could
not get the wallet. She was like a cat in his hands, getting away,
but he brought his knee into her, and she doubled over and he
nearly had the wallet, but she threw it against the train and the
money spilled into the wind.
He dropped to the ground, frantic to catch the money, and he
felt Tex push him onto the tracks. He rolled clear and lay still
with the wheel trucks thumping over the rail joints, shaking the
ground, but he was not frightened. All he could think was, Oh,
Christ, all that money, and he got to his knees and felt along the

ground but found only the empty wallet, and a few bills. He could feel the wind of the train's passage as the cars went by. Then they had passed and the engine was pulling away, its headlights flooding the tracks. He found a few more bills, twenties and a fifty. Can't be more than two or three hundred here, he thought, lucky if it's that. The wind had blown the rest into the water. Most of the money was gone, the check gone.

Suddenly Frenchy remembered he had been pushed under the train and he remembered to be frightened. I coulda been killed, he thought, she coulda killed me. He looked for Tex, but she was gone.

25

NICK rolled over on his face, and finally sat up. Before him was the glitter of open water. The water puzzled him and for a moment he did not know where he was. He felt dizzy and the pier floor was unsteady and kept dipping away from beneath him as he got to his feet and stood balancing himself on the narrow dock. The pier looked to be dangerously high, stretching a long way back to land. Below him the water rose and fell sickeningly. He reached for his wallet, but it was gone. He searched his pockets, but there was only the change from the broken ten. The rest was gone. Thirty-nine hundred gone.

I knew it was going to happen, he thought, I knew it and I had to let it. He wanted to punch himself. I had it in my hands, thirty-nine hundred smackers, and I let them take it, he thought. All gone.

When he reached the street, he had to sit down. You God damned sucker, he thought, you let them take you. Thirty-nine hundred bucks and you couldn't hang on to it. You let them roll you.

There was a piercing sound in his head, as though a gong had been struck and now it was still ringing. His shoulder was crippled and he could not raise his arm.

He got up again. The fog was thinning, and far off in the West he could see the enormous luminescence that was the setting moon. How long ago was it that he had seen it rising? So long ago that it seemed in some forgotten time. How excited he had been then. He remembered his excitement bitterly, as though it were something he had experienced to make him feel the loss of the money more keenly. He started to walk, but the dizziness came on him again.

As the fog thinned and lifted, he saw a hill sloping up and away from the Embarcadero, and in the cup of the hill he saw many small and box-like houses lining the narrow streets where an occasional light pinked the darkness. An overwhelming sense of disaster came over him when he saw the mausoleum-like row of houses and he began to think again of Ed. Where was he? He should have been in long before now. Why wasn't he in? Where are you, guy? he thought.

26

FIGLIA was eating in the Merchant's Lunch. There was a steak beside a mound of French fries on a plate before him.

The waiter, Joseph, slid a cup of coffee on the counter. "Steak all right?" he said.

"Steak's okay," Figlia said.

"You like me to French you some more potatoes?"

"No more potatoes."

The waiter nodded and spooned two heaping spoons of sugar into the cup of coffee and stirred it lazily for Figlia. While he was stirring, he looked toward the door where Nick had entered and was standing beside the counter. He made a motion with his hand and Figlia stopped eating.

"Here come the man who kill you," the waiter said.

Figlia turned. "Well, what do you know, it's the apple man," he said. "Did you get your ashes hauled?"

"He look like he get everything hauled," the water said.

Nick looked dumbly at Figlia. His face ached. He touched his nose and it felt like a shapeless blob.

"What happen to you?" the waiter said.

"I got rolled," Nick said. His voice sounded faint and far away. He saw the waiter shake his head sadly. He saw the men in the cafe watching him with the alarm that onlookers hold for the suffering who are about to die.

"Got any idea who did it?" Nick heard Figlia say. No idea, no idea, no idea, kept running through Nick's head. He had to sit somewhere and he fumbled himself to the counter and sat on a stool that seemed ridiculously high. He rested his head on the counter. "Didn't see a thing," he heard himself. Not a thing, not a thing, not a thing, ran through his head. Oh, Jesus, he thought.

"That's what you get for flashing all that dough," Figlia said at his elbow. "No telling who it was. You'd better wipe your face. Get him a towel, Joseph."

After a time, Nick felt his face upturned and the hot towel mopping his face. The moist warm towel soothed his face and made him sleepy. The water made the cuts in his cheek sting. The towel came away bloody and Nick thought, Oh, Christ.

"Up on his forehead," he heard Figlia say. "Here, let me." And now the towel was in rougher hands, mopping and wiping, cleaning away the blood that had caked into his brows and into his hairline.

Up to now, Nick hardly knew where he was. The hissing sound of the gas flame, the hard sounds of dishes in the sink, even the breaths of the men around him were loud and painful to hear. But this all passed, the room shifted and twisted into focus, the sounds assumed their proper loudness and Nick saw himself sitting beside Figlia.

"Lucky for me, it wasn't all in cash," Nick said. "Most of it was in that check."

The waiter shook his head. Figlia tossed the bloody towel across the counter to the sink.

"All you've got to do, is make out another check," Nick said.

"I gave you a check," Figlia said.

"Sure, but it's gone and I'll need another so I can collect."

"You collected," Figlia said.

"A check isn't paid until it's cashed," Nick said.

"Well, go ahead and cash it. Nobody's stopping you."

"I can't, I haven't got it. The guys that rolled me have got it."

"How do I know they won't cash it."

"You can put a stop on it," Nick said. "The first thing in the morning, you can go to the bank."

"Stop, hell," Figlia said. "By the time I get to the bank, that money'll be drawn."

"You're trying to get out of paying me," Nick said.

"How do you like that?" Figlia said to the room. "I paid the guy, you saw me pay him. He's got the guts to say I never paid him." He motioned to the waiter. "Bring him a cup of coffee, Joseph."

"I need that money," Nick said. "I can't get another load without it."

"Cut it out, I'm bawling," Figlia said.

Joseph brought the coffee and slid it over to Nick.

"You're going to make me out a check," Nick said.

"Sure, I am," Figlia said. He raised his cup and sipped coffee with a loud noise.

"You're God damned right you are," Nick said.

"I said I was, didn't I?" Figlia said. He put down the cup and cut himself a piece of steak with the paring knife. "Even the toughest steak looks tender, if you cut it with a razor," he said.

The waiter shrugged. "That's the way they come now days," he said. "Don't give 'em a chance to age. Knock a cow in the head and deliver the meat before it's cold."

"Best place to get a cut of meat is in Minnesota," Figlia said. "One time I was out to St. Paul, got a steak, it melted in my mouth. It was so tender, you could cut it with your thumb." He mopped up the blood from the rare steak and turned to Nick with the toast in his hand. "You better drink your coffee," he said to Nick.

"I want my check," Nick said.

"He wants me to give him his check," Figlia said. "I paid for his load once. He wants me to pay for it twice."

"It isn't like you paid," Nick said. "My name's on it. They can't cash it without my signature."

"They got ways," Figlia said.

"Mike," the waiter said, "he's going to make trouble. I don't want no trouble. Go outside with your trouble."

"So now you're kicking me out," Figlia said. "Two bucks for a no-good steak and I haven't even finished it, and you want me to move."

"All right, if it's no-good steak, you don't have to pay," the waiter said. He took the plate with the half-eaten steak on it and threw it into the sink.

"Okay, gang up on me," Figlia said. He got down from the stool. "I'll tell you what I'll do," he said to Nick. "I'll make you a deal. You need the dough. I'll pay you off, two dollars a box, less the five hundred cash I already gave you. Seven hundred bucks."

"Nothing doing. Thirty-four hundred bucks is what I want. That's what I've got coming and that's what I'm going to get."

Figlia shrugged. Standing, he finished his coffee, tipped his hand to the waiter and started out, but Nick caught him and turned him around. "What about my check?" he said.

"What about it?" Figlia said.

"You going to give it to me or aren't you?"

"I not going to give it to you."

Nick hauled Figlia up by the coat. The waiter came around the counter and tried to break them apart. Their bodies moved heavily in the confining space, stumbling against the stools.

"Let him hit me, if it'll make him feel paid," Figlia said.

Nick wanted to hit Figlia but something held his fist. He felt intimidated somehow and though he wanted to smash Figlia, he could not raise his arm. It was the thirty-four hundred dollars that was owed him. He knew he could kiss it goodbye if he landed one on Figlia. He let him down. "What the hell have you got against me?" he said.

"Why, not a thing," Figlia said. "You're a little dumb, but you look like a pretty good guy."

"Then why don't you pay me?"

"I paid you."

"Sure. If they don't cash the check, you'll be ahead thirty four hundred bucks."

Figlia straightened out his coat. "Okay," he said. "I'll be a square guy. If that check isn't cashed after a year, I'll give you the thirty-four hundred. Fair enough?"

"Sure, all I've got to do is stand around," Nick said.

"That's the best I can do," Figlia said. He stepped from the Merchant's Lunch and Nick watched him go. Anger was in him like a fire and he wanted to beat the money out of Figlia, but a feeling akin to cowardice stopped him. He saw the men in the restaurant turning away from him as though in shame and he felt ashamed within himself as though he had been given an opportunity to assert his manhood and had lost it. He had compromised himself for a little money. He knew he could not get it. So beat it out of him, he told himself. But if he beat him, he would surely not get the money. Then take the two bucks a box and get the hell out of here, he told himself. He stepped from the restaurant into the street.

Figlia was standing with Charles on the sidewalk. "You better go get the truck and bring her around," he said.

"We going to go up and get them apples?" Charles said.

"Yeah. I'm going with you. We'll take Dave along. Want to go, Dave?"

"This isn't going to be another tough buck, is it?" Dave said.

"Hell, no," Figlia said. "This one is going to be a cinch."

"Maybe we better take him along too," Charles said. He nodded to the swamper.

"Sure," Figlia said. "He'll pick one up and eat two. We want him like we want a broken head."

Nick came up and Figlia stood before him, his eyes hard and glassy. "You ready to take my offer?" he said.

"Not a chance of it," Nick said. "I just want you to know, I'm going to get that money out of you, if it's the last thing I do."

"Good for you," Figlia said. "That's the way I like to hear 'em talk."

The rage surged again in Nick and he wanted to swarm all over Figlia, but a voice inside him said, Sure, go ahead and louse up thirty-four hundred dollars. He knew he would never see the money, and if he did, he would earn it, every cent of it, fretting and worrying. He knew in the end he would have to beat up Figlia and that Figlia would still have the money. So beat him now, the voice said, go ahead, knock his head off, if that's the way you feel about it. But again he could not do it. Himself intimidating himself, standing in shamefaced self-betrayal. He went to the truck and got in.

"Any time you change your mind, let me know," Figlia called out behind him.

The swamper stepped to Figlia. "I don't think it's right for that kid not to know about what's going to happen to his partner's apples," he said.

"Too bad somebody doesn't tell him," Figlia said.

"Yeah, ain't it though?" the swamper said. He stepped toward Nick's truck. "Hey, Jack," he said.

Figlia brought out a five dollar bill and dangled it in his hand. "You must be hungry," he said. "Why don't you go get yourself a bite to eat?"

The swamper licked his lips. "I'll need a bigger bite than that," he said. He opened the cab door. "Hey, Jack," he said. But the truck was empty. Nick was gone.

Figlia stuffed the five-dollar bill into his pocket. "Beat it, you slob," he said. "We better take along some empties," he said to Charles. "Them apples'll be all over the hill. We'll need some boxes."

"How many do you think we'll need, Mister Figlia?"

"All we got in the back."

"Yes, sir, Mister Figlia. Come on, Dave."

Charles and the handler, Dave, went on down the block and Figlia went into the produce house. There was still traffic on Washington Street, but it was the thinning traffic of the late market. The night's rush was slowing down. The swamper ran, waddling, to the corner, looking for Nick. "Hey, Jack," he shouted. There for a minute it looked like I was going to eat, he thought. The thought made him hungrier. His voice sounded on the point of crying. He ran to the slaughter house, searching the dark street for Nick. "Hey, Jack!" The smell of coffee, strong and narcotic, came from the Merchant's Lunch, as he returned to Washington Street. The smell upset the swamper. It made him ache in the pit of his tremendous stomach.

27

NICK could hardly stand. His mouth was open and he closed it and tried to open his eyes. He made such an effort to open them that his head tilted back and a powerful compulsion to weep came over him and passed quickly before he could submit to it. He was tired. He had never been so tired in his life. Back, when he had sold the load and got the money, he had felt so awake and alive, but now he was dead. He felt drained and hollow. Sounds from the harbor rang in his head. The loss of the money and his gutlessness with Figlia made him feel drugged.

From where he stood on the stairs he saw Tex's door standing open and he rose to it, listening for any sound, but there was none. He stood before the door and still there was no sound and he touched the door and it swung back, slowly unfolding the room, and he saw the table with the whiskey bottle on it, over on its side, empty, and Tex's purse opened and spilled and beside it a torn letter pieced together like some desperate jigsaw puzzle. He saw the dresser with its bottles, and above it the mirror in which was the reflection of Tex's legs. He stepped into the room and saw her body in the mirror and when he went past the door, he could see her lying face down on the bed, drunk in that horrid loose way women have of being drunk. Her clothes were in a torn pile on the floor and when he picked them up they were still soaked with the warmth of her body.

Nick grasped her by the shoulder to turn her over, but it came free in his hands, as though coming apart, her body disjointed on the bed. He had to take her in his arms to pour her over and as she turned he got a noseful of the bitter half-digested smell of whiskey. The smell came away on his hands. He stood looking down on her body, graceless and sad. She looked like death warmed over with her hair in her face and her face ashen, the eyes open and blank.

"Tex," Nick said. He tried to shake her, but it was like shaking a corpse.

Tex closed her eyes. She said something he could not understand and he bent down. "What did you say?" he said. She said it again and it sounded like wanting a drink and he said, "I know you do and I'll get you one, but first you've got to wake up."

He stiffened his hand and slapped her and she stopped talking. He slapped her again, the flesh flushing where his fingers hit, and he said, "Tex, this is Nick, I'm Nick, remember Nick?"

Tex focused her eyes, the light in them sharpening to a point. "NickNickNick," she said. She moistened her cracked, parched lips.

Nick said, "Wake up, Tex. Come on, wake up."

Tex said something that sounded like profanity and Nick bent to hear her and she said it again, but he could not make it out and he bent down farther and he could feel the warmth coming off her and that whiskey smell. Suddenly she scratched him and he caught her hands and one was bleeding at the wrist where he had bitten her. She was the one. "You're the one!" he said and he slapped her and she said it again, and this time he heard her. "Kill me," she was saying, "Please kill me. Please, please, kill me!" He knew she had said it and he hit her again and her nose started to bleed and it was on his hands. She shouted it hoarsely, and he wanted to kill her. He got the bottle from the table and raised it and far off he heard the flushing of a toilet, the gulping, swallowing sighing of pipes, and he dropped the bottle and ran down the stairs and behind him he could hear the horrid wrenching crying that was like vomiting. He got to the street and was walking swiftly toward the harbor, drawn to the sound of the surf that came pounding through the piles, smashing and washing back, and now he could not hear Tex crying.

The moon was down. It had run through its orbit and sank below the horizon and the waterfront was dark. Nick thought of the moon swinging eternally about the earth, and the earth swinging about the sun, and the flaming sun with its rings of planets moving in an orbit to some unknown destination in space. When he looked up, he saw the stars far away and it made him swoon as though he were looking down from a great height. Somewhere, at the end of time, it was all going to end in fire, but he would be dead by then and out of it. He thought of the day his father was cremated. First there was the service in the church with the old man lying among a cluster of flowers and his mother touching the cold aged head. Then, as they drove away, he remembered looking back and seeing the tall brick chimney of the crematorium with its thread of smoke. And that night he had lain awake thinking of his father burning, the tired body coming to life in the flames, raising its arms, arching its back, stretching its legs, and a tremendous sigh escaping from the lungs as the fire raged and reduced him to a heap of ashes.

A truck came up behind Nick and the eyes of a cat blazed with light, suddenly extinguished when the truck went by. Nick thought of Ed coming in and of having to tell him about the load. I can't tell him, he decided. I'll get the truck and beat it out of town before I'll tell him. But he had no money. Just a little change in his pocket, maybe enough to pay toll on the Bay Bridge. How was he going to buy gas and oil? It never occurred to him to think of buying food. He could only think of keeping the truck moving. I can save the toll if I go around San Jose and take the Los Banos cut-off, he thought, but that makes the trip longer, so it's six of one and I might as well take the bridge and roll as far as I can. He wondered if his old job would be open, and if it was not, who would be on it, replenishing the canned goods on the shelves at Black's Package. Polly appeared in his mind, her face sad and pitying. You see, Nick, she seemed to say, I told you but you wouldn't listen. You're a baby, you're just a baby. He drove Polly from his head, but the spectre of failure would not leave him. He thought of the things that had happened to him since he had come to market. The petty little temptations. The hard-eyed laughing men who looked so much like butchers. His own timidity, as though this were some kind of physical conflict and he were flinching from being hurt. Soon daylight would be coming and the people in the city would be buying his apples and eating them, and he could see the smiles on their faces. How little they knew of how apples came to town. No idea at all. Some kind of magic had brought them there. Nick thought of the glint-eyed muscular men who walked with tight fists up and down the market street. Short, stocky, broad-chested men, who bared tobacco-stained teeth in laughter, while they cut out your heart. He had started so bravely, quitting his job and buying the truck and venturing to find a load, but now it was all gone, all the fine bravery gone. You had to be hard and shrewd, very hard and shrewd, more shrewd than he could ever be. It was not buying and selling. It was standing toe to toe and slugging at each other in a combat of such ferocity that he knew he would never be able to beat anyone down, but would always be the first to drop his arms, more in awe than in defeat that his opponent could put up such a fight for money, just money, not much money, not more than hardly enough for a person to live on decently, if one had the time to live at all, after grubbing for it.

Well, that's that, something within him said with sickening finality. You're sunk. He accepted defeat the way an old man accepts death, but there was a germ that resisted and squirmed and he knew that he had not accepted defeat completely. I'm going to hang around the waterfront until I find out who rolled me, he said to himself. He had no idea how he was going to find out, but he knew he would.

He walked along the dock, past the booze joints where the winos sat in a stupor, leaning on the counter like the stuffed figures in a crazy house. He went past the open doors of dark hotels, past the shuttered shops and shine joints, past the garbage-littered lots that bordered one side of the Embarcadero.

His foot kicked something and it skidded down the street. An old shoe, he thought, and he kicked it again and it opened and turned over. Too flat to be a shoe, he thought, and he picked it up and found that it was a wallet. His heart thumped when he saw it was his wallet. The money was gone, but Polly's face looked up at him from the window. He straightened and he saw high on the wall before him a sign that said, NEW HARBOR HOTEL. A light burned over the clerk's desk. The guy that got my wallet went into that hotel, Nick thought. He crossed to the entrance and saw the clerk asleep in his chair. The floor squeaked once as he crossed the lobby and went up the stairs to the second floor. The hallway stretched back in a cave that was faced with doors. A red light burned at the far end above the emergency stairs. The transoms were dark. Nick went to the third floor where again the transoms were dark. Dark too on the fourth. Somewhere a ventilator fan hummed. The sounds of sleepers, sonorous and appalling, hung on the air, but beneath them was the sound of voices, murmurous and faint. Nick went down the hallway, but the voices faded. He descended the emergency stairs to the third floor, with the red light bloody upon him. The voices returned. He went along the hallway, listening, and the sounds became louder, swelling upon him, leading him to a door. The transom was shut and only a narrow slit of light appeared on the rug. Nick stood listening to the voices which were blurred and disembodied by the thickness of wall and door, sounding to be voices from another world.

He knocked on the door and the voices stopped. He knocked again and there was a soft footfall and the slit of light disappeared. Nick stepped back and kicked open the door and instantly reached in and cut on the switch and in the swift blinding light, a man stood holding a small raw-skinned dog in his arms. Tex's friend. Behind him lying on the bed, but in the posture of rising, was the girl, Nadine. Nick stepped into the room and saw the dark man of the cafe, Frenchy. Beside him was a blonde girl.

"The hell with knocking," Tex's friend said.

"That's some key you carry," the man, Frenchy, said. "Just kick the door open and come right in."

"He came to see me," Nadine said. "Didn't you, Nick?" She took Nick's arm, but Nick brushed off her hand. "I want my money," he said.

"What the hell you talking about?" Tex's friend said.

"He must have lost some money," Frenchy said. "Maybe he thinks you rolled him," he said to Nadine, and the girl laughed and said, "If I rolled him, he'd know it."

"Somebody rolled me. I had thirty-nine hundred dollars in my pocket," Nick said.

"We saw you going out after Tex," Nadine said. "Maybe her and the old guy did it."

"No, they didn't do it," Nick said. "I know who did it."

"Let us in on it," Frenchy said. "Maybe we can help you get it back."

"Sure, sit down and have a drink and tell us about it," Tex's friend said.

"One of you did it," Nick said.

"Maybe he thinks I did it, Mitch," Frenchy said.

"If you did, you're three times the man I thought you were," the man named Mitch said.

"I want my money and I want it fast," Nick said.

"We all want it and we all want it fast," Mitch said. "But how are you going to get it?"

"I don't want to make any trouble," Nick said. "Just give me my money and I'll beat it."

Mitch opened his arms and the chihuahua leapt nimbly to the table where it stood with its rear crouched down, the tail with the vertebrae like knots in it curled delicately between its legs, and the legs trembling. Frenchy and Mitch separated so Nick was between them.

"I want my money," Nick said. He held out his hand. "I want my money," he said again, and he kept saying it in a quiet shaking voice. Frenchy came at him from the side and Nick swatted him into the wall. He tried to catch Mitch, but Mitch backed off. Frenchy came at him again and he batted him with the heel of his hand, his whole shoulder going into the blow, and he went after Mitch, but it was like trying to catch a fish in a bowl. He rushed him into a corner of the room and caught him and he could hear himself saying in a voice that was cold with rage, "I want my money."

When he could see again, he saw that the girl Nadine had his arm and Mitch was in his hand, with his head thrown back and the face broken. He dropped Mitch and turned to Frenchy, but the girl wrapped herself on his arm. He shook her off and he

heard her say, "Give him the money, Frenchy! Give it to him!" He
went to Frenchy, but Frenchy got away and he went to him again
and Frenchy had the money in his hand and was holding it out
like bait. There were three twenties and a fifty. Nick took them.
"There was five hundred cash and a check," he said. "I want it all."

"That's all there is," Frenchy said.

"Please give it to me. I don't want to make any trouble."

"I swear to Christ, that's all there is. I'd give it to you if I had it.
The wind blew the rest of it into the bay."

Nick caught Frenchy and went through him, but found nothing.
He returned to Mitch and searched him and found a wad of bills in
ones and fives, whore money.

"That's our money," the girl Nadine said, and Frenchy said,
"If you want to beat up somebody, why don't you beat up Figlia?
He's the one who made us do it."

"Sure, you go see him," the girl said. She came to Nick, clawing
to get the money, but he brushed her aside, intent on Frenchy, not
turning from him. "How did he make you do it?" he said.

"He told us we could have the five hundred, if we got rid of
the check," Frenchy said.

The girl went again to get the money, but the look on Nick's
face froze her. The look went beyond her, beyond the room, to the
market. She could not breathe, watching him; then he had gone
from the room and she could breathe and she saw the chihuahua
with its rodent face and protruding eyes, pissing on the table, the
wet spreading so it was standing in a little yellow pool.

28

FAR TO the East a faint smudge of light appeared and high up the sky was streaked with a long vaporous cloud. In the Valley, roosters had been crowing for an hour, cheering the morning. The air felt brisk and cold. A flock of seagulls went by, gliding on unsteady wings. A rumble of traffic stirred beyond the market and somewhere a streetcar clattered down the tracks, the sounds echoey and distant.

The swamper clasped his hands under his armpits. His eyes were pinched and his face was drawn.

Washington Street was empty. A pale milky light hung on the air and through it the buildings and warehouses looked wan and far away. The sidewalks were littered with wilted produce and rotting fruit and already beggars were searching the gutters and the big garbage cans in the alleys, picking through the night's refuse before the sweepers came. Men were hauling the unsold produce back into storage vaults. Only a few trucks were parked along the curb, the trucks of late buyers. Soon they too would be gone and all the stall doors would be pulled down, the market closed.

The night's fog had precipitated upon the street and the pavement was wet. The swamper toddled down the glistening walk, his shoes scraping. One box of Hale peaches, each one big and flushed with ripeness, was on the curb. The swamper looked around to see if he was being watched and stooped quickly to get one, but a voice said, chidingly, "Aah-aah." The buyer stepped from a produce house and picked up the box and carried it to his truck. The swamper moved away.

The Merchant's Lunch was crowded with market workers. The

sound of their voices and laughter trickled into the street. Up over the door, the exhaust fan blew out the odors of cooking, making the swamper's stomach churn, his pig eyes brightening and rolling. He could not bear to watch the men eat and his mouth puckered and tightened like a child's.

In the middle of the block, three Negroes were standing in a line, relaying rattlesnake melons from a pile on the walk to a bed of sawdust in the produce house. The swamper stood beside them. Down at the bottom of the pile was a big one. The swamper kept his eye on it. The watermelons made him think of early Summer: *The time I was swamping for Pete Brustow hauling melons out of Turlock, acres and acres of melons, making one big spread of vines coiling in a jungle tangle on the ground, the watermelons like fat bellies in the leaves and the pickers slapping them so you could hear it clear in the yard and cutting the pigtail stems of the ripe ones and the field trucks hauling them in.*

The Negroes got to the big one and the swamper reached over and patted it once and it rang hard and firm. Ripe. Sweet ripe. Red ripe. When they sounded too firm they were green, and over-ripe when they sounded dull, but this one was perfect. The Negro picked it up and the swamper stepped forward, his hands out as though to catch it. "You can throw me that one," he said.

"Out of the way, man," the Negro said. He threw the melon, but the swamper had confused the rhythm of the line and the melon floated fat and ponderous through the air and broke apart upon the sidewalk.

"Hey," the produce dealer shouted from the cashier's cage.

The swamper stepped quickly to the melon and grabbed up the heart and ran into the street. The heart had a coating on it that was like frost and the red meat was shot through with black shining seeds.

The produce dealer stepped to the sidewalk. "Hey, you, put that down," he shouted.

"He's putting it down," one of the Negroes said.

"Man, look at him put it down."

The men stood watching the swamper eat the melon, stuffing and sucking and gulping, his eyes darting to the side to see if the produce dealer was going to interfere, his body agile and ready to parry him, the juices dripping from his chin, running down his neck into his shirt and soaking through his shirt. He finished the melon and looked about, his eyes sharp with greed.

"He might as well kill the rest of it," the produce dealer said.

The Negroes carried the pieces of broken melon to the swamper and watched him eat all of it, and when he was done, he wiped his hands on his shirt and dried his mouth with his sleeves. There was a fullness in him. The ache was buried in watermelon, insubstantial food. His gut would be aching again within an hour, but it was soothed for now. The swamper belched and grinned. "Next time you miss, give me a call," he said.

"Ah, you God damn—" The produce dealer stopped, profanity inadequate. "Okay, boys, get the rest of 'em in," he said.

The Negroes returned to the melons, relaying them into the produce house. The swamper toddled on down the street. If I can get a ride out, I'll shake this town, he thought. By now the sun had risen and the one streak of cloud was bright with light, white and wispy against the blue.

The swamper saw Nick run to the stall where the doors were pulled down. He saw him pound on the doors and heard him shout, "Figlia!"

The swamper crossed the street. "Looking for Figlia?" he said.

Nick turned and the swamper saw the fury pent within him. "Where is he?" Nick said, his voice like a whip.

The swamper grinned. "They went out a while ago," he said, "him and the handler and that guy who works for him."

"When will they be back?"

"Don't know. They're closed for the day, I guess. But he oughta be here tomorrow night. Maybe you can catch him then." The swamper watched Nick squirm in impatience. "Maybe I could tell you where they went," he said.

"Where did they go?"

"What's it worth to you?"

"It's worth a lot to me. Where did they go?"

"All I want is to swamp for you," the swamper said. "I'm a good driver. You can ask Steve Ferguson. I used to swamp for him.

I'll spell you off when you get tired. You're new at this game. I'll show you some of the ropes."

"Tell me!"

"Okay," the swamper said, "but you better get set. This is gonna knock you."

"Where is he?" Nick said.

The swamper nodded. He looked at Nick, but he did not know how to say it. "What's your partner's name?" he said.

"Ed," Nick said. "Ed Kennedy. What about him?"

"Figlia went to him," the swamper said. "He went to pick up his load."

"Did Ed come in?"

"No. He ain't coming in."

"Did he break down? Did he send word he broke down?"

"He broke down alright, but he didn't send no word."

"Then how do you know?" Nick's voice was quiet but it gave the effect of screaming. The swamper opened his mouth to tell, but he could not say it. He saw the anxiety gather in Nick's face and he wanted to tell, but he did not know how and his big face slobbered and puckered and his voice trembled.

"Jesus," he said, "I'm trying to tell you, but I don't know how."

"Tell me!" Nick said.

The swamper waited until his voice was steady and he said, "He cracked up. Happened up at Altamont. Truck went off the road and burned."

"Is he dead?" Nick said.

"Yah! He burned too. Not enough left of him to fill a bucket." And now the swamper could tell it. "But his load's all right. One of the trucks come in, the driver seen it. Apples all over hell, but none of 'em hurt."

Nick's face became aghast. Ah, Ed, he thought. This was the dream turned into reality. Ah, Ed's wife. Ah, Ed's kids. He thought of Ed's charred body crammed into a bucket, how it must have happened, the truck going over and over down the hill and across the meadow and slamming against the rocks and Ed waking to find himself locked in the torn cab, with gasoline raw on his body, trying to escape, but hardly time to escape, the tank exploding and Ed screaming in the midst of fire.

"Figlia went to pick them up," the swamper said. "He said nobody'd know they wasn't his apples."

A look of rage flushed over Nick's face and the swamper instantly regretted his words. He saw Nick run to his truck.

The swamper waddled after him. "You're going to let me swamp for you, huh?" he said. "You said you would." He saw Nick trying to start the truck, but he was blind with rage and kept fumbling the key in the lock.

"You said you was going to let me swamp for you," the swamper said. "Remember, you said it?"

Nick could not get the key into the lock and he cursed it. He threw it against the panel board and it bounced into the street and the swamper picked it up. "You better move over and let me try," he said. "Go on, move over." He pushed Nick from the wheel and got in behind it and Nick watched him in a frenzy, the way a dog watches a man eating, as the swamper struggled with the key and the lock. He watched him struggle to start the truck and now the engine was running. He watched him hit the clutch and made movements with his hands as the swamper shifted into gear, clashing it painfully, and the truck pulled away from the curb and drifted past the men working on the pile of watermelons, past the beggars in the street. The swamper waved his hand. "So long, you jokers," he shouted.

The truck reached the Embarcadero and passed through the tunnel and on up to Mission. The swamper saw Nick staring ahead, his eyes furious and unseeing.

On Mission was a cluster of kids going to school, the girls with their clean pink scalps showing beneath crisply parted hair, the boys skylarking on bikes. They caught Nick's eye. Up to now he had been one of them. He had been growing away from it all the time, but he had come to the market with the vestiges of youth and innocence still within him. Now the last of it was gone. One startling, frightening thought of his mother passed through his head but he squashed it. There was only meanness and hardness lumping like grief in his chest and he knew if he looked into a mirror he could see his eyes cold-hard and his face turned to stone.

The truck took the ramp to the Bay Bridge, not the lower deck where trucks were supposed to go, but the top deck among the fleet passenger cars.

It was a beautiful morning and the swamper felt good. He thought of what was going to happen to Figlia and he felt wonderful. The sky was clear and there were few clouds, clean and white and very high. The bay looked bright green, breaking in rows of whitecaps along the surface. The skyline of the city of Oakland was sharply limned, even to the smallest detail on the tall buildings that stood above the waterfront. The wind that blew in from the Golden Gate was fresh and strong, blasting stiffly against the truck. It gave an edge-of-the-world feeling, as though the truck were flying through the sky. The Swamper knew that Figlia would not give up the load easily and that there was going to be a fight. Oh, what a fight! He sat tensing himself, feeling a marvelous and childlike elation. He could not wait until they got to Altamont. "We won't walk right in, when we get there," he said to Nick. "We'll wait until they bring the load out to us on the road. And then we'll take 'em. Won't we?"

Nick did not answer and the swamper said, "We are going to take them, aren't we?"

Nick looked briefly to the swamper, and the swamper saw his eyes and smiled quietly to himself. After a time, he stopped smiling and looked again to Nick, but Nick had turned and was looking straight through the windshield.

The truck went swiftly down the road.

AFTERWORD by A. I. Bezzerides

Swindle

Here I am, somewhere past 88, and my third book, *Thieves' Market*, published nearly fifty years ago by Scribner's, is about to be published again by the University of California Press.

Simultaneously, a French edition, introduced by Philippe Garnier, is to be published for the first time by Gallimard in Paris.

I had not read it for years; thought I should, just to see how it went. As I opened it, I remembered something that happened long before I wrote it, before I had accumulated the experience that would enable me to write it.

I had just written my first short story, *Passage into Eternity*, sold it to *Story* magazine. Soon after it was published, the editor wrote me a letter in which he said that my writing had a long breath, that I should be writing novels.

This reminded me of another experience I had years later, while working at 20th Century Fox Studios, writing scripts for movies. I had just given my secretary some pages to type. A few minutes later, she came into my office with the pages in her hand. I remember thinking, poor thing, she can't read my handwriting, I can hardly read it myself. I asked her:

"Are you having a problem?"

"No," she said, "oh-no."

She told me she always read whatever I gave her to type before she typed it, that there were times when what she read made the pages shake in her hands.

"Why would it do that?"

"Because you're a wonderful writer; you shouldn't be wasting your time writing scripts."

234

As I clutched the book, I found myself pondering what I had said to her.

I didn't write books, because few of them, even the best, ever became bestsellers, and I needed the exorbitant bucks that studios were willing to pay even lousy writers in order to support my parents and my family.

The books that I have written thus far, *Long Haul* in 1938, *There Is a Happy Land* (far-far-away) in 1942, *Thieves' Market* in 1949, all deal with an identical ingredient: the swindles and privation that life had inflicted upon me.

Etched into my soul was the poverty that had surrounded me when I was a child: From as far back as I could remember, the endless wranglings of my mother screeching for money-money-money, the endless efforts of my father, to "mehk-de-mohney" by exploring neighborhoods with his horse-and-wagon, peddling fruits and vegetables. Somehow he bought a truck, not a multi-tired, half-block-long twenty-tonner, but a scrawny ton-and-a-half four-wheeler. He didn't buy it paying cash, because he didn't have any; he bought it by promising to pay, with money he hoped to earn by dealing with produce markets in distant big cities.

By then I was old enough to work with him, during summer and Christmas vacations and times in between, to help load the truck, to drive it, to serve as a built-in mechanic, repairing it whenever it broke down, which was often, hauling produce north and south, along narrow no-lane highways. As a consequence, I became a startled witness to the swindles that went on, initially the puny-primitive swindles that were inflicted upon ordinary people like my father, swindles that became less puny, less primitive, became ever increasingly sophisticated, as I passed through high school and went on to college.

I drifted from job to job, until I became so disgusted that I found myself sitting before a battered old typewriter that my wife had got from God knows where and placed on a table in a corner of the shack we lived in on Sycamore street in Hollywood.

"Write," she kept telling me, "write! You'll feel better."

I kept holding my breath as I typed-typed until the pile of blank paper on one side of the table had become the manuscript of a book titled *Long Haul*, stacked on the other side of the table.

William Saroyan, whom I had known since early childhood, who had graduated from selling the *Daily Examiner* on Market Street in San Francisco into becoming a writer, suggested that I send *Long Haul* to his agent, Ann Watkins, in New York, who sold it to Carrick and Evans, who published it.

Despite the review in *Time* magazine, the book did not sell.

Even so, a Hollywood agent, William Dozier, phoned me, told me he had read the book, liked it, wanted to represent me, to offer the book to all the motion picture studios in Hollywood.

Of course, I agreed, and what do you know, miracle-of-miracles, the next day he phoned me, to say he had *sold* it! To whom? To *Warner Bros.!* For how much? For *fifteen hundred dollars!*

My reaction? I was excited, but I contained my excitement, because I had a problem, although I doubted he could solve it.

I found myself asking, did he think he could talk them into paying twenty-five hundred, because I had just bought a house in Manhattan Beach, had borrowed that much from my mother-in-law to pay for it, and if possible, I would like to pay her back.

"Oh, sure, that'd be a cinch."

The next day he called back, to announce jubilantly that he had talked them up to *two grand!*

My reaction? I let my emotions fly:

Two-thousand dollars! For *words!* Just *words!* Horribly typed on yellow sheets of paper! Wow!

It wasn't until a week or so later that I was contacted by a writer, Meyer Levin, who later became a friend, and collaborated with me on a presentation we titled *Power-House*, about the crews constructing power-lines, which was swindled by Warners, who made a picture about crews constructing telephone-lines, despite our selling *Power-House* to Paramount Pictures, who never made it, stymied by the Warners production.

Meyer, who had read in *Daily Variety* that the book had been sold, told me that a script had already been written, based on my book, that a movie was in the process of being shot with Humphrey Bogart and George Raft and Ida Lupino, together with many of the studio's contracted actors in the cast, that the title, *Long Haul*, had been changed to *They Drive By Night*, all this long before they had bought the book.

He asked me how much they had paid me, and when I told him, he said, "*What?*" Which provoked me to ask how much he thought they should have paid. He said they would have paid many times that, had the agent represented me instead of Warner Bros.

I had no idea whether it was guilt and conscience, or greed to swindle more stories out of me, for peanuts, that motivated Warner Bros. to offer me a seven-year contract, with options to be exercised every six months.

Whatever their reason, I grabbed their offer, so I could quit my putrid career as a communications engineer, by becoming a writer, writing scripts in an entirely new world.

After I signed the contract, I found myself wondering, was I offered a job because the studio thought I might sue them, because of the swindle they had inflicted upon me, hoping to assuage the swindle by assigning me to a story that I was to adapt into a script?

The first script I wrote was written only after I had read dozens of scripts, to see how it was done, driven as I was to write scripts that would be better.

I was given a story about an immigrant farmer who was being swindled by a produce-house. I kept the farmer, but chose to do a story about the Oklahomans who had abandoned their sun-scorched farms to migrate to California, where they hoped to harvest crops for San Joaquin Valley farmers.

I had seen a lovely young Oklahoma girl playing a guitar and singing a song in a juke-joint filled with Oklahomans.

I involved her as a character in the story, and changed the title of the script to *Juke Girl*. I wrote lyrics for a song, even whistled a tune to fit the lyrics, wrote the script in such a way that the pangs and pleasures of the story emerged from the pages it was written upon.

Juke Girl was made into a picture in which Ronald Reagan played the leading role of a liberal-minded trucker. Ha!

The picture became such a box-office hit that I went to the Chinese Theater in Hollywood, where it was playing, to watch the audience as it came out, to witness the expressions in their faces that would say better than words whether or not they had enjoyed the movie. I saw that they had, they certainly had.

Jack Warner, the chief-executive of the studio, was standing beside the ticket-booth, also searching faces. I saw him shake his head as he gestured toward the crowd, and heard him say to his associate who was standing beside him, watching too, "I can't see . . . why *anyone* . . . would want to see . . . this picture!"

Later, after Warner and his associates had departed, I saw an old-old-old woman come tottering across the lobby, supported by the hands of her two old-sons, the three of them Oklahomans who were far from home. As they drew near I heard her say in a heavily accented Oklahoman voice: "Whoever writ this story, sure knew his folks."

Needless to say, the studio did not fire me; they picked up my options, because they saw they could make a buck out of me.

In my next book I intend to write about the vast variety of swindles I have witnessed, not only when I was working with my father, and later when I worked alone, but ranging from far back into my childhood, in my encounters with my mother—who failed, despite numerous efforts, to abort me—through my life at home, then through grade school, through high school, through the produce markets, through the trucking trips I made to all the big cities in California, through college, until I dropped out days before graduation and began shifting from job to job, through all of the swindles I encountered first as a night engineer for Electrical Research Products, then as a sound-man for a public address outfit, as a sound-mixer for a big jazz band's radio broadcasts, as an engineer for the Mitchell Camera Corporation, then as a writer for the Motion Picture Studios, then, when TV arrived, as a writer for television producers: swindles described in such vivid detail that they will point like a long finger toward the sky-scratching high-rises that cluster in the hearts of all big cities, not only in California or the United States, but in the world, towers destined to metamorphose into tombstones that will mark the end of MAN-CONCOCTED CIVILIZATION.

I will write this book, I will, even as I keep the tip of my right forefinger in touch with the pulse in my left wrist.

FILMOGRAPHY

1940: *They Drive By Night*. Warners. Writers: Jerry Wald, Richard Macaulay. Producer: Mark Hellinger. Director: Raoul Walsh. Novel basis only.

1942: *Juke Girl*. Warners. Writer: A. I. Bezzerides. Producer: Hal B. Wallis. Director: Curtis Bernhardt. Based on the story "Jook Girl" by Theodore Pratt.

1943: *Action in the North Atlantic*. Warners. Writer: John Howard Lawson. Producer: Jerry Wald Director: Lloyd Bacon. Based on the novel by Guy Gilpatric. Joint additional dialogue, in collaboration with W. R. Burnett.

1943: *Northern Pursuit*. Warners. Writers: Frank Gruber, Alvah Bessie. Producer: Jack Chertok. Director: Raoul Walsh. Based on the story "Five Thousand Trojan Horses" by Leslie T. White. Joint additional dialogue; occasional credit as co-writer.

1943: *Background to Danger*. Warners. Writer: W. R. Burnett. Producer: Jerry Wald. Director: Raoul Walsh. Based on the novel *Uncommon Danger* by Eric Ambler. Joint additional dialogue.

1946: *Desert Fury*. Paramount. Writers: Robert Rossen, A. I. Bezzerides. Producer: Hal B. Wallis. Director: Lewis Allen. Based on the novel by Ramona Stewart.

1951: *Sirocco*. Columbia. Writer: A. I. Bezzerides. Producer: Robert Lord. Director: Curtis Bernhardt. Based on the novel *Coup de Grace* by Joseph Kessel.

1951: *On Dangerous Ground*. RKO. Writer: A. I. Bezzerides. Producer: John Houseman. Director: Nicholas Ray. Based on the novel *Mad With Much Heart* by Gerald Butler.

1952: *Holiday for Sinners*. MGM. Writer: A. I. Bezzerides. Producer: John Houseman. Director: Gerald Mayer. Based on the novel by Hamilton Basso.

1953: *Beneath the Twelve Mile Reef*. Fox. Writer: Original screenplay by A. I. Bezzerides. Producer: Robert Bassler. Director: Robert Webb.

1954: *Track of the Cat*. Warners. Writer: A. I. Bezzerides. Producer: John Wayne, Robert Fellows. Director: William Wellman. Based on the novel by Walter van Tilburg Clark.

1955: *Kiss Me Deadly*. Parklane/United Artists. Writer: A. I. Bezzerides. Produced and directed by Robert Aldrich. Based on the novel by Mickey Spillane.

1955: *A Bullet for Joey*. United Artists. Writers: A. I. Bezzerides, Geoffrey Homes. Producers: Samuel Bischoff, David Diamond. Director: Lewis Allen. Based on the story by James Benson Nablo.

1959: *The Jayhawkers*. Paramount. Writers: A. I. Bezzerides, Frank Fenton, Melvin Frank, Joseph Petracca. Producers: Norman Panama, Melvin Frank. Director: Melvin Frank.

1959: *The Angry Hills*. MGM. Writer: A. I. Bezzerides. Producer: Raymond Stross. Director: Robert Aldrich. Based on the novel by Leon Uris.

Television:

William Faulkner: A Life on Paper (feature documentary)
DuPont Theatre
Meet McGraw
Sunset Strip
Wells Fargo
The Virginian
Rawhide
Bonanza
The Big Valley (series creator)
Great Adventure

California Fiction titles are selected for their literary merit and for their illumination of California history and culture.

Photo by Garrett White, 1992

A. I. Bezzerides was born in Turkey in 1908 and raised in Fresno, California, the son of an Armenian mother and a Greek father. He is the author of many screenplays, including the film noir classics *On Dangerous Ground* (Nicholas Ray, 1951) and *Kiss Me Deadly* (Robert Aldrich, 1955). He is also the author of the novel *Long Haul* (1938) from which a film, *They Drive by Night*, was made by Raoul Walsh in 1940. He lives in the San Fernando Valley.